I0758480

Face of Danger

UNDERCOVER MAGIC BOOK TWO

ISBN: 978-1-951738-98-3 (Paperback Edition)

Cover Design by CReya-tive Book Design

Edited by Dawn Yacovetta

Proofread by Dominique Laura

For Melissa,

*You help me tear it all apart and then show me how
to put it back together so it's better than before.
Thank you for braving the trenches with me and pulling my ass back out.*

*"The world is full of monsters with friendly faces
and angels full of scars."*

-Unknown

Face of Danger

CHAPTER ONE
LINA

Lina's memories returned with the force of a jackhammer to her brain. She was only distantly aware of her physical body slumped down in one of the Tempest Lounge's booths. Her attention was consumed by her past.

It was all there, laid out like a sumptuous buffet for her to pick and choose from.

Her name.

Her family . . . well, what was left of it.

Her fifteenth birthday when she received her first kiss.

Her eighteenth birthday when she received her first tattoo.

But there was one memory that outshone all the others. The one that had been powerful enough to pierce her dreams when she'd been cut off from everything else that made her whole. She focused on that memory now, immersing herself in those final, terrifying seconds, and watched them play out like some kind of twisted snuff film.

And she was its star.

Through the slashing rain and darkness, she ran into the alley, only to crash into a wall moments later. Dazed, she struggled to lift herself from the ground.

She needed to keep moving because he was right behind her.

Mataius Drake. The boy she'd grown up with. The man she was promised to.

It was too late. Above the sound of the pouring rain, she heard his dark chuckle.

"Evalina," his terrifying voice crooned. "You know there's no escape. While I do love a good chase, playtime is over. I'm here to collect what's mine."

She opened her mouth and screamed for help. But she knew there were no heroes in her story. Only devils disguised as men.

Something crashed into the back of her head, and Lina crumbled to the ground once more.

Consciousness returned, steeped in the pain of hundreds of invisible needles stabbing her eyes. The instinctive need to lift her hand to her head was halted with a rattle of noise. Confused, she squinted through the throbbing pain and looked down at the heavy, silver chains that lashed her to a chair. Her vision blurred, and she shivered at the feel of the icy rivers of blood dripping down her face and neck.

She tried to make out where she was, but the flashes of lightning outside the windows and the flicker of a dozen candles laid out on the floor revealed nothing familiar.

Harsh whispers came from somewhere behind her. She tried to call for help, but a tortured moan emerged instead. The whispers fell silent, replaced by the scrape of boots over the floor.

Mataius hit her hard across the face then fisted a hand in her hair, pulling her head up and back.

"Did I tell you you could speak?" The heat of his breath washed over her cheek. "I'm growing impatient. I've been waiting for this day for what feels like my entire life." His hand trailed down the side of her face in a macabre imitation of a caress. "Just a little bit longer now, and then you won't be my problem anymore. In fact, you won't be anyone's problem.

"The others are coming. And then . . . well, let's not ruin the surprise, shall we?"

He pressed against the weeping wound on the back of her head. She screamed against the pain, and then the world faded to nothing until a cool breeze over her damp clothes woke her.

Wax pools had formed beneath the flickering candles around her, and the sound of footsteps filled the room—too many to belong to one person. A low throbbing beat joined the footsteps. Her terrified brain recognized the source of the sound as a drum.

She tried to cry out, call for help, but something coated in the metallic taste of her blood had been shoved into her mouth.

The drumming grew louder, and a chorus of deep voices started chanting a demonic symphony. The candles guttered, and some blew out entirely. The unmistakable sound of metal scraping against metal joined the sounds.

A sob choked her as the wet slide of a tongue began to trace the damp tracks on her face.

"I don't believe I've ever tasted anything as delicious as your fear," Mataius whispered against her ear as he freed the gag from her mouth. "Go ahead and scream as much as you want, sweetheart. It only makes it better."

A dagger glinted, and fiery pain ignited just above her heart. She sucked in a shocked breath, and then her screams joined the unearthly chorus that rose in a crescendo around her.

"Beautiful," Mataius said, twisting the blade and dragging it lower. "So fucking beautiful."

Mataius carved into her chest with his dagger, drawing the symbol that would complete whatever ritual he'd initiated. She knew he intended to kill her, and there'd be nothing left for her father to find except her mutilated body.

Darkness swelled, and she welcomed the relief of oblivion.

Sound returned too soon though. Voices whispered, and Lina groaned. The burning in her chest was muted, but she could still feel the throb. Like a toothache. She tried to open her eyes, but they refused to obey.

"Shh. Quiet now, Sweetling. It will all be over soon."

A new voice but a familiar one.

"Un-uncl . . ." her tongue felt too thick to form the words.

"Yes, Sweetling. I'm here. You just rest now. You've done more than enough."

Alistair was here. She was safe.

Then another, softer voice spoke. Quinn. "We don't have much time. The damage they did was fatal. We cannot stop the severing. Already, the soul is trying to leave the body."

Whose soul? Her soul? Lina struggled to make sense of the conversation.

"Do what you can."

"Are you . . . are you sure?"

"It must be done."

"It could take decades before the spell breaks down enough to call her back. Left untethered for that long, she'll become . . . unstable. What is left when she does return . . . she'll not be the woman we know."

"Is there a way to prevent it?"

"Yes, but—"

"Do it."

"She won't remember us."

"Perhaps it's better that way."

"Alistair."

"Do as I say, heir. Or leave."

"Hold her steady. This is going to hurt."

Lina screamed as her right forearm began to burn. The pain ignited behind her eyes as memories rose to the surface only to smolder and burn like photographs. There and gone, leaving nothing in their wake.

"It is done," Quinn said, her voice heavy and flat.

"And now?"

"And now we wait and pray to whatever god will listen that it wasn't too late."

The world tilted, and Lina grew weightless as if she was floating or *being carried. Then, it stopped. Something cold and wet seeped into her back.*

"Until we meet again, my dearest friend." Quinn's voice was so sad.

Water splashed onto Lina's face, and something warm pressed against her forehead.

"Sweet dreams, my beautiful Evalina."

More warm drops of water. And then something else started to tickle her face and neck. Dirt. They were burying her. She started screaming in her head that she was still here. But no sound emerged. There was nothing but the weight. It pressed against her on all sides, and she drifted out of consciousness, welcoming nothing at all.

"Evalina?" Alistair croaked.

Lina snapped her head to the side, zeroing in on a voice she never thought to hear again. With his appearance having been changed by the Brotherhood, it was a little easier to pretend that her beloved uncle—the man who'd cuddled her when she scraped her knee and gave her her first banana split—wasn't the same person who helped shovel dirt over her mutilated body.

"Hello, Uncle."

She looked away from the man who had buried her alive.

The empty tavern had fallen mostly silent, the lone bartender keeping herself busy behind the bar. Given the slightly bored expression on her face, Lina was willing to bet this wasn't the first time she'd witnessed some kind of supernatural blowout at work. Nor would it be the last.

For her, it was probably just a typical workday at the Tempest Lounge, perhaps even one with slightly less bloodshed than usual. At least, so far.

The night was young.

Part of Lina wished she could claim the same, that this was just another bullshit Tuesday. Maybe it was in the sense that her entire life seemed to be turned inside out on a regular basis—especially recently—but that kind of constant upheaval wasn't exactly something one ever gets used to.

Just when it seemed like she was starting to get her life on track, the universe went and slapped her across the face just to remind her who was in charge. Hint: it sure as shit wasn't her.

"Lina?" a deeper, slightly accented voice called.

Her eyes shot to the grief-ravaged face of her Guardian.

"Are you . . . all right?" he asked, voice tentative, pale blue eyes searching.

She wasn't sure there was a word in existence that adequately explained what she was feeling right now, so she nodded.

"Do you remember?" her uncle asked.

"I remember *everything*. You buried me alive. Why?"

"These two were the ones responsible for killing you?" Finley asked, his eyes burning with hazel fire as his voice dropped to a dangerous pitch.

"My fiancé—" Nord sucked in a shocked breath, and Lina's gaze shifted to his horrified face as she continued, "—was performing some kind of ritual, and I was his unwilling sacrifice. These two found me at death's door, stole my memories, and buried. Me. Alive." The words were ground out and dripping with anger.

Nord was ashen, staring at her in horror.

Alistair was the first to speak, dismayed when he asked, "Mataius did that to you?"

"Yes."

He shook his head as tears dripped down his cheeks. "All this time, we didn't know who was responsible. There was a ransom note. It was addressed to your father, but I got home first. I'd suspected something was going on and left the banquet early. I tried to call him, but he didn't answer. Quinn arrived not five minutes later. You two had plans that night. Do you remember?" He faltered, waving a hand like he was getting off-topic. "There was no address, but we knew a spell that could track you. We—" his voice broke "—didn't get to you in time. All that was left was your body."

Alistair cleared his throat, fighting hard to keep his voice even as he continued his explanation. "When we first arrived, you weren't even breathing. I managed to get your pulse back, but it was clear we were too late. Your body was already shutting down. We had to do what we could to salvage what was left. In order to preserve your physical self and reverse the damage—"

"My body had to be returned to the earth," Lina guessed, sensing where his explanation was going.

Her uncle nodded. "But the bigger issue was your soul. It couldn't stay tethered to a damaged vessel, and after what Mataius did . . ."

"My soul was already trying to flee its damaged vessel by the time you found me," Lina said, her voice wooden as she filled in the horrific blanks.

Again, Alistair nodded. "Quinn knew of a way to buy you time. The magic allowed your soul to heal. However, it also freed you from the pain of your past."

"If you'd retained your memories, you would have been little more than an avenging spirit," Quinn chimed in softly. "We didn't want that for you. If we could keep your mind intact while my spell repaired your soul, you would be whole when it finished. Mind, body, and soul."

That's when the last piece of the puzzle fell into place. The ball. The rooftop. Those shocked gray eyes.

"Mataius knows I'm alive," she whispered. "He's the one I saw at the ball."

Finley and Nord exchanged a look.

"We'll find him," Finley promised.

"He's been missing for years," Alistair said, his voice hollowed out. "We'd thought he'd met the same fate as Ev—as Lina. It's one of the reasons the rest of the heirs went into hiding."

Finley's eyes narrowed with interest at the mention of the heirs, but all he said was, "We'll find him."

Her head was still swimming with all the knowledge it now

contained. She knew there were questions she should ask, answers she should demand, but it was hard to focus on anything besides her anger.

As if he could sense her need, Nord held out a hand, which Lina accepted gladly. He pulled her into his body and ushered her away from the others. Even though they were out of hearing range, he dipped his chin so his mouth was right beside her ear.

"You will tell me what he did to you in detail so that I may repay each blow tenfold. He will not walk this earth much longer."

Lina pressed herself into Nord's warmth as she shook her head. "I'll tell you, but not so you can avenge me."

"Please, Kærasta. It would be my honor to serve his heart to you on a platter."

"No. When we find him, Mataius is mine."

She welcomed the chance to shove a dagger into that bastard's shriveled excuse of a heart.

Nord's arms tightened around her. "I would never deny you your vengeance. Though, I hope you'll accept my offer of assistance in meting it out."

Lina's lips twitched with the barest of smiles. She pulled back to meet his gaze. "I'm not sure I can trust you to walk away and let me finish the job. You don't have the best track record with maintaining control during a fight . . ."

He returned her words with a dark grin. "That's a fair assessment. But for you, Kærasta, I'd at least try to resist."

His willingness to stand back and simply be an accomplice to murder if she wished to commit one shouldn't have been sweet, but it was. Some girls liked flowers and chocolates. Apparently, she was into casual offers of murder. It touched her that he was willing to deny his own needs to ensure hers were met, and it was definitely a sign of his affection.

Her tumultuous emotions began to ebb, her Guardian's unflagging support comforting Lina in ways she hadn't known she needed. Nord was her safe harbor as the tempest of her past raged, but she knew, no matter what hard truths she had to confront, he'd be there with her every step of the way. No matter what. Not because of his vow to protect her but because he was hers.

Her nose scrunched as a thought occurred to her. "I guess you were right after all."

"Oh?" he asked, lifting a brow.

"I did belong to someone."

His eyes looked pained as he nodded. "So you did."

Lina lifted up on her toes and pulled his head down so their eyes were level. "But I was right, too. My heart never belonged to anyone but you."

Nord's eyes flared brightly and then fluttered closed. "Lina," he breathed, resting his forehead against hers.

"This isn't the right time or place for us to have this conversation, but I wanted you to know," she said softly. "In case there was ever any doubt."

"Thank you," he whispered, his breath gently fanning her face as they regretfully pulled away from each other. As his hands dropped, he tipped his head to the booth where the others were waiting. "So . . . what do you want to do about them?"

Lina had plenty of ideas but none she was ready to act on. She knew she needed to hear the rest of what they had to say before making any decisions.

"I guess it's time to hear the whole story."

CHAPTER TWO
LINA

Lina turned back to face Alistair and Quinn with a sigh, bracing herself for the next round of emotional blows.

"Just say the word, and we're out of here," Nord whispered.

She dipped her chin in the barest hint of a nod to let him know she'd heard him and closed the distance between her and the back booth. Knowing she had an escape route made it easier to face what was left of her past.

Alistair slumped back down in the booth, his hands clasped in front of him on the table, his shoulders hunched and eyes downcast.

For her part, Quinn looked unimpressed. She sat with her back ramrod straight and her chin slightly raised. It was an expression Lina found eerily familiar. One she witnessed countless times before. Although, she couldn't recall a time she'd ever been on the receiving end.

Lina reclaimed her seat beside Quinn. Finley remained standing while Nord grabbed a chair from a nearby table and placed it at the end of the booth. After spinning it around, he dropped into the seat, straddling it, his arms draped across the back. Through all of this, Alistair kept his head down, but Lina knew he was tracking absolutely every detail.

It didn't escape Lina's notice that she was sandwiched between the most important people from both her old and current life. Not sure how or where to start, she let her eyes drift between the loved ones from her past. She could just make out the tear tracks on her uncle's cheeks while her oldest friend sat stiffly, barely daring to draw in a breath.

Of the two, it was almost less painful to look at Alistair—almost.

With Quinn, there was no escaping the barrage of memories. Those deep plum and raspberry eyes had always been uniquely hers. Right now, they peered warily at Lina, anticipating the worst. It occurred to her then that she wasn't the only one at this table carrying invisible scars.

Time had done a number on them all.

The realization provided her with the final push she needed.

Licking her lips, Lina forced her words out. "I'm ready to hear what you have to say."

Quinn's gaze turned hopeful, and her rigid posture became more relaxed.

Alistair sucked in a ragged breath, his head jerking up as he said, "Thank you. If our positions were reversed, I'm not sure I'd be so forgiving."

"Well, let's not forget the part where we did successfully save her soul," Quinn said. "I think we deserve a little credit for that if nothing else."

"If you're looking for a gold star, I'm fresh out," Lina said.

Quinn grinned. "There's my Queen E."

The need to correct her was fierce, but Lina managed to swallow the words. What she remembered of the girl she used to be wasn't exactly filling her with the warm and fuzzies. In so many ways, she'd been sheltered and spoiled by her family, knowing only what they wanted her to and never stopping to question what she'd been told. Her world had been so small and she, utterly oblivious. She may look the same, but she wasn't that girl anymore. Her eyes were wide open now, and there was no going back.

Getting murdered had a way of changing one's perspective.

Her head pounded from the onslaught of memories and questions battling for her attention. It was too much to try to sort through, let alone process. That would have to come later, once she was alone. For now, she decided to start with something simple.

"So," she said, glancing between Alistair and Quinn, "how long have I been . . . gone?"

"It's been almost twenty-seven years to the day since we found you in that basement," Alistair said.

Finley let out a low whistle. "The heirs were first reported missing around that same time."

"What heirs?" Nord asked.

"The heirs of the Mobius Council," her uncle answered. "It's comprised of five families—The Cuskas, Drakes, Satori, Thortons, and Alinari. Each family holds one seat on the Council. Lina is the heir to the Cuska seat. Mataius was the heir to the Drake's."

"Was?"

Her uncle nodded. "Additional security measures were put into place after Lina's death. When Mataius couldn't be located, we assumed all the heirs were under attack and sent the others away for their own safety."

"What's so special about the heirs?" Nord asked. "Why would anyone want to target them specifically?"

"It has to do with the way our kind inherit power," Lina answered.

If anyone else was surprised that she was the one providing the answer, no one's expression gave them away. The novelty of it wasn't lost on her though. It was a nice change of pace.

"What do you mean 'your kind'?" Finley asked.

"We're animagi," Lina said as if that should be answer enough.

Finley snorted, clearly thinking she was joking. When no one else joined in, his expression sobered and he said, "I always thought they were a myth."

Lina raised a brow at him. "Myths all stem from somewhere. Surely, your Brotherhood with their renowned archives must know that."

Nord smothered a grin with his hand. Quinn, however, didn't bother hiding her amusement.

"First of all, the extent of my knowledge does not represent that of the Brotherhood as a whole. Secondly, I think I might have liked you better before you knew who you were," Finley said lightly, his slight smile removing any potential sting from his words.

"To be fair, that rumor is intentional. We are the ones who started it," Alistair said.

"Fair enough, but since my knowledge is clearly lacking"—Finley shot Lina a droll look—"would you mind filling me in?"

Alistair eyed the bartender as he considered the request.

"Don't worry about her," Quinn said. "I'll take care of it before we leave."

Translation: she'd remove the woman's memory of them being here. Whatever she happened to overhear would be forgotten before it could ever be shared.

"I am here to answer my niece's questions, but so long as she doesn't mind a brief history lesson . . ."

"By all means," Lina said, waving a hand for him to proceed. She wasn't in a hurry to find out why he and Quinn had felt it necessary to bury her alive. Maybe she should have been, but her mind was already overflowing with regained information as it was.

Her permission seemed to satisfy whatever lingering doubts her uncle might have had. He turned his attention to Finley and Nord.

"Animagi are an ancient magical race whose ancestors walked this earth long before the dinosaurs. Our power is not simply elemental. It stems from creation itself, evolving from the animal counterparts we share an affinity with." Alistair pointed to himself and then Lina. "Cuska, snake. Satori," he continued, pointing to Quinn, "sphinx. And so on."

"So you are all, what, shifters? Or do you mind-meld with animals or something?" Finley asked.

"Some of us can shift. It's rarer to have a connection—what you refer to as mind-melding—with a familiar, but both are more the exception than the rule," Alistair explained. "Our gifts are less specific than that. The power manifests differently in all of us though certain abilities seem to stay within family lines. The Satori's power is tied to intelligence and mentalism, but memory weaving, for example, is a rare and powerful gift that only appears once every hundred years or so."

"All Satori have some kind of mental ability, but not all are memory weavers," Nord summarized.

"Exactly."

Finley smirked. "Bum luck, Lina."

"Excuse me?"

"Out of all the animals you could have been tied to, you got paired with a snake. Hardly exciting."

It was Lina's turn to smirk. "Really? Why do you think one of the oldest stories in the world centers around a snake in a garden? I wouldn't underestimate me if I were you."

Finley's eyebrows flew up. "Touché."

"Quite right." Alistair winked at her. "Our family has given rise to some of the most powerful animagi of all time."

"What's the Cuska line known for?" Nord asked.

"We have the ability to change the world," Alistair said with a small shrug.

Quinn rolled her eyes. "Please. Overstating much? You create things with magic; that doesn't make them real. There is nothing more real than what someone believes to be true. Come talk to me when you can control that," she said, adding under her breath, "pretentious prick."

Lina snorted. The five families had always fought over whose gifts were most impressive.

"We are best known for our transformational and regenerative abilities. It's similar to what you do as a Guardian," Lina said softly to Nord. "Except, where you change the nature of something that already exists, those in my family can create something out of nothing. The bigger the item, the more power required. Many of my ancestors were gifted healers, the best of which were able to bring men and women back from the very brink of death. It is even rumored that some were able to achieve true mastery over death, only crossing over to the next life because they wanted to."

"Selective immortality?" Finley breathed.

Lina shrugged. "I've never heard it referred to as such, but sure. Well, apparently. It's hard to confirm something I've never witnessed. So you see," she said, giving Finley a mocking smile, "we snakes may not seem as impressive as the majestic sphinx, but our ability to control and manipulate reality makes us one hell of an opponent."

Finley gave Lina a considering look. "So it would seem. Glad we're on the same side."

It looked like he wanted to say something else, but Alistair interjected, steering the conversation away from the Cuska line and back to Nord's original question regarding why anyone would want to harm the heirs.

"As I was saying, the Mobius Council is comprised of the five remaining animagi families. Our power is passed down from generation to generation. When a new generation comes into their power, they replace the previous Council members."

"And by 'come into', he means inherit," Quinn explained. "The bulk of a family's particular branch of magic resides in the patriarch or matriarch of each family. That power flows into their heir during their Awakening."

Alistair nodded and added, "If an heir is killed before the Awakening is complete, the power dies with them. It's essentially magical genocide, and it's why we started the rumors that our kind were extinct. Animagi have always been very powerful. Many do not like knowing we exist in the world, so they hunt us. Pretending to be basic—albeit strong—mages is how we've survived until now."

"And this is what you think happened to Lina? Mataius killed her before she could inherit her full power?" Nord asked.

"That is what we assumed. Although, that was before we found out Mataius was her murderer. Lina hadn't shown any signs of entering her Awakening. So if his intention was to cripple the entire line, Mataius struck too soon. But he would have known that. As an heir himself, he would have been intimately aware of the signs of the Awakening and would have known to wait if that was indeed what he was after."

Goosebumps formed along Lina's arms and neck as she recalled Mataius' dark ritual. She was transported back to that basement, her heart pounding in time with the drums while the sound of chanting filled her ears.

"Is there a way to induce the Awakening?" she asked, interrupting the conversation taking place around her.

"None that I know of," Alistair said, his eyes flashing behind his glasses as his head spun back to her. "Why do you ask?"

She shivered, her voice hollow as she said, "Mataius' ritual had to serve some greater purpose. Perhaps he discovered a way."

Alistair shook his head. "It's not possible, Mataius doesn't have that kind of power."

"Mataius didn't act alone. He had help. The magic they used, it wasn't like anything I'd ever seen . . ." Lina trailed off and shivered again.

Nord pressed his leg against hers beneath the table, offering her his strength.

Lina blinked rapidly, forcing herself to focus on the present and finish her thought. "It was dark—twisted."

Alistair frowned, clearly disturbed. "If he did manage to initiate the Awakening, your father would have been severely weakened by the magic transfer, but his power was unaffected. Unless," he said, his voice dropping as his mind worked through the possibility, "the fact that your spirit was bound to the earth kept the ritual from being completed . . ."

Out of the corner of her eye, Lina caught Nord and Finley exchanging a pointed glance. She was willing to bet they were carrying on a conversation of their own via their telepathic link. Given the topic of conversation and last night's events, she was pretty sure she knew what they were discussing, too. She'd made the same connection herself.

Regardless of when it started—with Mataius' ritual or her spirit's return to her body—last night was the culmination.

Her Awakening.

It hadn't been her magic that had returned to her. Well, not just her magic. She'd inherited the full reservoir of her family's power.

Lina was no longer an heir.

She was now the head of the Cuska family and, as such, the rightful leader of the Mobius Council.

Not ready to explore what that meant for her—or if she even wanted to claim her birthright—Lina changed the topic. "Speaking of my father, where is he anyway?"

Quinn stiffened, her eyes darting to Alistair, who awkwardly started to clear his throat. They exchanged an uneasy glance before Alistair's eyes shifted back to Lina's face.

That single act told her everything she needed to know.

Feeling numb, she answered her own question, "He's dead."

"Sweetling, I'm so sorry—"

Lina shook her head, cutting off his flow of words. She and her father had never been close. Any love and fatherly affection she'd received in her childhood had been provided by her uncle.

Anatoly Cuska had never forgiven his daughter for her mother Katarina's death. Nor had he wasted an opportunity to let her know that her only value in his life was the blood running through her veins. As his only child, she'd always been the future leader of their family. Much to his disappointment.

He must be turning in his grave right now.

Conflicting emotions surged up within her. A child's desire to please her father. A heartbroken girl's pain due to constant rejection. A woman's grief at the loss of a parent.

Lina balled her hands into fists and trapped them between her knees to hide her trembling. Nord's knee brushed against hers, reminding her once more that he was there. That she was not facing any of this alone.

"When?" she asked, proud that her voice remained steady.

"Two years after you," her uncle said. "It was an assassination. I believe, but could never prove, that the Drakes were behind it."

"Wait, you're saying you think someone connected to the Mobius Council assassinated their own leader?" Finley asked.

"I am," Alistair confirmed. "It's why I gave up my seat. A cover-up of that magnitude would require inside help. First, Evalina and then, my brother . . ." He shrugged. "I no longer trusted anyone."

"With me dead and you and my father gone, who's holding the Cuska seat on the Council?" Lina asked.

"Your cousin Nikoli."

Lina frowned, trying to place a face to the name, but all she had was a hazy memory of a little boy covered in dirt.

"What do you think about all this?" Finley asked Quinn.

"I think the Drakes have always abhorred the power dynamics of the Council. The Satori have a long memory, but the other families have forgotten why the Council was formed in the first place."

"Care to elaborate on that for the rest of us?" Finley asked.

"Not really."

Silence stretched as they stared at one another.

Meanwhile, Lina's head throbbed. She wasn't sure how much longer she could sit here. Her brain felt like it was seconds away from imploding. Between what had happened the night before with her magic returning and then today with her memories, she'd put a lot of strain on her body.

"Wait," Finley said, looking at Quinn accusingly, "something you said isn't adding up. If Lina really has been dead for almost thirty years, you should be in your fifties."

"Look at you, already up to double-digit addition in your head. Well done," Quinn said, folding her arms across her chest and leaning back against the wall. "Would you like to try subtraction now?"

Finley glared at her. "Why haven't you aged?"

"Animagi possess an extended lifespan," Alistair answered. "Our physical aging slows significantly in our mid-twenties, and we don't tend to look like this," he gestured to himself, "until well into our second century."

"So thirty years wouldn't make much of a difference, physically speaking," Nord said.

"Not unless they were glamoured as I was," Alistair confirmed.

Finley frowned, still unhappy about something. "Okay, that explains the looks, but what about your magic? Shouldn't you have inherited the rest of it by now? Entered your Awakening or whatever? Why haven't you—or any of the other heirs for that matter—replaced your parents on the Council?"

Quinn blew out a breath, looking bored. "Not that it's any of your business, but I requested a suppression spell. All the heirs did. The Awakening can be . . . intense. It leaves us weakened, magically, until the power stabilizes. None of us wanted to be a bunch of sitting ducks if there really was a threat out there. It was safer to wait. Besides," she said, her voice softening as she turned to Lina, "we didn't know when you might return, and I didn't want to be chained to the Council if you needed me."

She reached out and gripped Lina's wrist, squeezing tightly.

"I know you may not believe me, but everything your uncle and I did, it was to keep you safe. Lina, when we found you—" she broke off, pain shining in her eyes. "It was the worst day of my life. Seeing you like that . . . burying you. The only thing that helped me get through it was knowing that you'd be back. That we would seek vengeance. That's all I've ever wanted, and when I saw you last night —" She blew out a watery breath. "It took everything in me not to throw my arms around you and weep like a child. When I performed that spell, I knew the damage was bad, that it would take time for your soul and body to rejoin, but I never imagined you'd be gone so long."

Tears pricked her eyes, and Lina's throat got tight. "I believe you."

Quinn dipped her head, her eyes falling closed as a tear spilled down her cheek. "I'm so sorry that you thought, even for a second, our burying you was malicious. If there'd been any other way to save you, we would have done it. But I swear it was the only way. I could not love you more if you were my blood."

"I know."

Quinn threw her arms around Lina, hugging her hard. "I'm so happy you're back. The world is a truly boring place without my partner in crime."

Lina returned the embrace, giving in to the tidal wave of emotion that had been threatening to overtake her since her memories returned. Her eyes blurred from her tears, and her shoulders shook from some combination of sobs and laughter.

Lina blew out a breath as she pulled away, exhaustion tugging at her. The last few hours—days, really—had been a rollercoaster of emotion, and she could no longer hold the effects of it at bay. She started to sway where she stood, and Nord's hand shot out to steady her.

"We should get you home," he said.

She nodded her agreement and then let out a muttered curse.

Nord raised a brow. "Something wrong?"

"I left a driver waiting for me outside. I'd completely forgotten about him until you mentioned going home."

"Fin, see if he's still there, and make sure he's appropriately compensated," Nord ordered softly. "And get his card. Never hurts to have a driver on the payroll."

"On it," Finley said, heading for the door.

"You have everything you need?" Nord asked her.

"Wait, you can't leave yet. There's still so much more she needs to know," Alistair protested.

"Look at her. She's barely able to stay upright. Is there anything you need to tell her that can't wait until tomorrow? Any immediate danger that she's in without this information?" Nord asked.

"She's right here and can speak for herself," Lina muttered.

Nord ignored her, but Quinn caught her eye and smirked.

Alistair considered the question before shaking his head. "No, nothing that can't wait a day or two."

"Good. Then I'm taking her home so she can rest. She'll let you know when she's ready to continue with your conversation."

Lina opened her mouth to say that she didn't have a way to get in touch with either of them, but Nord was already holding his phone out to Quinn.

"If you give me your numbers, I'll make sure they get programmed into her phone as well." His eyes flashed as they caught hers. A not-so-subtle reminder that she was still due a lecture about losing her phone. Again.

Her uncle finished inputting his information and handed the phone back to Nord, but his eyes were leveled on her. "Until tomorrow, then."

Alistair had been reserved this whole time, keeping his distance until she gave some sign that she was ready. She could see that it was costing him. Leaning down, she wrapped her arms around him.

His body trembled in her hold, but he didn't waste a second before returning the hug with his own. His voice was gruff as he whispered, "I look forward to getting to know the woman that you are now, but I want you to know that I could not be more proud of the little I've seen so far."

Hot tears trickled down her face. Approval. Acceptance. Unconditional love. It was a balm to her wounded heart. If there was any residual anger left, those words erased it. But, deep down, Lina knew she'd already decided to forgive him before she sat back down.

Too overwhelmed for words, Lina pressed a kiss to her uncle's stubbled cheek, knowing he would understand the gesture for what it was. After a moment, she stepped back and placed her hand in Nord's.

"Let's go home."

CHAPTER THREE
NORD

Nord's eyes flicked up to the rearview mirror, seeking out Lina's sleeping form in the backseat. She'd curled up and drifted off almost immediately once the car was in motion.

"How's she look?" Finley asked softly, eyes focused on the road in front of him.

"Exhausted, her sleep seems peaceful though."

"Hardly surprising after everything she's been through." Nord allowed his eyes to caress her reflection a moment longer before training them on his partner. "How much of what was said tonight did you already know?"

"Not as much as I'd have liked, but they did confirm a few things I'd already suspected."

"Such as?"

"The division within the Council. That Anatoly's death wasn't due to natural means. That the truth about their abilities is only the tip of the iceberg when it comes to their secrets."

"Do you think Alistair and Quinn are hiding something?"

"From Lina or from us?" Finley asked.

"Either."

He considered the question. "No. Not intentionally. He made it pretty clear there was more he wanted her to know, and he didn't seem to have any qualms speaking freely in front of us."

Nord hummed his agreement. He'd sensed the same. "Any guesses as to what else he wanted to tell her?"

"Could be anything," Finley said. "If I had to guess, I'd say it might have something to do with why she was targeted. But he was genuinely surprised to learn about Mataius' involvement, so I'm not sure how much insight he has into the events leading up to or surrounding her death."

"What do you know about the ex-fiancé, other than he comes from a family of murderers?" Nord forced the question from his lips, his rage spiking to dangerous levels at the thought of the man who dared betray Lina.

"Mataius?"

Nord gave a terse nod. Just the bastard's name had his beast rattling its chains.

"As much as I know about the other heirs, which is to say very little."

They were silent for a moment before Nord asked, "What about the other two families?"

"The Thortons and the Alinari. The Thortons are pretty quiet, the Alinari less so. When a body shows up, the Alinari are usually behind it."

"And their heirs?"

"Naya Thorton and Emmerson Alinari."

Nord stared expectantly for a few seconds before he realized Finley wasn't going to say anything else. "That's it? That's all you've got on them?"

Finley shot him an annoyed glance. "What do you want me to say, mate? They're names in a file. I already told you they disappeared without a trace a few decades back. That's the extent of what my clearance covers. Everything else is redacted and may as well not exist as far as I'm concerned. I don't know if you've figured it out yet, but this is big shit we've stepped in. Any information we get from here on out is going to have to come from the source."

They both looked back at Lina. It was hard to picture her as the daughter of a well-known criminal, let alone as the heiress to an underworld kingdom.

"What are we going to do about Mataius?"

"Is that an actual question?" Nord asked, eyes flashing as his head snapped back to his friend.

Finley rolled his eyes and hit the turn signal. "He's a dead man, obviously. But we have to find him before we can kill him. Outside of Lina spotting him at the ball, no one has seen him in decades. That's one cold trail for us to follow."

"Someone has to know something. Maybe someone inside the Council?"

Finley snorted. "Someone willing to talk to us? Doubtful."

"People can be persuaded," Nord said, his voice holding a violent edge.

"I doubt, even with your methods of 'persuasion,' we could make one of them talk to us."

"What about Quinn or Alistair? Surely, they have viable contacts."

"Quinn . . . maybe. Alistair? That's a harder call. He betrayed them when he faked his death and became an informant for the Brotherhood."

"It's worth asking, at the very least."

Finley nodded. "It's a starting point if nothing else." They drove in silence for a few blocks before Finley asked, "Do you think she has any idea how much danger she's in?"

Nord's eyes returned to Lina's slumbering form. "I don't know. But she has something far worse in her life than anything out there waiting for her in the shadows."

"What's that?"

"Me."

"The weapon they never see coming?" Finley asked.

Nord's lips curled in a feral grin. "Exactly." His thumb brushed over the cool surface of one of his rings. "I think it's well past time I added a new trophy to my collection."

The car slowed, and Finley clicked a button to open the metal gate protecting the entrance to their private garage.

"Did you ever stop to think that she might be powerful enough to handle things herself?" Finley asked, his voice more curious than combative.

"Doesn't matter. My being hers means she'll never have to."

NORD ADJUSTED HIS HOLD ON LINA, TWISTING HIS SHOULDERS AND ANGLING his body sideways so that he could squeeze them both through the door to her room without smacking against anything.

She made a soft sound, and he winced, worried he'd woken her with all his jostling. When he glanced down to check, he was half-expecting to find her looking up at him, but her eyes remained closed.

Straightening, he crossed the room in a handful of measured strides, coming to a stop beside the bed. Supporting her full weight with one arm, he tugged the comforter down. That done, he slowly lowered her to the bed, carefully untangling her arms from around his neck.

He allowed his fingers to trail along the exposed skin from her elbow to the tips of her fingers as he lifted, not quite ready to leave her side. He had to admit she looked peaceful lying there with her hair fanned out on the pillow like a golden cloud, her lips slightly parted as she took deep, even breaths. The two purple crescents beneath each of her eyes were the only hints of her inner turmoil.

Remembering that she still wore her boots, Nord deftly removed them and set them on the floor beside the bed. That done, his eyes returned to her face, wanting to confirm one final time that she was still resting easily.

He knew he should leave her, that right now sleep was the one thing she needed above all else, but he was loathe to do it. Selfish as that was.

After everything they'd been through, the one thing he needed right now was her. Her in his arms, the feel of her heartbeat against his hand, the soft sound of her breaths filling his ears—each one a reminder that she was alive. That she was safe.

That she was his.

But her needs, as always, came before his own. So instead of lying down beside her and curling his body around hers as he desperately wished to, he pushed the need away and settled for letting his knuckles graze her cheek.

That small touch was not quite enough to sate him though, so he bent down and gently brushed his lips against her forehead.

"Sleep well, Kærasta," he whispered, pausing with his lips against her velvety skin to breathe in the honey-and-lavender scent of her before finally forcing himself to stand and turn away.

Her hand shot out and gripped his wrist, halting his movement.

"Stay," she whispered.

"You're supposed to be sleeping."

"Sleep and I have a troubled history."

His lips twitched, and he turned back. "How so?"

"We don't like each other very much. Sleep's like the little boy in grade school who pulled my pigtails and tripped me. Basically, it kicks my ass under the guise of innocence."

"Need me to beat it up?"

"Definitely."

Nord was smiling as he climbed into the bed next to her. He reclined against the pillows, lifting an arm so she could curl into his side and rest her head on his chest. Once she was settled, he wrapped his arm around her waist, allowing his hand to idly trace random patterns against her skin.

"Afraid the nightmares will return?" he asked after a moment.

Lina sighed. "Maybe. Mostly, I'm tired of being in my own head. There's a whole lot of me in there right now. A whole lot of everything, really."

"It must feel a bit like another person took up residence inside your mind."

Lina craned her neck to peer up at him. "You sound like you're speaking from experience."

"I'm no stranger to having someone else's memories in my head. It's unsettling, to say the least."

"Yes, that's it exactly. Like, I know they are mine, but it feels like everything I remember happened to someone else. The only memories that actually feel like they belong to me are the ones involving you."

Her words washed over him, warming him from the inside out. His free hand lifted to curl around her neck. "We have that in common then."

She held his stare, her pulse spiking beneath his palm. "I find that hard to believe."

"Lina, I may have existed for centuries, but that's all it was. Existing. Until I found you, I didn't know what it meant to be alive. Don't you see? Everything I've done has led me here, to this moment. To you." He ran his thumb along her bottom lip. "I was born to be yours."

Her lips parted on a soft exhale, and tears shimmered in her eyes. "Nord, I—"

He shifted, swallowing her words with his kiss. Each brush of his lips over hers was a promise, an echo of the vow he made the first night they met. He would be her protector. Her weapon. Her lover. Anything and everything she needed him to be. His body—his soul —was hers to use however she saw fit.

Until she drew her last breath.

She protested as he pulled away. "Wait. Don't stop."

He rested his forehead against hers, his eyes trained on her swollen lips as he willed his thundering heart to slow.

"If I don't stop now—"

"Who's asking you to?"

He chuckled, and his left arm tightened around her waist while he ran his fingers down the side of her face with his other hand. "There's nothing I want more than to finish what we started last night, but what you need right now is rest."

"But—"

He cut her off with a swift kiss. "Sleep, Lina. We have plenty of time. The rest of our lives, in fact. But to say you've been through a lot in the last twenty-four hours might be the understatement of a lifetime. Give yourself time to recover and adjust." He tipped her chin up, forcing her to meet his gaze as his voice dropped to just above a whisper. "When I claim you, I'm going to spend hours worshipping your body. First with my hands, then with my mouth. I'll make you cry out my name as you come at least half a dozen times before I ever slide into you. So you see, my Lina. I need you rested. I need you whole. With what I have planned for us, I'll accept nothing less."

Her eyes were glazed, and her skin flushed when she finally managed a reply. "Sweet mother of God, you don't do anything by half measure, do you?"

"Not when it comes to loving you."

She tilted her chin up for a kiss, and he obliged. Unfortunately, with the way his body immediately reacted and demanded more, he was forced to pull back far sooner than he wanted to. Settling back into the pillows, he pressed her head back to his chest.

She toyed with his rings. "Nord?"

"Hmm?"

"Will you keep talking to me?"

"About what?"

"I don't care. Anything as long as it's not about me. As soon as it gets quiet, my mind starts racing. I just . . . want to shut the voices up for a while."

He squeezed her once and kissed the top of her head. "I can do that."

She let out a relieved breath. "Thank you."

His fingers played with her hair while he searched for a topic.

"My father took me on my first hunt when I was nine years old. There was a wild boar that had killed one of the villager's children. It was his duty to see that the threat would not claim any other innocent lives. I was big for my age and foolishly thought of myself as more man than boy. I begged my father to let me take care of it. I wanted to do something for the people that would one day be mine, prove my worth as their future leader.

"He didn't say anything at first when I asked, just stared at me in this iconic way of his. Like he was weighing and measuring me by thought alone. Finally, he looked straight into my eyes and asked me, 'Are you ready to take a life?' I laughed. Told him of course I was, that this was a beast that deserved to die; it would be an honor to do so."

Nord paused, shaking his head at his youthful ignorance. His fingers remained in her hair, stroking the strands as he continued.

"My father had to explain that all creatures acted on instinct and that the boar, while a mere beast to us, was probably frightened and trying to defend itself or its family. He asked me whether I would condemn someone from our village to death if they killed in order to protect their young from an intruder. 'Of course not!' I answered, horrified by the idea. That's when my father placed one hand on my shoulder, leaning down until our eyes were level, and asked, 'Then how can you condemn any creature to death for doing the same?'

"I was stunned. Nine years old, and he'd just rocked my entire world. 'Why must we kill him then?' I'd asked. My father explained that just as the beast must protect its family, so too did we. But that before one ever takes a life, they must first understand what it was they were doing. The weight of the act. 'All life has value and purpose. If you do not honor it, you are not worthy of ending it.' It was one of the most important lessons he ever taught me."

Nord fell silent, the sound of their mingled breathing the only noise in the room for several heartbeats.

"After that, we went on our hunt. My father showed me the proper way to take a life. How to end it as painlessly as possible. Later, I would learn how to prolong it. How to make it hurt. But that day, I learned mercy. Once he deemed me ready, he sent me to deal with the boar on my own. Afterward, when it was done, he showed me his rings. Told me how each one represented an important battle fought and a life taken. He pointed to the smallest, the one he wore around his neck, and told me about the time my grandfather had helped him craft it after he returned from his first hunt. Then, he did the same with me."

"He sounds like a wonderful man," Lina said.

"He was."

"What did he think of you joining the Brotherhood?"

"He was not alive to witness it. Although, I like to think he'd be proud. I joined shortly after he was killed. My heart was too filled with anger and the need for bloodshed to be the kind of leader my people deserved. After seeing that his death was avenged, I stepped aside."

"What did the rest of your family have to say about that?"

His hand went still on her head. "They were not around either."

Lina breathed heavily. "Oh."

"It was a long time ago."

She moved her arm so that she could weave her fingers through the ones he rested on her hip. "Time doesn't negate loss. It just helps us learn to live with it." She swallowed. "I never knew my mother. She died giving birth to me."

"I'm sorry about that."

"So was my father. Actually, enraged is a better word than sorry. I don't think he was sorry for a single thing in his life."

Nord swore at himself. Here he was supposed to be providing a mindless distraction, and he was inadvertently dredging up painful memories. "I'm sorry, I didn't mean to poke at old wounds. It was just the first story I could think to share."

"No, no. You didn't. I promise. It's a great story. I love getting to know more about you. Will you tell me another?"

"Are you sure?"

"Definitely."

Comfortable silence stretched between them as Nord considered and dismissed various possibilities. Eventually, with a soft chuckle, he asked, "Would you like to hear about the time my brother accidentally turned my father blue?"

Lina snickered. "Uh, yeah?"

Smiling, Nord cuddled her closer, his hushed voice filling the room, moving from one story to the next. Before long, the woman in his arms fell into a deep and peaceful sleep, but he kept talking to her just in case the sound of his voice staved off any potential nightmares.

It wasn't until the first rays of day shone through the window that his voice faltered and he finally joined her.

CHAPTER FOUR

LINA

A subtle tickle preceded the brush of something soft and warm on her cheek. Then again. Tickle. Warmth. Tickle. Warmth. It took Lina's sleep-fogged brain awhile to recognize the feel of Nord's beard scraping her skin as he trailed kisses along her jaw and down her neck.

Fully alert now, she pretended to still be asleep to see how long she could draw out the moment. His kisses were languid as he continued to pepper them over her skin. He began alternating between little nips and kisses, using his tongue to soothe any sting as he moved lower.

"I know you're awake," he murmured once he reached the hollow of her throat.

"No, I'm not."

He chuckled, the sound rolling through her like quiet thunder. "Ah, that's too bad. I was hoping we could have breakfast in bed." He pressed an open-mouth kiss right above her collarbone. "I thought you could be the main course."

Fuck. Yes.

Her eyes flew open. "I'm awake."

Nord's eyes lifted, twinkling with laughter as he brushed his lips lower. Her breath hitched when he grabbed the top of her tank with his teeth and started tugging the white cotton down.

Then, all hell broke loose—and not in the 'Nord is having Lina for breakfast' kind of way.

Sirens rent through the air, their shrill screeches piercing the quiet stillness of the morning.

Lina's hands flew up to cover her ears. "What is that?"

Nord was already on his feet, weapon in hand. She hadn't seen him grab it, but the blanket was missing, so he must have used his magic to create it as he jumped off the bed.

"One of the wards has been breached," he told her, crossing the room to crack open the door and peer into the hallway. "Stay here while I check it out."

"The fuck I will." Lina had been alone most of her life. Now that she had Nord, she wasn't willingly letting him out of her sight any more than he'd let her out of his.

"Lina," he growled, spearing her with glowing azure eyes. "This is not the time to test me."

"Did you forget?" she asked, swinging her legs over the side of the bed. "I'm not useless anymore. I can help. I've got my power back."

"Untested power."

She threw her hands up. "What does that matter? Magic is magic. I can be an asset."

"We aren't having this conversation right now. Sit your ass down, and stay here. I'll deal with it."

Lina cocked a brow and placed her hands on her hips, ready to unleash on him. The siren cut off, and the sound of racing footsteps preempted her rant.

Nord twisted to face the door, using his body to shield hers.

"You guys okay in there?" Finley called, his voice just loud enough to be heard over the ringing in her ears.

Some of the tension in Nord's shoulders eased.

"Yeah," he called back.

"It was the elevator's ward. Someone's on their way up here. I'm heading to the door to intercept them."

"I'll go with you," Nord said, pushing the door farther open.

"Me too," Lina said.

"Lina—"

"Try to stop me again, Viking, and we'll both find out just what this untested power of mine can do."

He glowered at her, his eyes burning with blue fire. "Fine," he bit out, reaching out to fist a hand in the neck of her tank. He gave a sharp tug, and she stumbled forward, going up on her tiptoes as his lips crashed into hers.

Much to her disappointment, the kiss ended as abruptly as it began.

"But for the love of Odin, stay back."

"S-sure thing," Lina stuttered, a little dazed as she followed a short distance behind them.

Finley and Nord exchanged a glance once they reached the front door. Nord gave a quick nod, and Finley pulled the door open just as the elevator chimed its arrival.

The Guardians moved into the reception area, weapons ready, while Lina stayed just inside the door, feeling like she'd forgotten how to breathe as she waited for the elevator to slide open.

Seconds crawled by, feeling like hours until the elevator's metal doors finally revealed its occupants.

It was hard to say who was more surprised. The trio prepared for battle or the two peering out of the elevator at them.

"Is this how you welcome all your visitors?" Quinn asked, stepping into the reception area.

"Only the uninvited ones," Finley snapped, lowering his gun.

Lina's uncle looked contrite, but Quinn's eyes traveled to Nord, and she smirked. "Nice ax."

His lip curled in a snarl. "If you think that's my only weapon, you'll be dead before you realize your mistake."

Quinn winked at him, totally unfazed by the threat. She shifted her attention to Lina, breaking out into a full-blown grin as she took in her disheveled state. "Morning, sunshine. Did we interrupt your" —her eyes darted between Lina and her Guardian, and her smile turned wicked—"beauty sleep?"

Lina could feel the heat flooding her cheeks and knew she was probably crimson. She hadn't given any thought to her sleep-matted hair or the rumpled state of her clothes when the threat of danger loomed.

At least she wasn't naked.

"We're sorry to have intruded so early," Alistair said.

Clearing her throat, Lina lifted one shoulder in a nonchalant shrug. "You didn't. I was actually just about to have breakfast."

One of Quinn's brows lifted in amusement. "I'm sure you were."

Finley saved Lina from having to respond.

"How did you two even get up here?" he asked, scrubbing a hand over his face.

Quinn held up her index finger. "I . . ." she trailed off on a dramatic pause, "pushed the button."

Finley groaned as Quinn started laughing. "Hate to break it to you, Guardian, but an elevator is hardly a sophisticated security system. If that was supposed to stump us, you might want to reconsider."

"No one but the three of us should be able to access this floor unescorted," he replied tightly.

Quinn shrugged, feigning innocence. "I don't know what to tell you then. Must have been magic!" She wiggled her fingers for emphasis.

Finley's eyes narrowed. He was far from amused, and Lina found it hard not to smile. Quinn had always loved outsmarting their security teams when they were younger. She'd had a saying for it. Something about how penises weren't an asset but a weakness.

"Never trust anything that can be taken out by a nut shot," Lina whispered, remembering.

Quinn beamed. "Right? If men really were the superior creature, they wouldn't have something so delicate between their legs. Now, a vagina, those know how to take a pounding."

She was talking to Lina, but her eyes were trained on Finley, who was turning an interesting shade of purple.

Lina snorted. Quinn had always been unapologetically inappropriate, but witnessing her in action now, while two highly trained killers still held weapons that had just been drawn on her, was beyond unexpected. She wasn't sure if she should clap or throw her body in front of her oldest friend and plead her case.

Alistair coughed and dipped his chin, trying to hide his smile. This was familiar ground for him, having spent years overhearing similar conversations. He'd learned not to interfere when Quinn went off on one of her tirades. He tried, once, but Quinn's rather colorful comeback had him blushing so hard he'd never repeated the experience.

Finley and Nord were less prepared. Lina was pretty sure one of them would have knocked Quinn out by now had she been a man. As it was, they had to be contemplating the best way to shut her up.

Nord opted for taking control of the conversation. He turned to her uncle, his voice glacial as he asked, "What part of she'll call you when she's ready to talk did you not understand?"

Alistair shrugged. "The situation changed. When you left last night, you asked if what Lina didn't know was the difference between life and death. I didn't think so then. Now I do."

Any lingering mirth fled as reality came crashing back down around them. Even Quinn looked properly sobered by the words.

So much for breakfast.

With a sigh, Lina pushed the door all the way open. "Why don't you guys come inside? This sounds like a conversation I should be sitting down for."

"What changed between last night and this morning?" Nord asked once everyone was seated with their beverage of choice—black coffee for Nord and Finley, Earl Grey for Alistair, and water with lemon for Quinn. Lina's stomach was a ball of nerves, so she didn't trust herself with anything at the moment. A shot of tequila sounded promising though.

Alistair set his cup down carefully. "Well, we'd always assumed that Lina's death was inherently tied to her position as an heir. Learning that Mataius was her murderer made that unlikely. So I started to consider other potential motives."

Lina broke out in a cold sweat. Rubbing suddenly clammy palms on her knees, she leaned forward. "And? What did you come up with?"

"That," he said, pointing to the tattoo on her forearm.

Her eyebrows snapped together. "What?"

"Maybe I can help explain this one," Quinn said, tucking a long strand of black hair behind her ear.

"As long as someone does," Nord said.

"Cool your jets, Viking. I'm getting to it."

A vein in his neck throbbed in response.

"Yesterday, I mentioned there was a reason the Mobius Council originally formed. That," she said, mirroring Alistair and pointing to Lina's tattoo, "is the reason. The Ouroboros Prism."

Lina searched her memory banks but came up empty. Nord and Finley looked equally confused.

"I'm sorry, was that supposed to mean something?" she asked.

Quinn gave her an apologetic smile. "Not if I did my job correctly, which I'm guessing by your expression I did."

There was a beat of silence, and then what she said clicked. "You removed the memory."

Quinn nodded. "You can't tell someone something you don't know."

Her voice was casual, but the implication behind the words was so dark that Lina shuddered. There was only one scenario where she would unwillingly tell someone something that she was supposed to keep secret.

Torture.

Nord must have reached the same conclusion. He all but vibrated with tension as he snapped, "Speak plainly."

"We needed a hiding place. Lina as the future head of the Council was ideal," Quinn said.

"Wait, back up. I feel like I'm missing a large piece of the puzzle here. What exactly did you do?"

"*We* do," Quinn corrected.

"Quinn," she said, warning heavy in her voice, "I love you like a sister, but if you don't tell me what the fuck is going on, I'm going to stab you in the eye."

"So violent," she muttered. "The berserker is rubbing off on you —and not in the fun way."

"Quinn."

This time, it was Alistair with the note of censure in his voice. He shook his head and then said, "The Mobius Council formed to protect the secrets of the animagi, specifically the Prism. It is the last of the original animagi artifacts, and its power is unparalleled. In the wrong hands, it could be catastrophic. Rather than allow that to happen, the Council hid it to ensure that no one person could ever wield its power.

"In the year just prior to your death, I had . . . concerns that the safety of the artifact was in question. Your father was behaving irrationally, making comments about needing to protect it from the others on one hand and then turning around and suggesting he steal it and use it himself. Rather than risk either of those scenarios, I," Alistair paused and then grimaced. "Well, I beat my brother to the punch. I stole it, and with Quinn's help, I hid it . . ." His eyes bored into Lina's. "In you."

"*In* me?" She stared at the crystals inked into her skin. "My tattoo? So my memory of going with Quinn to get it is a plant? That never happened?"

Her uncle winced. "I'm sorry about that. It was my idea to use you to hide it. I needed Quinn to ensure that you never realized it. It was the only way to make sure no one could get their hands on it."

"How would Mataius have figured it out if you two are the only ones who knew where it was hidden?" Nord asked.

"I don't know," Alistair said with a deep frown. "But if he did, there's no telling how many others did as well."

"Call me crazy," Finley said, "but if he knew what the Prism looked like, wouldn't the tattoo be a bit of a giveaway?"

Alistair looked insulted. "As if I would do something so foolish. Not that it would have mattered. Until I stole it, no one, save the original Council members, had set eyes upon the Prism." His expression turned considering. "But, assuming Mataius did somehow figure out where I'd hidden the artifact, he must have thought Lina's death would negate the spell concealing the Prism. What he couldn't have realized, though, was that by its very nature, the Prism would keep her from truly dying."

Lina blinked. That was . . . a lot. Instead of trying to understand the whole, she focused on the one detail that confused her the most.

"If that's the case, why did Quinn have to"—she waved her hands around—"do whatever it is she did when you guys buried me? I thought you were the ones who made it so I would come back?"

"I mean, we did. Technically," Quinn said. She blew out a breath, looking frustrated. "Think of it this way. What we did ensured that you would still be *you*."

Lina shook her head, feeling frustrated herself. "I'm not following."

Alistair leaned forward. "Perhaps it would be easier to understand what she's trying to say if you knew more about the Prism itself."

Great. More information to try to shove inside her already overstuffed head. She gestured for him to continue.

"Do you know what an ouroboros is?"

"It's a circle, right? Usually depicted by a snake swallowing its tail."

"Or a dragon," Quinn muttered.

Alistair shot her a look, and she mimed zipping her lips.

Returning his attention to Lina, he said, "Exactly, it's an infinite loop. The Prism is so named because it is an object of pure magical potential, infinite in its capability. It absorbs magical energy, stores it —almost like a battery—so that it can be used later. But, unlike a battery, the Prism can never be depleted. Once absorbed by the Prism, that magic will always exist within it. And not just that, it can also be accessed by whoever uses the Prism. Do you understand what that means?"

She swallowed. "I think so. Whoever is in control of the Prism can tap into all the power it has absorbed over the centuries. They'd have unlimited access to a never-ending supply of magical energy."

Alistair nodded grimly. "And so you understand why it needed to be kept hidden. Why I couldn't take the chance someone would get their hands on it?"

Lina nodded. No one should have that much power. The potential for misuse was too high.

"Well, as you can imagine, hiding an object with that much power is no easy feat. It took the combined efforts of all five animagi families to create a box capable of muting its signature. I had to get a bit more creative since I did not have their resources. So instead of muting it, I realized I needed to disguise it."

"I get the feeling we're not talking glasses and a mustache here," Finley said.

Alistair glared at him.

"Sorry," he said, but it lacked sincerity.

When Finley winked at her, she realized the joke had been for her benefit. She smiled at him before returning her attention to her uncle.

"So how do you disguise something like the Prism?" she asked.

Nord shocked her by answering. "You make it appear like something else." At her confused look, he continued, "Do you remember when I told you all magic leaves a trace?"

She nodded.

"It's sort of like planting someone else's DNA at a crime scene. If you can muddy the trace so that it appears to have originated from a different source, then you can throw someone off-track."

"Is that even possible?" she asked.

Nord nodded. "An artifact like the one your uncle described would take on the magical signature of whoever's power it absorbed. Once combined with someone, it would be almost impossible to tell its magic apart from the original magic owner—even for a Guardian—because they are ultimately the same."

"Like a clone," Lina said.

"Precisely," Alistair said. "The only way to hide it was to make it appear like there was nothing there at all. It had to blend in."

"By seeming like it was just my magic," she said.

He nodded.

"So you, what, fed it some of my power?" she asked.

"Well, it's a little more complicated than that. You see, I didn't just create the illusion of the tattoo. The Prism is quite literally merged with you—like ink in your skin."

Lina felt a headache building behind her temples.

"Are you saying that *I* am the Prism?"

"No—" Her uncle laughed as if that was the funniest thing he'd ever heard. "Your body could never contain that much power. The Prism and the power it holds are still confined to its original form. You are simply the container it now resides in; two distinct objects that are in constant contact."

Lina relaxed a little. She didn't think she could deal with the mindfuck of being some kind of living artifact. It was just too out there.

"All right, that makes sense, I guess. So I'm not the Prism itself. I'm just the fancy new box it's hidden in."

Her uncle nodded, so she continued with her summarization.

"But the spell you used to camouflage the Prism's presence in me linked us together. And because of this magical coexistence, when Mataius tried to kill me, the Prism's power kept me alive?"

Alistair cleared his throat. "That is more physics than magic, actually. Energy is never destroyed, merely transformed. As a source of pure energy, the Prism cannot be destroyed. Since you and the Prism are bound to each other, the same currently goes for you."

"But I died."

"Your body died," Alistair corrected. "Your essence—or soul if you prefer—did not. You were simply existing in a different state."

"So if all of that was because of the Prism, what did you and Quinn do?"

"Your uncle took care of your body, and I handled your mind," Quinn said. "Together, we worked a spell that would allow your body to eventually return, and I took your memories so that while you existed separate from it, you didn't go batshit crazy. You're welcome, by the way."

Lina stared at them. It was an incredible turn of events. There's no telling what would have happened if they hadn't gotten to her in time.

"Well . . . fuck," she finally said, shaking her head. "Let me make sure I got all of this. I'm alive—but probably shouldn't be. The Prism is fused to me. Mataius might not be the only one who wants me dead to get their hands on it. Is there anything else I'm missing?"

"I think that about sums it up," Alistair said.

"Great, in that case, I need a drink."

CHAPTER FIVE
LINA

Lina returned to the living room in time to hear Finley ask, "So were you the ones responsible for the curse that killed that saleswoman?"

Alistair sighed. "Standard protective measure, I'm afraid. Anyone who works for the Mobius Council receives it to ensure they never repeat information they shouldn't."

"I'm sorry, was I not clear that we're now on the drinking stage of this impromptu family reunion?" Lina asked, an open bottle of tequila hanging from her hand. "You want to drop more bombs, count me out. I'm at capacity for the decade."

Not waiting for them to reply, she took a deep swig straight from the bottle.

"You planning on sharing that?" Quinn asked.

Lina eyed her. "That depends. You gonna make me talk about serious shit?"

"Nope."

She handed Quinn the bottle. "Bottoms up."

Quinn accepted the bottle with a wide smile and took a deep pull before handing it back.

"You sure that's a good idea?" Nord asked.

"I think the question you meant to ask was: Do I care?" Lina said, lifting the bottle back up to her lips for another sip. "I think I've earned a bit of a break, don't you?"

Nord looked conflicted. "If that's what you want," he finally said.

Lina smirked, the alcohol already loosening her limbs—and her lips. "It's not at the top of my list, but it'll get the job done."

Nord's eyes heated, and the azure flecks ringing his pupils pulsed. It was obvious he'd prefer she blow off steam some other way, but unless he planned to let her take him for a ride, liquor was the quickest way she was going to shut off her brain.

Alistair cleared his throat, reminding Lina he was there.

"So much for that idea," she said sadly, taking another sip. The once full bottle was now half-empty.

"I think I'm needed . . . um . . . I'll just be . . ." Alistair trailed off. After his attempt to come up with a plausible excuse to leave failed a second time, he gave up all pretense and simply stood and strode from the room with a muttered, "Right, then."

"Where's he going?" Lina asked.

"Don't think he wanted to watch his niece eye-fuck her Viking," Quinn answered, plucking the tequila bottle from Lina's hand.

"Hey!"

"You're supposed to be sharing," Quinn reminded her.

"Well, this is devolving quickly," Finley muttered.

"What are you, the morality police? Just because you have a stick shoved up your ass doesn't mean we all have to," Quinn replied tartly.

Quinn and Finley glared at each other.

Lina snickered. "You two should just get naked already. Might take the edge off."

"Maybe you should take your own advice," Quinn shot back, amusement shining in her eyes as she held out the tequila.

"I'm working on it, trust me."

Nord stole the bottle before Lina could, lifting it to his lips and holding her gaze as he finished it.

Lina stared at him with no little hunger. "That was mine," she finally managed when he set the empty bottle down.

"I was thirsty."

Quinn plucked at the silk of her camisole. "Holy hell. I'm hot just watching him. It's a mystery to me how you manage to ever get anything done. I'd be too busy climbing him like a tree to ever let him leave the bed. Or the shower. Or the floor . . ." She shrugged. "Wherever, really. I'm not picky."

Lina snorted as Finley scowled.

"I'm not either," Nord said with a smirk. Then he wrapped an arm around Lina's waist and shocked the hell out of her by proceeding to give her the most erotic kiss of her life—both of them.

When he was done, Lina blinked up at him as her heart pounded in her chest. "Wh-what was that for?" she whispered.

He brushed his nose against hers. "Just making a point."

"And what point was that?" Quinn asked, her smile huge.

"That I'm spoken for," he told Quinn with a wink. "So you'll have to look for something else to climb."

"It's cute that you think I need to look."

Finley's scowl deepened.

"How about we get out of here and give you two space to relax and catch up," Nord offered.

I'd rather we kick everyone out and finish what you started this morning.

He must have read the thought in her eyes because his lips quirked, and he ran his thumb over her lips in a pale imitation of a kiss. *Later*, his eyes seemed to promise.

"I'd really like that," she said after a beat, realizing as she did that the words were true.

A day off, with nothing more serious to worry about than what she wanted to drink next, sounded amazing.

She needed a day. Just one where she didn't have to think about the shitshow that her life had become.

Yes, she had a psychotic ex and an unknown amount of other potential murderers hunting her, but she'd be perfectly safe in the penthouse with Quinn. Figuring out what to do about them could wait. Dealing with the consequences of her inherited magic, and the title that accompanied it, could wait. The unwanted artifact playing hide and seek in her body—or was it her soul?—all of it could wait.

Just for a day.

Then, she'd strap on her lady balls and deal with it.

"Consider it done," Nord said, brushing his lips over hers one last time before pulling away. "Finley, let's go."

"But—"

"Now."

"How is it I'm getting kicked out of my own house?" he asked Lina.

"We let you pretend you're in charge, but none of us actually believe it," she told him.

He scowled at her, but the expression didn't last long before morphing into a smile. Leaning down, he gave her a kiss on the forehead. "If you need anything, just give us a call."

"I will," she said.

He started after Nord but paused in front of Quinn.

"Gonna give me a goodbye kiss, too?" she asked sweetly.

For half a second, Lina thought Finley might actually be considering it.

Instead, he growled, "If anything happens to her, I'm holding you responsible."

"Hey!" Lina protested, not appreciating the implication that she was a child in need of looking after.

Something suspiciously like respect glimmered in Quinn's eyes. "All I've ever tried to do is keep her safe, Guardian, but fair enough."

They shared a long look before Finley broke it off with a nod. "Glad we understand each other."

"So," Quinn said once they were alone, "where do they keep the rest of the liquor?"

FOUR HOURS AND SEVERAL EMPTY BOTTLES LATER, LINA AND QUINN HAD finally dissolved into giggles on the floor. The amount of alcohol they'd consumed would have been problematic if they were mortals, but their supernatural metabolisms required steady drinking if they wanted to maintain any kind of prolonged buzz.

"You think that ghost story is bad? How about the time the guy occupying my apartment forgot his girlfriend was coming back from her work trip and brought his date home with him? He had his face planted in her bra and her panties in his hand when she walked in, but it wasn't until his girlfriend cleared her throat and peeled the purple thong off her face that he realized his mistake. I swear, that chick handled it like a boss. The way she laid into him was better than any show I ever got to watch when one of the people I haunted left their TVs on."

"Men are pigs," Quinn declared, punctuating the statement with a hiccup. Her hand flew up to cover her mouth. "Excuse me," she said before bursting into peals of laughter.

Lina laughed so hard she snorted, which set them both off again.

It was awhile before Quinn sobered enough to ask, "What was it really like? Being a ghost, I mean?"

Lina considered the question. "Lonely, mostly. People always say they want to be invisible so they can observe without others knowing, but the novelty of it wears off fast. I had lots of roommates to watch, and that was entertaining at first. You can learn a lot about people when they think they're alone. But it's not the same as having someone to spend time with, you know?"

Quinn reached over and squeezed her hand.

"I didn't understand, at first, that they couldn't see me. I kept trying with each new resident, hoping I'd eventually find someone who could see or hear me. After a while, when I finally accepted that wasn't going to happen, I started talking to them, pretending like we lived together and were carrying on a conversation. I'd complain about stupid things like when they didn't put the toilet seat down, or pick up their socks, or wash the dishes, their movie choices—anything. Just to feel like I was still part of the world."

"Oh, Lina," Quinn said, her eyes misty.

Lina waved the words away. "It's fine. Better than the alternative, right? Mostly, I just watched the world keep going on around me, wondering if anything would ever change. And then it did. And now here we are."

Quinn continued to stare at her, making Lina feel like she was a wounded puppy. The comparison made her squirm. She didn't want anyone to see her as a victim. As someone who should be pitied.

It was her reality. She'd lived through it, and now it was over. Why dwell on it?

"Do you remember that time we snuck out of my house to go to the Desecrated Graves concert?" Lina asked suddenly, desperate to change the subject and get back the lighthearted mood they'd been enjoying.

"Oh my God! Your dad was so pissed. I've never seen anyone with literal steam coming out of their ears before."

Lina rolled her eyes. "He was always doing shit like that. Trying to scare me into behaving with parlor tricks."

"And did it work?"

Lina gave her a look. "What do you think? You were right there alongside me."

Quinn grinned. "That would be a big, fat 'no,' then."

"You think he would have realized I could easily get around any magical barriers he put in place. I mean, hello, he wasn't the only one that could modify reality."

"But just think about how much fun we had because he *didn't* give you enough credit."

"True. Very true," Lina said, reaching for the bottle of vodka they'd started on, only to find it empty. "Shit. That was the last one," she said with a pout.

"Blasphemy!" Quinn shouted, standing unsteadily. "We must remedy this at once."

Lina stared up at her. "We're hardly in any state to go to the store."

Quinn put her hands on her hips and stared at Lina. "We don't need a store. We've got you."

"Me? Oh! Right." Lina pushed herself upright and tried to picture row upon row of bottles appearing on the coffee table beside her. In her mostly inebriated state, it was much harder to concentrate than usual, and the images in her mind blurred and swayed.

She bit down on her lip. *Hmm. Maybe it'd be easier with just one bottle.*

Lina pictured the unique shape of the tequila bottle and its golden lid, holding her hands out in front of her and willing it into being. The image flickered in her mind, most of the subtle details lost. She opened one eye. Her hands were still empty.

"I was able to summon drinks just fine yesterday." Letting her hands fall to her lap, she looked up at Quinn, sounding slightly heartbroken as she said, "I think my magic is broken."

Quinn laughed. "I think you're just drunk."

"Pfft. I've used my magic drunk plenty of times before."

"Yeah, okay, but things were a little different then. First of all," she said, holding up a finger, "you hadn't just been dead for a couple of decades. Second," she continued, talking over Lina before she could interrupt, "you know the Awakening leaves us vulnerable."

Lina let out a gusty sigh, not feeling overly comforted by the reminder.

"Don't worry about your magic, Lina," Quinn said, holding out a hand to help her stand. "It's there. With as much magic as your body just acquired, it must be like trying to fit the entire ocean into a hot tub. Your body is just . . . recalibrating."

"How long will that take?"

Quinn shrugged. "Hard to say. It's different for all of us. I was down for a couple of weeks before it kicked back in. One day, barely more than a fizzle; the next, it was back like nothing happened but, you know, ten times more powerful. Sort of like I traded in my magic for the upgraded model, but I had to wait for it to be shipped across the country before I could drive it home."

"Since when do you go with a car metaphor?" Lina asked with a laugh. Then the meaning of what Quinn said penetrated Lina's drunken fog. "Wait—you've been through it too? I thought last night you said you hadn't."

Quinn arched a brow. "Is that what I said? I remember telling Mr. Stick Up His Ass that I suppressed it—which I did. He didn't need to know that the spell wore off after a couple of years. My mother knows, obviously, but she is retaining the seat on the Council until I'm ready. We thought it was best."

Quinn's mother, Cora, was a truly gifted woman. While she wasn't a seer in the traditional sense, she often had hunches that panned out. If Cora thought it safer she and Quinn maintain the status quo, then she had a valid reason.

"Does she know what happened to me?"

"Not the full story. We agreed that was for the best, too."

Lina blew out a breath, reality momentarily intruding on the happy bubble she'd fought so hard to get lost in. She shoved it away and refocused on the problem at hand. "Do you think if I call the doorman, he might bring up a couple more bottles?"

"Screw the doorman. I bet Finley keeps the good shit in his room."

Before Lina could think better of it, Quinn was already pulling her along. "Which room's his?"

"Uh, that one," Lina said, pointing.

Quinn gleefully rubbed her hands together and opened the door. She paused in the doorway, shaking her head with an amused snort. "Man, even his bedroom has a stick up its ass."

Lina peered around, not seeing anything wrong with Finley's room. "What makes you say that?"

Quinn was already beelining for his dresser, but she gestured over her shoulder. "Look at the way he makes his bed. I don't think they even worry about folds that tight in the military. He probably uses a ruler." Quinn glanced back at Lina and rolled her eyes. "Also, I bet if you look through the drawer beside his bed, you'll see that he color-codes his sex toys. Or alphabetizes his lube at the very least."

Lina found herself walking over to his bedside table, curious if Quinn's theory was accurate.

"And seriously, what guy have you ever met doesn't leave clothes strewn all over the floor? Finley doesn't have so much as a sock out of place," she continued as she started to pull open drawers. After a loud snort, she held up a ball of navy-blue silk and tossed it in Lina's direction. "He even rolls up his ties, for God's sake."

Lina caught it with a giggle, creating a makeshift headband as she wrapped the silk around her head and tied it in a big bow.

Quinn threw a couple more ties onto the floor for good measure, seeming to enjoy her innocent demolition of his careful handiwork. She didn't even bother to close the drawer before moving on to his bookcase. There, she gave a happy shout. "Now we're talking."

Lina's interest in the contents of Finley's bedside drawer fled as Quinn started to wave a mostly full bottle of deep purple liquid in the air. "I knew he'd keep the magic-laced stuff in his room."

She uncorked it and took a deep pull straight out of the bottle. After a few sputtering coughs, she offered it to Lina. "Careful, it's potent."

Lina gladly accepted but took a more conservative sip. Her eyes immediately watered. "Holy balls, what is that?"

Quinn shrugged. "Does it matter if it gets the job done?"

"Guess not," she said, taking another sip.

Quinn had been right. The liquor was far stronger than anything they'd been drinking thus far. Even so, it wasn't long before they'd emptied the bottle and discarded it on the floor. It was also probably why Quinn decided it would be a great idea to rearrange the contents of Finley's closet. She was currently mispairing shoes inside of their shoeboxes.

"It's official," Quinn declared, slapping the last lid on its box. "I'm an evil genius. He's going to lose his shit when he finds that."

Lina shook her head. "You're something, all right."

"You have to admit that was pretty fun. Not to mention a totally successful scavenging trip."

"It was," Lina agreed, "but now we're out of alcohol again."

Quinn started to step out of the closet and then reconsidered, reaching back to grab a pristine, white button-up. "Temporarily. I know a guy."

Lina removed her headband. "Uh, unless you're hiding him somewhere, I don't see how that helps us."

Quinn pressed her crimson lips to the inside collar of the shirt and then hung it back up with a mischievous grin. "Who said anything about staying here? Darling, we're going out."

"Oh my God, yes!" Lina shouted, throwing her arms up in the air. The silk slipped from her fingers, forgotten as it fell to the floor like a lone party streamer. "That is a *great* idea. It's been forever since we've had a girls' night out."

"That's right, baby. This was just the pre-party. The fun is just getting started. We have a lot of years to make up for."

"You've always been a terrible influence," Lina said happily, coming to stand beside Quinn and resting her head on Quinn's shoulder.

"I know," Quinn said with a grin. "It's why you love me." She slapped Lina on the ass, startling a gasp out of her. "Now, let's go get you sexed up."

"What do you mean 'sexed up'?" Lina asked, slowing her steps until Quinn was practically pulling her down the hallway.

"You know, hair out to here, face painted for the gods, itty bitty dress, sky-high heels." She gestured dramatically with her free hand as she spoke. "Sexed. Up."

Lina bit her lip. "I'm not sure I own anything that fits the criteria."

Quinn stopped dead. "And you don't have an ounce of magic you can use to fairy godmother yourself something." She pouted. "Tragic."

"Wait!" Lina said, slapping her forehead with her palm. "Yes, I do. I still have the dress I wore the night I met Nord. It's practically transparent and looks painted on. Will that work?"

"That'll do! Besides, it doesn't really matter what you wear. Tonight, you need to look totally fuckable. Not that you don't already," she added with a wink, "but by the time I'm done with you, not even your Viking will be able to keep his hands—or other parts—to himself."

"Let's hope so," Lina groaned.

She'd already filled Quinn in on her born-again virgin status and the number of failed attempts she'd gone through, trying to rectify the situation. In typical Quinn fashion, she'd pledged herself to the cause. There were now officially two brains behind Operation Get Lina Laid.

"It's the least I can do after accidentally clam-jamming you this morning."

"Clam jam?" Lina asked, fairly certain her mental image of a long table with buckets of seafood dumped out along the middle was not what Quinn was referring to. Memories she might have, but there were a lot of modern sayings and gadgets she was still catching up on.

"It's the female version of a cock block," Quinn explained, tugging her into the room she'd indicated was hers. "You know. When someone swoops in and ruins someone else's chance at getting off."

Lina threw her head back and laughed, wiping a tear away as she said, "At this rate, my poor ovaries will always be blue."

"Nope. Not if I have anything to say about it. Now, come on. Get outta those jeans and into that dress so I can see what I'm working with."

She rushed to obey, the thought of a proper night out filling her stomach with thousands of happy butterflies. Quinn never did anything halfway, which meant there was a high probability they were going to get into trouble tonight. But that was nothing new for them. They'd learned how to talk themselves out of just about anything by the time they were teenagers.

And if that didn't work, well . . . she knew a berserker who could probably intervene on her behalf. For some reason, that thought only made her more excited about the night ahead. She'd been cooped up for so long. It was time to go out and raise a little hell.

CHAPTER SIX
NORD

Since looking into the Mobius Council was technically working outside of the Brotherhood's strict purview, Nord and Finley had opted to continue their strategizing somewhere more private. Namely, the heavily warded bunker situated deep into the earth and accessed only via their private garage.

Finley had dubbed it the Berserker Bunker, rationalizing that all the best superheroes had a badass secret lair. Nord was certain the name had more to do with the fact it made his eye twitch every time Finley found a reason to utter it—which was far more often than he had any need to—and was always accompanied by a shit-eating grin.

"Somebody has to know where to find the cocksucker," Finley said, slamming a file he'd 'borrowed' from the Brotherhood's records down on the table. Hands fisted, he pressed his knuckles into the cherrywood table in the center of their workroom and leaned forward, head hanging down.

Alistair shrugged apologetically from the wing-backed chair he was occupying. "If there is, I don't know who to ask. All my contacts in the Council think I'm dead."

Nord swallowed a frustrated groan. It wasn't completely the old man's fault that he was entirely useless. After all, it was the Brotherhood's request that he cut off all ties before they offer their protection. He'd just been following orders.

Stupid move, looking back. A double agent would be really useful right about now.

Nord pushed off the wall he'd been leaning against, drawing Finley's attention as he started pacing.

"All right," he said, "so if we can't come out and ask the Drakes about their missing heir, who can we ask? There has to be somebody we know who has connections. It's not like the piece of shit is still in hiding. Lina saw him at the ball, which means other people did too. Someone, somewhere, has to know where he is."

Finley and Alistair grew thoughtful, their gazes distant as they mentally weeded through possibilities.

Nord continued to pace, coming to an abrupt stop when a face popped into his mind. He *really* didn't want to have to ask that asshole for help again.

Finley shot up from his hunched position. "I've got it."

"Who?" Alistair asked, leaning forward in his chair.

Don't say it. Don't say it. Don't—

"Crombie."

Fuck.

Nord's jaw clenched. If they were thinking the same thing, then there was no escaping it. They were going to ask the fae bastard for another favor. It wasn't like they had another viable option; Finley wouldn't have mentioned him otherwise. Not after what happened last time.

That didn't mean Nord had to be happy about it.

Finley caught Nord's scowl. "I don't like him any more than you do, mate."

"I know, I know." Nord sighed, a headache building at the base of his skull. "He's the first legitimate lead we've managed to come up with. And with his underground connections, he's the most likely person to know where to start asking around for information about Mataius."

"If you rather wait and see if Quinn has any ideas . . ."

"She doesn't," Alistair interrupted. "At least, not as of this morning. We were discussing it on our way over. That might change in the next couple of days though."

"Why? What's happening in a couple of days?" Nord asked.

"Quinn's offered to come out of hiding—"

"Not that she's been doing a very good job of it since she's running around all over the damn place," Finley said.

"Well, it's not like anyone knows who she is," Alistair pointed out. "And if they do, she can easily make them forget. By dropping her anonymity, she'll draw unwanted attention to herself and her actions, but the upside is she might be able to learn more by officially reclaiming her spot in the Council. She's already requested a meeting with her mother to discuss it."

Finley studied Nord. "It's your call. We can wait to go to Crombie until after we see what Quinn learns."

Nord shook his head. As much as he wanted another option, he knew this was the path they needed to take.

"We risk losing any upper hand we may still have if we wait. Once Quinn starts asking questions, word can—and probably will—get back to Mataius. Right now, he doesn't know we're looking for him. It's better for us if we can keep it that way." Nord sighed as another thought occurred to him. "Besides, Crombie can go places and talk to people that we can't due to our affiliation with the Brotherhood. For all the power and freedom that comes with being a Guardian, there are also chains. Crombie isn't bound by the same rules."

"And you think that word won't spread if we go through Crombie?" Alistair asked.

"I think the people who work for Crombie are smart enough not to risk his wrath," Finley answered. "You don't ingratiate yourself with the King of the Cretins by sharing all his secrets."

Alistair ran a hand over his chin. "Isn't that also true of the Council?"

"Maybe it used to be, but if there's as much division as you've suggested, information is likely being offered to the highest bidder. People will want to be in good favor with whoever ends up winning that war. Even if it means they're playing both sides."

"You raise a good point," Alistair said with a frown. "In times of war, enemies often hide behind the mask of an ally."

Nord found himself agreeing. How many times had he used the same tactic? It was so much easier to deal the killing blow when everyone was looking in the opposite direction.

"We need to move fast," Nord said. "We can't sit around and wait for his next auction."

"Agreed," Finley said. "If we head to The District, somebody there can get word to him. It might take a day or two, but it's the quickest way to get in touch with him."

"How can we be sure he'll respond to our summons?" Nord asked.

"We can't, but I have a feeling if we mention it has to do with Lina, he'll come willingly enough. You saw how interested he was in her the other night."

Nord felt the sudden need to punch something.

Repeatedly.

He forced himself to take a deep breath and shoved the image of Crombie's hands on Lina as far from his mind as he could. The fae prick wouldn't survive to see the sunrise otherwise—and like it or not, they needed his help. Which meant they needed him alive.

"Now?" Alistair asked, glancing out the window where the sun was already setting.

Well, glancing at the enchanted wall that mirrored what was happening outside. Windows weren't exactly functional below ground, but people tended to get a bit cagey if there was no source—or illusion—of natural light.

"You have more important things to do tonight than track down your niece's murderer?" Nord asked, some of his temper leaking into the words.

Alistair blinked owlishly behind his glasses. "When you put it that way . . ."

"That's what I thought," Nord said, picking up the older man's cane from where it had fallen on the floor and holding it out to him.

The hissing silver serpent that made up the handle glinted under the florescent lights. There was something familiar about that snake. Before Alistair could grab it, Nord pulled the handle closer, inspecting it.

It didn't take long for him to remember where he'd seen it before. The snake was a perfect match to the one in Lina's tattoo, down to the M-shape created by the reptile's tongue.

That wasn't entirely surprising since their family claimed an affinity with snakes. The identical nature of the images meant there was a special significance though, which was harder to decipher.

"What does the M stand for?" he asked, offering the cane once more.

Alistair stared at Nord, reaching his hand out carefully as if he didn't fully trust him not to pull the cane away at the last second again. Once the cane was firmly in his grasp, he stood and asked, "It isn't obvious?"

"If it was, do you think I'd bother asking the question?"

Alistair's lips twitched up in a smile. "I suppose not. It's our crest. The M stands for Mobius and the snake represents our family's integral connection to its mission."

"Do all the families in the Council have one?"

Alistair nodded. "The Drakes incorporated their dragons, the Thortons their thunderbirds, the Alinari have their gryphons, and the Satori use their sphinx—but all five of our crests showcase the letter M in some fashion."

Nord tucked the information away, curious what he might discover hidden in the archives regarding those images. If he could learn what to look for, it would offer yet another way to try to track down Lina's murderer. Right now, they needed all the help they could get. That meant any lead was helpful—even if it was an asshole fae prince with boundary issues.

"Right, so we just need to take care of one last thing before we can head out."

Nord's eyes narrowed on Finley's smirking face. There was only one reason the bastard ever wore that particular expression. He was going to make Nord dress up. The warm tingle of magic rushing across his body confirmed his suspicion.

Nord glanced down, eying Finley's handiwork.

"No. Absolutely not."

Finley shrugged, entirely unrepentant. "No getting around the dress code, I'm afraid. Coats and ties are required for entrance after dark."

Nord pinched the maroon fabric between two fingers. "The floral shirt is bad enough, but is velvet really necessary? I look like a prig."

Finley rolled his eyes and used his magic once more to transform Alistair's outfit from tweed to something classic and black.

Nord shook his head, not about to go out in public wearing Finley's abomination. While Finley was distracted with his own clothes, Nord called on his power to turn the velvet and floral monstrosity into a more traditional black suit, white button-up, and simple black tie.

"There," Finley said, once his navy suit and silver tie were in place. "Now, we're ready to go."

Nord was halfway out the door when he felt the familiar tingle of magic roll over him once more. He didn't even have to check to know the velvet was back.

"You motherfucker," he growled.

Finley's laughter was his only answer.

CHAPTER SEVEN
LINA

Lina eyed the familiar green and silver awning with only the briefest flicker of trepidation. When Quinn mentioned they were going to see her 'guy', Lina hadn't anticipated that meant going back to Crombie's nightclub. Before her nerves—or good sense—had a chance to take root, she spotted a familiar mountain of a man standing just outside of the door.

"Kiko!" she squealed, waving and rushing over like The District's bouncer was one of her long-lost friends.

He blinked at her a couple of times as if trying to ascertain whether she was drunk off her ass or just plain crazy. In Lina's case, it was probably a bit of both.

Before she could launch herself at him and give him a totally unwanted hug, Quinn caught her arm and hauled her backward. "Easy there, tiger. I'm not sure who you think this is, but *Linc*," she emphasized the name, "doesn't do hugs."

Lina waved the name away. "No, no. This is Kiko. It's the nickname I gave him in my head while he was doing his broody gatekeeper act last night, and then I completely embarrassed myself by using it out loud. Remember?" Lina asked him with a self-deprecating laugh.

The bouncer blinked at her once more and then informed her in a voice that sounded like he'd swallowed a bucket of gravel. "My brother worked the door last night."

Quinn was trying hard not to laugh as she whispered, "Lina, this is Linc. Nox's twin. You can tell them apart because Linc has a scar running through his eyebrow, and Nox doesn't. See?"

If she'd been fully sober, Lina might have spent more than a second to process her faux pas. Instead, the only part her mind registered was that this guy didn't have a special codename, and that meant he was left out . . . which probably hurt his feelings.

"Huh. Well, that's not fair. You definitely deserve a cool name, too. Let me see, let me see . . ." she murmured, tapping a finger on her chin.

"Lina," Quinn said in a low, warning tone. "I don't think—"

"I know," she said, beaming at the stone-faced bouncer. "Since your brother is King Kong, you've gotta be Godzilla. I hereby dub you Zilla!"

Lina looked around for something to knight him with—royals were always doing that when they gave somebody a new name or title. Not seeing anything that would pass as a sword or scepter, Lina quickly pulled off one of her rhinestone stilettos and tapped him on either shoulder with the six-inch filigree heel.

"There! It's official."

Quinn watched all of this play out between splayed fingers, her shoulder shaking with suppressed laughter as Lina slipped her shoe back on.

The bouncer formerly known as Linc, who hadn't budged throughout Lina's impromptu speech or ceremony, shocked the hell out of them both by taking one of Lina's hands and executing a perfect courtly bow. Eyes holding hers, he pressed unexpectedly soft lips to the back of her hand before dropping it and returning to his previous position.

"Thank you for the name. I'll use it with pride."

Heat crept into her cheeks as she stared at his stoic face. There was nothing, not even a slight creasing near his eyes or twitch of his lips, to indicate that he was teasing her. All signs seemed to suggest that he was being entirely genuine although it was hard to know for sure since his expression hadn't changed once since they arrived.

"You're welcome."

Quinn was still gaping when Lina's eyes found hers to silently ask, *what now?*

Recovering first, Quinn gave him her trademark smirk. "Well, now that we got that out of the way, care to let us up, Linc?"

"Zilla," he corrected, the boulders he called biceps bulging as he crossed his arms over his chest to glare at her. After a second, he turned to wink conspiratorially at Lina, who grinned up at him. Jutting his head back toward the stairs, he said, "Go on up. You ladies have fun. Holler if you get into any trouble."

Quinn shook her head and muttered something inaudible under her breath as she moved inside.

Lina hesitated by the door.

Zilla raised a brow. "You need something, beautiful?"

"I know Quinn said you don't do hugs, but I—oh, fuck it," she said, placing her hand on one of his forearms to help steady her as she pressed a kiss to his cheek.

True surprise registered on his face. "What was that for?"

Lina lifted one shoulder in a shrug. "You could have been a real dick, and instead you were a gentleman. It means a lot to me."

He stared at her for a moment before dipping his chin. "Meant what I said. You find yourself in need, come find me. I've got your back, no matter what."

It was Lina's turn to stare, his declaration warming her from the inside out. "Just like that? Don't get me wrong, I appreciate the offer. More than you know. Hell, I'll probably have to take you up on it the way things have been going lately. But you don't seem like the kind of guy to make a promise like that lightly."

"It's a rare person who stops to consider the feelings of someone she doesn't even know. Rarer still if that someone looks like me. Anyone singular enough to do that deserves loyalty and protection." He offered her something that might have been a smile. "You better get in there. Your friend is waiting for you."

It wasn't until Lina was halfway up the stairs that she realized she'd never mentioned not wanting to hurt Zilla's feelings out loud. No wonder the half-giant, half-orc brothers guarded the door. They could read minds—at least to some capacity—which allowed them to identify potential threats before they ever set foot inside.

It also meant there was no such thing as secrets at The District.

⁂

Lina lost track of the number of people Quinn greeted by name as they wove through the throng of bodies on their way to the bar.

"How often do you come here?" she asked once they'd flagged down a bartender and ordered a cocktail and two shots each.

"Oh, two or three times a week. It's a good place to see and be seen or listen and be unseen as the case may be. Plus, the drinks are strong and the eye candy limitless."

"The Quinn I know would never let her eyes have all the fun."

Quinn cackled. "You know me so well. What can I say? Hiding got boring pretty fast. I needed to find some way to pass the time."

Remembering what Finley said about the kind of people that frequented Crombie's events, Lina cast her eyes around and lowered her voice before asking, "You're safe, right? You make sure you're not inviting the wrong kind of person into your bed?"

"Honey, have you forgotten? We *are* the wrong sort of people. As far as everyone else is concerned, the members of the Mobius Council are little more than thugs and thieves—powerful and well-connected ones, to be sure, but criminals all the same. And those are the people that actually like us."

"True, but everything we've done has always been in the name of protecting our kind. We may not always be on the right side of the law, but that doesn't mean what we're doing is wrong," she argued, feeling a long-forgotten sense of righteous anger surge forth at her friend's words. It had always rubbed Lina the wrong way that her friends and family had been cast as the bad guys when all they were doing was trying to keep the rest of their kind safe.

"*I* know that. You don't have to convince me. But I also have the benefit of knowing the why behind our methods. Others—your Viking's Brotherhood, for example—don't have that luxury. To them, the magical weapons we provide and other questionable services we offer only paint us one way. It's rare for heroes to live anywhere but the light, and we, my darling, have become creatures of the dark."

Lina rolled her eyes and downed one of her shots. "That's a matter of perspective. One person's hero is just someone else's villain."

Quinn followed suit, downing one of her shots as well. She made a face as she slammed the glass back on the bar top. "Too true, Queen E. Too true. But enough of the serious talk, I thought we were supposed to be out having fun, not debating the ethics of whether or not the ends justify the means."

"You're the one who brought it up," Lina said, staring at her friend pointedly as she sipped her cocktail.

"No, I'm not," Quinn said with a laugh. "You did."

"I did not! I was just making sure you weren't bringing home a bunch of scheming douche buckets and putting yourself in danger of being murdered in your sleep. You were the one who had to go and bring all that other baggage up."

Quinn was openly laughing at her by the time she'd finished her mini-rant.

"What?" Lina snapped.

"What the hell is a douche bucket?"

"I don't know! But it sounded appropriately awful."

Quinn wrapped an arm around Lina's shoulders and gave her a

kiss on the temple. "You don't need to worry about me. I can take care of myself."

Lina slid her arm around Quinn's waist and squeezed. "True, but I'll worry anyway. As tough as you are, you can still be hurt."

Something flickered in Quinn's eyes, but it was gone before Lina could identify it.

"I don't let anyone get close enough to do real damage," she replied, flashing a smile that looked a bit forced.

Lina wanted to ask why, but Quinn was right. They were supposed to be out having fun, forgetting about all the serious shit, not dredging it up.

"Here," Lina said, holding out Quinn's second shot. The women clinked glasses and downed the amber liquid. Lina coughed, the liquid leaving a trail of fire down her throat. "What was that anyway?"

"We call it Fire Water, but it's just some fancy scotch from a distillery run by a bunch of druids outside of Edinburgh. I don't remember the burn being quite so aggressive though," she added, still grimacing slightly as she set their shot glasses down. "But then, I never order it for the taste."

"Oh? Why order it then?"

Quinn gave Lina a look. "The high, obviously. Nothing like a little magic-infused alcohol to get the job done. It takes half the number of drinks for twice the buzz. Now that's my kind of math."

"Explains why my head feels like it's trying to detach itself from my body."

Quinn grinned. "Excellent, that means it's kicking in."

"Yeah, I'd say so." Lina did a full-body shimmy, laughing at the tingling sensation rippling through her arms and legs. The more she moved, the more euphoric she felt. "I want to dance," she declared, shaking her shoulders and hips like they were already on the dance floor.

Quinn whooped. "Yes, girl! Get it!"

A few other patrons whistled appreciatively as she worked her way down to the floor and then back up. Snagging her drink, Lina downed the rest of it and grabbed Quinn's hand. "Come on. Let's get out there."

Quinn rushed to kill her drink, passing her empty glass to a nearby waiter as she stumbled along, trying to keep pace with her over to the sunken area that had been converted into a dance floor. The tables that had filled the space last night had been cleared away, leaving a wide-open place for the guests who wanted to bust a move.

As soon as her foot hit the top step, the music swelled around her, the volume cranking up from a two to a twenty, its throbbing beat settling inside of her chest until its pulse was indeterminable from her own.

"Oh, hell yeah!" Quinn shouted behind her. "I love this song!"

Arm's up, Quinn started rolling her hips and shoulders in a serpentine fashion that had the other patrons looking her way.

Lina followed suit, letting the rhythm flow through her. With the first whip of her hair, she ceased being Lina, ex-ghost and current Prism locker, and transformed into Lina, living song. She was completely lost to the music, her hands in her hair as she moved her head side to side, her hips creating invisible figure eights, her body swaying as she existed in her own little bubble.

Strands of hair plastered themselves to her face and neck. Beads of sweat dripped down her back. Her feet and calves were already protesting the height of her heels. She was enjoying every second of it. This was exactly what she needed. A perfect, mindless escape.

When a pair of hands gripped her hips and pulled her back into an obviously male body, she twisted away and reached for Quinn, who was ready for her.

As soon as they clasped hands, Quinn pulled her forward and simultaneously spun her around so that by the time Lina came to a stop, they'd switched places. It was an instinctual reaction, a move they'd used countless times in the past whenever they wanted to escape gropers disguised as dance partners. The women grinned at each other, both loving the way they fell back into sync after so long apart.

Time lost meaning as one song seamlessly transitioned to the next, allowing them to keep dancing without missing a step. After a few more songs, Lina noticed Quinn's lips moving but didn't catch the words over the roar of the music.

"What?" she asked, shaking her head to show she didn't understand.

Quinn mimed taking a drink, raising a brow like she was asking a question. Realizing her friend was asking if she wanted something, Lina nodded eagerly. Quinn winked and danced her way back to the bar.

Lina continued to groove, mostly ignoring the other dancers except to check once in a while that she wasn't about to accidentally whack someone in the face with one of her arms as she waved them around her body.

The song shifted again, and she faltered as it turned into something slower and darker.

"Please, don't stop," a voice crafted from midnight and shadows crooned in her ear. "I've enjoyed watching you."

Lina spun around. "Crombie."

His storm-cloud-colored eyes flashed with amusement. "Is that any way to greet a friend?" he asked, needing to invade her personal space in order for her to hear him.

She crossed her arms. "Only the admitted stalkers."

"Ah, but I watch all my patrons. It comes with owning the place. So, you see, I'm not stalking, just working." He tapped the tip of her nose.

She slapped his hand away. "Sure you were."

His lips quirked up, not remotely offended. "You can't blame me for noticing you. You're the most captivating woman in the room, especially when you dance." He glanced around like he was searching for someone. "Looks like you've lost your partner. Care for a new one?" He held his hand back out, this time palm up.

Lina eyed it like it was about to bite her. "I don't think that's a good idea."

"Why not?"

"I'm not supposed to trust you."

Crombie tilted his head back and laughed. "No, you're definitely not. But since when do you do what you're told?" he asked, tilting his head to study her.

"When it aligns with what I want to do."

Both of Crombie's eyebrows lifted. "I see. Well, in that case, if you won't dance with me, at least have a drink with me. I insist," he said, cutting her off before she could decline by taking one of her hands and wrapping it around his arm.

"But Quinn—"

"I have no doubt our little weaver will find us easily enough," he said, patting her hand in what she assumed was supposed to be a reassuring manner as he led her to one of the shadowed alcoves along the wall.

Walking next to Crombie was a much different matter than trailing after Quinn. People openly stared at her as they moved to the side to clear a path. She could practically see the wheels spinning in their minds as they tried to figure out what made her special enough to warrant his undivided attention.

He gestured for her to take a seat. Lina eyed the U-shaped pleated leather couch and discretely tugged the short skirt of her dress down though it merely crept back up her legs as soon as she sat.

"I have a confession," Crombie said once she was settled.

"Just one? Surely your sins are more numerous than that."

His answering grin was wicked as he sat across from her. "Sin is merely the sign of a life well-lived."

Lina raised a brow. "Sounds like something a sinner would say."

He chuckled. "Doesn't make it less true."

"What did you want to confess?"

"I noticed you as soon as you came in. I wasn't going to interfere in your evening, but then that cretin put his hands on you—"

"Just how closely were you watching?"

He flashed her a wolfish smile. "I merely intended to come to your rescue if the need arose, but it seems you didn't require a white knight after all." He sat back and rested an arm along the top of the couch. "Which, frankly, I must say is a relief. I'm shit at pretending to be one."

"So which is the confession?" Lina asked, finding herself leaning closer. "The part where you aren't a white knight? Or the part where you wanted to be?"

For a second, Crombie froze, an incredulous expression taking hold—as if he'd never considered the possibility of being one of the good guys before. In that one suspended moment, he looked torn, vulnerable. The illusion of humanity shattered as he laughed. It was a soft sensual rasp that wrapped itself around her as he leaned forward, elbows on each of his knees as he took one of her hands in his.

"My dear Lina, we just established that I'm a lifelong sinner." With his other hand, he reached out and tucked a strand of hair behind her ear, his fingers lingering on her jaw. "There's no reforming me."

She'd suspected all along that she was going to get herself in trouble tonight—had looked forward to it even. But it wasn't until she was locked into a staring contest with the fae prince that she knew he was going to be the reason.

CHAPTER EIGHT
NORD

Nord had given up trying to undo Finley's handiwork by the time they arrived at The District. It wasn't worth the effort to keep changing himself back into something less flamboyant. He'd resigned himself to a night spent clad in velvet, but Finley had surprised him by opting for a more understated maroon suit with a black shirt and tie as his final selection for Nord.

He raised an eyebrow at Finley. "Compromise? That's not like you."

"I know. Best not to get used to it."

Nord shook his head as they made their way up the stairs and into the nightclub. It was just after seven, but it was already packed with supernaturals more than ready to blow off some steam.

The club had undergone a transformation since last night, the main seating area giving way for a dance floor, and the overhead lights swapped out with emerald green strobes and a glittering disco ball. If last night had been all about showcasing the space's—and attendees'—opulence, tonight was about indulgence.

Everywhere he looked, there was something else to see. Some new scandalous offering to revel in. The food and drink—mind-altering substances from both the mortal and supernatural worlds—were only the beginning of what was on offer. No matter the vice a guest might be after, The District had them covered.

Instead of acrobats, the guests themselves were tonight's entertainment. Evening gowns and tuxedos were replaced by outfits that would have been at home on a Paris runway or BDSM clubs alike. The center of the room was filled with writhing bodies, some couples not even pretending to dance as they lost themselves in each other. More discreet partygoers were making use of the room's many shadowed corners and alcoves, but the sounds coming from within left no doubt as to what its occupants were doing.

"Place hasn't changed a bit," Alistair said.

Nord and Finley glanced at him.

"What? I haven't always been a stodgy old man," he said defensively, placing both hands on top of his cane and straightening to his full height. "Believe it or not, I was quite the lady killer in my day. Take it from me; seduction starts on the dance floor."

Nord put a hand on Alistair's shoulder. "Hate to break it to you," he said, gesturing to a nearby couple. "That's not seduction."

Alistair snorted. "I should say not. Their mindless humping lacks all the subtlety and nuance of a proper seduction."

"Nuance, huh?" Nord asked, finding his offended yet dignified reaction amusing.

"You really trying to get sex advice from Lina's uncle?" Finley asked.

Nord stilled. "Who said anything about needing advice?"

Finley slapped Nord on the arm. "I mean, it's been a while, mate. Might not hurt to take a few notes. If you berserkers fu—"

Nord grabbed one of Finley's fingers and bent it back as he pulled his hand off of his arm. "I'm going to suggest you stop right there unless you want to eat your teeth."

Finley shook his hand out. "I think I'd prefer to keep my teeth where they are, thank you."

"Good call," Nord said. "Now, how about we do what we came here to do?"

"Fine," Finley agreed, eyes scanning the crowd. "This way," he said after a moment, leading them to the far corner where two of Crombie's lackeys stood in front of a roped-off area.

Glamours were optional at The District outside of auction nights, meaning most people showcased a hybrid form instead of a human one. There were fairies showing off multicolored wings, leopard shifters whose spotted patterns were replicated as full-body tattoos; there was even a water nymph with pale blue skin who left a trail of watery footprints in her wake.

The two gargoyles they were walking toward, however, didn't bother with glamours at all. They stared at the trio as they approached, their black eyes and mottled gray faces expressionless. If not for the way their eyes shifted as they tracked the trio's movements, they would have appeared like the statues they inspired.

"We need to get a message to Crombie," Finley said without preamble.

"I look like a secretary to you?" the gargoyle on the left asked. He pointed to the row of alcoves on the other side of the club. "Tell 'im yourself."

Nord's eyes flared as he called on his power, using it to see the occupants hidden by the shadows.

"Fair warning, I wouldn't bother him while he's with the blonde," the gargoyle on the right added. "He's as likely to kill you as he is to talk to you if you try to get between him and one of his conquests."

Nord's eyes landed on the blonde in question not half a second later.

"Lina."

His rage surged forth, begging to be unleashed.

"Where?" Alistair asked, moving to stand beside him.

Blood roared in his ears, drowning out the man's question. He couldn't look away from Crombie's hand caressing Lina's face. His jaw clenched tight, a vein in his neck pulsing wildly.

"Why is it every time he's alone with her, that fae bastard can't keep his fucking hands to himself?" Nord snarled.

Rationally, Nord couldn't really blame Crombie. Lina was stunning, her hair a wild tangle of curls falling down her back. Her eyes shining, cheeks flushed, lips twisted up in a wry smile as she laughed at whatever the piece of shit was saying to her.

And she was wearing that dress. The one that clung to her curves and made her legs look miles long.

It gave him ideas, that dress. Ones where her back was pressed up against the wall, the scrap of fabric pulled up to her waist, and her legs wrapped around his hips as he drove relentlessly into her.

Yes, rationally, Nord understood exactly why Crombie couldn't help but touch her.

But Nord was far from rational.

The berserker within continued to claw its way to the surface, already planning the best way to eliminate the threat.

"Far be it from me to interfere," Alistair began.

"Then don't."

"I may have only just come back into her life, but I know my niece, Guardian. If you go over there and start a fight, she's going to think you don't trust her."

"He's the one I don't trust."

"I get that, and she will too . . . eventually. But what will be lost in the time it takes for her to forgive you?"

The words of warning pierced through the first vestiges of his bloodlust, helping him keep it at bay a little longer. Nord didn't think Lina would be truly upset by an intrusion, nor did he doubt her commitment to him. But just the possibility of her thinking he might was enough to make him reconsider his next move.

Spying a waiter holding a tray full of drinks, another option presented itself.

Nord ran a palm over a discarded cocktail napkin, leaving five crisp hundred dollar bills in its place.

"Are we bribing someone?" Finley asked.

"Something like that," Nord said, holding the cash out to the waiter and taking the loaded tray from his hands. "You guys might want to go find Quinn. If Lina's here, she won't be far away, and I'm not sure how much longer we'll be welcome."

Finley muttered something under his breath, but Nord barely heard him. He was already moving across the room, tray hefted in one hand, lips curling up in anticipation.

This was going to be fun. . . even if it was plan B.

CHAPTER NINE
LINA

"That's too bad." Lina tilted her face to the side, forcing Crombie to drop his hand and break the contact between them. "I've already reached my lifetime quota for dealing with douche buckets."

Crombie's eyes narrowed infinitesimally. "Is that judgment I'm sensing? Just because I freely admit to who I am? Morality is just different shades of gray, Lina. Here I was, thinking you of all people would understand that. Weren't you just talking about perspective? Something about how villains are just someone else's hero if I recall."

Lina's mouth fell open. "I *knew* it. You weren't just watching out for me. You've been spying on me."

His eyes dropped, and he adjusted the cuff of his jacket, his voice taking on a bored quality as he replied, "There's nothing that goes on in this club that I don't know about."

Her earlier realization came back to her. There really was no such thing as a secret at The District, which meant Crombie knew a whole lot more than he'd been letting on.

There was a muffled shout and then the distinctive tinkle of glass hitting glass. Before she could turn to see what was going on, icy liquid rained down on her, creating dozens of tiny rivers racing down her neck and back.

Lina spun around, finding a smirking Viking standing directly behind her, a lone white napkin held out like a sad peace offering.

"I'm so sorry," he said, sounding anything but as he repeated his words, and his maneuver, from The Monster Ball.

She snatched the napkin out of his hand and began dabbing at her skin. "I think you've used that line on me already."

The azure flecks that ringed his pupils flared white-hot, sending her pulse skyrocketing.

"It worked so well for me the last time."

"I hope, for your sake, he's not that clumsy in bed," Crombie drawled, pulling her attention back to him.

Lina bit the inside of her cheek hard to keep from laughing. Crombie, dark, dangerous, king of the criminal underground, looked like a drowned rat. He was covered, head to toe, in sweet-smelling liquid. His hair was plastered to his face, eyelashes spiked together, the wet fabric of his shirt and pants molding to his chiseled body. His lap was littered with ice cubes, slices of fruit, and one cocktail skewer that somehow managed to land directly on his crotch and offer her the world's tiniest salute.

"Oh, I don't know," Nord said, eyes dropping meaningfully to the mess in his lap, "I think that was executed with flawless precision. Just like everything else I do."

Crombie stood, sending the various garnishes—except for one tenacious olive—to the floor. "If you'll excuse me, I find I'm in need of a clean shirt."

"No need to rush back on our account," Nord replied. "You won't be missed."

"If you think I'm just going to overlook this prank of yours, you clearly don't know who you're fucking with."

Nord's answering smile was little more than a baring of teeth. "If that was supposed to be a threat, princeling, I think you're the one who's uninformed, but I'd be happy to educate you."

Lina felt the first pinpricks of alarm as Crombie glared at Nord for a long, drawn-out moment. She'd never seen Crombie fight, but she knew what Nord could do—had witnessed the blood-spattered aftermath. There was no way this would end well for any of them if these two came to blows.

As it turned out, she needn't have worried. The fae prince spun on his heel and stalked off, disappearing into the crowd. If not for the dry Crombie-shaped imprint on the couch, it was like he'd never been there at all.

"Well, you certainly know how to make an entrance," Lina said, giving up on trying to reach the damp places on her back.

Nord took a step toward her, crowding her back into the darkness of the alcove. Heat shot through her at his unexpected nearness, and she was oddly thankful for her wet, albeit sticky, dress as it helped cool her down. He wasn't touching her, but there was no ignoring the electricity arcing between their bodies.

"What are you doing here, Lina?"

She blinked up at him, startled by the harshness of his tone after the almost playful way he'd dealt with Crombie. His face was mostly obscured by shadows, making it impossible to read his mood. Was he mad at her or just worried?

Deciding it didn't matter because she was too damn old to feel like a naughty schoolgirl, Lina went on the offensive.

"Me? What are *you* doing here, Nord? You following me now?"

"That's not how this works, Kærasta," he said, tilting her chin up with a finger. His voice was hard and his eyes glowing as they bore into hers. "I asked you first."

She jerked away from his touch, oddly hurt to hear his name for her in such an angry tone. "Don't call me that."

He flinched as if she'd struck him, and Lina's temper started to thaw.

She'd spoken without thinking, her defensiveness and, yes, even a bit of guilt for not letting him know where she was going, causing her to lash out. She knew the word held special meaning to him, that it was an endearment his father used with his mother. Her rejection of it must have felt like something far more personal than she'd intended it to be, perhaps even a rejection of Nord himself.

Hoping to undo whatever damage she inadvertently caused, she added in a gentler tone, "Not when you don't mean it."

His expression softened, and the glow in his eyes dimmed. "How about we start over?"

"I'd like that."

Nord cupped her cheek, his thumb lightly stroking her cheekbone. Leaning forward, he brushed his mouth against hers, tasting of spice and mint. Pulling back just far enough to meet her eyes, he asked, "What are you doing here, Kærasta? I thought you were at home, enjoying a night off."

"Well, I am enjoying a night off. Just not at home. I think I, uh, might have forgotten to tell you that."

Both his brows lifted. "You think?"

She grimaced. "Sorry. I know how you worry—" Nord made a face, so she rushed to add, "And rightly so, given everything going on, but I got a bit caught up in the moment."

He ran his fingertips from her forehead to her jaw, sending tingles down her body. Running his thumb along her bottom lip, he asked, "How can I protect you if I don't know where you are? Do you have any idea what it would do to me if something happened to you?"

Guilt, regret, and something that felt a whole lot like love swirled in her chest and clogged her throat. "Probably the same thing that would happen to me if our roles were reversed."

Nord rested his forehead against hers. "I hope you know it's never been my intention to clip your wings. I want you to soar, Lina. I'm just trying to ensure that you have a safe place to fly." He sighed. "I guess I'm just asking you to be extra careful, at least until we deal with Mataius."

"I suppose that's reasonable," she said, pressing her palm to his cheek.

"I have my moments," he said, lips ghosting up.

"Infrequent though they are," she teased, sliding her arms around his neck and drawing him closer. "We should probably commemorate the moment."

"Oh?"

"Mmhmm," she murmured, lips already descending on his.

Their kiss was like a piece of tinder catching flame. Scorching, insatiable, and seconds away from blazing completely out of control.

"There you are," Quinn called.

Lina and Nord unwillingly moved apart, the former breathing deep to try to calm her racing heart.

"I almost didn't recognize you with the Viking-size growth on your face," she added with a knowing smirk as she set two nearly overflowing glasses down on the low table.

Nord continued to devour Lina with his eyes, all sorts of promises shining in their burning depths.

Lina swallowed and forced herself to step away before she made a complete spectacle of herself and jumped him right there, voyeurs be damned.

"Quinn, I thought you promised to stop acting like my human chastity blanket."

"Belt," Nord corrected under his breath.

"Right," Lina said with a nod, pointing in his direction. "That."

Quinn snickered.

"Keep laughing, Satori. You do anything else to interfere with the *plan* again, and I'm going to have to start accepting applications for your replacement."

"What plan?" Nord asked at the same time Finley, who'd just reached them, asked, "Who are we replacing?"

"You would never," Quinn said, ignoring them both.

"Try me."

Quinn's eyes narrowed with mock anger. "Evil. I approve."

Lina grinned.

"Oh, you want to replace Quinn," Finley said. "Excellent. I volunteer." He slapped Nord on the shoulder. "This guy will vouch for me."

Lina snickered. Her eyes traveled to where Finley stood just behind Nord and then flared wide when they landed on her uncle.

"H-hi," she stammered, praying hard that he hadn't witnessed her practically dry-humping Nord mere seconds earlier. That would be embarrassing on a level she would never recover from.

"Ha, like you could ever replace me. What are you guys even doing here?" Quinn asked, hands on her hips.

"Same thing as you, I'm guessing," Finley said dryly.

"Came to blow off some steam, huh? Big dancer, are you?" she asked, her voice barbed. "What's your favorite move? I'm guessing you're a finger guns kind of guy," she said, performing a series of body rolls and shooting at imaginary targets on the dance floor. "No?"

Finley glowered at her. "Cute."

"Come on, big guy. Show me what you got."

"Hard pass."

"Oh, I see," Quinn said, patting him on the arm and nodding sagely. "That's okay. Not all of us are rhythmically inclined. I wouldn't want to embarrass myself either."

Alistair let out a loud bark of laughter he quickly disguised as a cough.

Quinn winked at him. "Now I know you have moves, hot stuff."

Even in the dim light, Lina could make out her uncle's blush.

"Must you always insist on alienating everybody?" Finley asked.

Quinn smirked up at him. "Why? Can't handle a little ribbing?"

The metallic flecks ringing Finley's pupils flared silver, and a vein began pulsing wildly in his neck. Lina took that as her cue.

"So, what brings you guys here, really? I highly doubt it had anything to do with dancing and cocktails."

"We needed to get a message to Crombie," Nord said.

"A message?" she asked, eyes darting between the three of them. "About what?"

"These two think he might know the best way to track down Mataius," Alistair answered.

Lina shot Nord a look. "Don't you think you should have asked him for help before you threw a tray of drinks at him?"

"Probably."

"Not very good at buttering people up, are you?"

His lips twitched, and he discreetly ran his hand down her spine until he was cupping her ass. Her dress was so short that his fingers grazed the back of her thigh.

"I don't know. You tell me."

Liquid heat spiraled through her belly and pooled in her core. She pressed her legs together to try to ease the building ache.

"Not fair," she gritted out.

He dipped his head, his lips moving against her ear as he whispered, "We've already been over this. Life rarely is."

Lina swallowed. "I think I hate you."

"That's not hate you're feeling."

She drew in a shaky breath. "Could have fooled me."

He chuckled in her ear, the sound doing all sorts of delicious things to her insides.

"So, um . . ." She coughed a little to clear her throat—and her mind. "Why do you think Crombie would have that information?"

"Because he's built himself an empire around finding lost things," Finley answered.

"And people. Don't forget them. Although oftentimes, they don't tend to be lost as much as they're just trying not to be found," Crombie said, looking perfect and polished once more in a fresh suit with nary an olive or cocktail skewer to be found. "But why are we talking about me?"

"I thought nothing went on here you didn't know about," Lina said with a tight smile.

"It doesn't. I'm just being polite. I like to give people a chance to tell me things on their own terms. It also allows me to see how honest someone really is. You learn a lot from the details people try to hide."

Lina barely suppressed a shiver as Crombie's stormy eyes met and held hers. He was studying her intently, his eyes searching for something in their depths.

Nord made a low, growling sound beside her.

"Well, if you already know why we're here, let's stop playing games. Will you help us?" Lina asked.

"Why would I want to do anything to help you?" he returned, his eyes moving to Nord and then straying to the discarded garnishes that still littered the floor.

His body went rigid beside hers. If Crombie denied them this favor out of some stupid alpha male attempt to establish dominance, things would go very, very badly. Nord's berserker would not react well to a challenge like that.

Not.

At.

All.

She couldn't let Crombie refuse.

"Please," she said, allowing some of the desperation she'd been trying so hard to ignore since last night creep into the lone word. And then, sensing Crombie would savor hearing her admit it, she added, "We need you."

As she suspected, Crombie's attention snapped back to her. Curiosity turned his eyes a burnished silver.

"Well, now we're getting somewhere. Let's head up to my office so that we may speak freely."

CHAPTER TEN
LINA

"I believe we left off with you telling me how much you needed me," Crombie said, eyeing Lina over his steepled fingers.

Lina suppressed the urge to roll her eyes. *What is it with men and their overinflated senses of self-importance? The guy oversees a network of petty criminals and thieves. What's he want, a parade? A street named in his honor? Come the fuck on. It's not like he's some sort of god.*

Her eyes drifted over his perfectly sculpted face, and that palpable aura of danger she'd picked up on last night slammed into her as soon as her gaze met his.

Right?

What did she really know about Davis Crombie that didn't stem from a bunch of secondhand rumors?

Mouth suddenly dry, Lina licked her lips. "It's hard to know where to start when I don't know what you know."

"Assume I know nothing."

"We'd save a lot of time if I didn't have to start at the beginning," she hedged.

He waved a hand in the air. "Start with why you're looking for this Mataius."

Quinn snorted. "Come on, Crombie. Enough with the games. You know exactly who Mataius is. Just like you know exactly who Lina and I are. Isn't that the whole reason you made a point to collect me? Because you wanted access to my connections on the Mobius Council?"

Crombie's brow quirked. "And here I thought we were friends."

"What you are is a necessary evil. Friends trust each other. I tolerate you."

A muscle ticked in his jaw. "I've taken it easy with you. Don't forget that I can call in my favors at any time—or what I do to people who can't pay their debts."

Quinn shrugged and sat back in her seat. "So do it, and then I'll call in mine. You're not the only one owed something here, Crombie."

A low clap of thunder rolled around the room. "Careful how you speak to me, little weaver. You might have the backing of a powerful syndicate, but no one is untouchable."

Quinn gave him an exaggerated pout, wholly unaffected by his display of temper. "The truth hurts, doesn't it, Crombie? This whole time you thought you had me in your pocket, but I was merely biding my time." She uncrossed her legs and leaned forward, dropping her voice as she crooned, "It's no fun when you realize that, for all your puppeteering, you're the one being used, is it?"

Finley snickered from his perch in the back of the room.

Lina cleared her throat. "I think we've strayed a little off-topic."

"Nah, we were just establishing some pertinent facts," Quinn said with a smirk. "But I think we're all on the same page now."

Lina eyed her best friend with no little measure of respect. No matter her opponent—or whether or not she had the actual upper hand—Quinn was utterly fearless. Not to mention ruthless. The woman always went for the jugular.

"Remind me never to get on your bad side," Lina muttered.

Quinn winked, her voice warm as she said, "I love you too much to let that happen." And then she proved Lina's musings to be undeniably true when she turned back to Crombie and said in a noticeably cooler voice, "Help us find Mataius, and I'll consider your debt to me paid in full. Or don't, and I'll convince Lina to let her berserker have his way with you."

Holy shit, did she really just say that?

For one hopeful second, Lina thought she might have misheard. Then her eyes darted to Crombie's irate face, and the blood drained from hers.

Oh fuck.

She really did.

Lina couldn't help but wonder if this was the part where she died for good. From the look in his eyes, Crombie was definitely contemplating murder.

The room was deathly silent while they awaited Crombie's answer. Mind racing, she scrambled to think of a way to salvage the negotiation before Quinn's ultimatum got them all killed.

A quick glance at Nord beside her confirmed he'd be no help in that regard. The flecks in his eyes hadn't stopped pulsing with power since Crombie showed up. If anything, the azure had only grown brighter in response to Quinn's suggestion. He'd welcome the opportunity to go toe to toe with the fae prince.

Do something, she mouthed to her uncle, who was standing on Nord's right.

Alistair shrugged back at her helplessly.

Finley was standing almost directly behind her, which meant she couldn't look to him for help either.

Lina started looking around the office for something she could use as a weapon. She spied a few sharp-looking pens and one potentially lethal letter opener, but they were all within reach of Crombie's fingers. In the end, her eyes landed on a heavy-looking bust on the corner of his desk.

She was still working through how she'd jump up from her seat and grab it by the base, then spin and bash Crombie against the side of his head in one flawless move, when his voice interrupted her planning.

"It's going to take some time," he said, proving that he did, in fact, know exactly who they were looking for.

"Time is a luxury we don't have," Nord said.

"That's not my problem. You're the ones requesting my help. It takes as long as it takes."

Nord pressed his lips together, clearly unhappy with the response. But what could he say? Crombie was right.

"If I may?" Alistair said, stepping forward. "You and I have never officially met, although our organizations have had many run-ins with one another over the years. I'm Alistair Cuska."

Crombie nodded as if this was not new information to him even though the name her uncle just claimed was widely believed to belong to a dead man. Was there anything Crombie didn't already know?

"Mataius murdered my niece, Mr. Crombie. Tortured her. For hours." Alistair paused, looking down to collect himself before continuing. "After he tired of playing with her, he left her to bleed out. Can you imagine, Mr. Crombie, what it does to a man, finding someone they love more than life itself unmoving in a pool of their own blood?"

He was trembling with rage, his voice giving life to the grief Lina had sensed ever since she found him that day in the archive.

Crombie opened his mouth, but Alistair was not finished.

"Since you know who we are, I trust you understand *what* we are and what it is we are capable of. Let it suffice to say that, had we not managed to find what was left of my niece when we did, Mr. Crombie, the woman you've taken such interest in would not be sitting before you now. I think we can both agree the world would be a far darker place without her in it. I think we can also agree that the man who dared to perform such depraved acts of violence on an innocent such as her does not deserve to walk free. He is a blight on this world.

A plague that must be extinguished. All we seek is the opportunity to right that wrong. To mete out the vengeance that is rightfully ours."

Tears clogged Lina's throat even as a small part of her balked at being called innocent. To her uncle, the man who was more father to her than her own, she'd always be the little girl who came running anytime she had an ouchie—real or imaginary—that needed fixing. In his eyes, maybe she was still innocent.

Crombie looked to Lina, his expression thawing slightly. "After all you have suffered, I certainly understand your desire for haste. While it does not mean I can make things happen any faster, I can promise that I will put feelers out tonight. As soon as I know something, you will."

"Thank you," Lina said, thinking that perhaps Crombie was not as averse to playing the hero as he believed.

He nodded, his expression hardening once more as he stood. Crombie may ignore his heritage, but there was no denying the air of royalty emanating from him now.

"If you would have simply asked instead of threatened, you would have found my answer the same. But since you did not, let me make something very clear." He looked first at Finley, then to Nord, and finally leveled the full weight of his icy gaze on Quinn. "If any of you step into my club uninvited again, I will consider it an act of outright hostility and will respond the way I do to all threats."

There was no need to ask for him to clarify. The simmering fury in his eyes was impossible to misinterpret.

"I believe that concludes our business. Now, get the fuck out of my club."

Crombie blew out of the office like a thunderstorm.

Lina was stunned he would leave them alone in his personal space until she realized that while private, it was far from personal. She doubted there were more than a handful of people alive that could ever claim to know Crombie on a truly intimate level. For a moment there tonight, she might have been one of them. She caught a glimpse beneath his carefully crafted façade before the mask slammed back down and shut her out. Probably for good, considering how the evening ended.

"He was talking about you two," Finley said, gesturing to Nord and Quinn.

Quinn rolled her eyes. "If you're so sure of that, why don't you put it to the test?"

"You're the one who went and blackmailed him," Finley said.

Lina shook her head at their senseless bickering. "What does it matter who started it? You heard him; he wants all of us out of here."

Quinn gave Lina a shrewd look. "Something tells me he'd make an exception for you."

"Yeah, well, let's not risk it," she said as her head started to feel like it'd been caught in a vise.

Tension had settled in her neck and temples as soon as Crombie found her on the dance floor, and it had only grown as the night progressed. She'd tried to shrug it off as a side effect of Quinn's druid drink, but that was just her way of stubbornly clinging to the last vestiges of her denial. The truth was harder to ignore once sobriety made a full comeback.

Her attempt at a day off had been doomed from the start. She should have known better. There was no escaping her past. Her dreams had proven that easily enough. No matter what she did—or what was done to her—it would always find her.

Mataius would always find her.

Nord's fingers brushed her back, making her shiver. "You okay?"

He must have sensed the growing unrest within her. There was no hiding her feelings when it came to him. Her Viking missed nothing. Hell, he was so attuned to her he'd probably notice if she lost an eyelash.

"Yeah," she said with a tight smile. "Just ready to go home."

"I can help expedite that," Finley said, creating a portal in the middle of the room. "You guys head out, I'll drop Quinn and Alistair off on my way back with the car."

"You Guardians might not know how to have fun, but having a portal maker at our disposal is definitely useful," Quinn said.

"Careful, Satori. That almost sounded like a compliment," Finley said.

Quinn shrugged. "Don't get too excited. If the Viking could summon a portal, we'd have no use for you at all." She tossed Nord an apologetic smile. "No offense, but it really is your only shortcoming."

Nord suppressed a smile. "None taken. We all have parts to play."

Lina rolled her eyes. Finley and Quinn could make a fight out of anything. Her gaze fell on the shimmering door beyond the portal, and she suddenly longed for her bed.

"I'm all for a quick escape, but I thought you guys weren't allowed to use those here," Lina said.

"Technically, no one is supposed to use magic of any kind at The District since it's a registered sanctuary, but, well, we've already completely disregarded that rule if you consider what happened last night," Finley said. "And as far as the Brotherhood is concerned, what they don't know won't hurt them. Besides, think of how much it'll piss Crombie off when he doesn't see you two leave. We've already done such a great job ruining his night. Why stop now?"

"Only you and Quinn would think it's a good idea to poke an angry bear," Lina said with a sigh.

"That surprises you?" Finley asked, looking between her and Nord. "I spend the better part of each day taking the piss out of this guy, and he's far scarier than any bear."

Lina huffed out a little laugh. "Because you're certifiable."

"I prefer the terms 'thrill-seeker' or 'adrenaline junkie' but sure. That works too." He rubbed the top of her head affectionately. "Go get some sleep, love. We'll take care of things here and deal with the rest of it in the morning."

She gave him a quick hug and then turned to give one to Quinn as well.

"I can already tell I'm going to hate you in the morning."

"Somehow, I doubt that," Quinn replied mysteriously.

Lina gave her a sharp look as she pulled back, wondering what the hell that was supposed to mean.

Before she could ask, Quinn offered her an enigmatic smile and said, "Enjoy the rest of your night." Then, to Finley, she added, "Do anything stupid while I'm a passenger in your car, I'll make you forget your own name. I expect to get home in the same or better condition than when I left."

Finley gaped at her as she sauntered out of the door. Throwing an exasperated look over his shoulder, he asked, "Has she always been this way?"

"'Fraid so," Lina confirmed, trying hard not to laugh.

"Why are the beautiful ones always so bloody mental?" Finley asked under his breath as he stalked out after her.

Still snickering, Lina craned her neck around, expecting to find her uncle sharing her amusement, but Alistair was gone.

"He snuck out while Finley was making an ass of himself," Nord said. "Asked me to tell you he'd check in on you tomorrow."

Lina frowned in the direction of the door, not liking that he left without saying goodbye. But then, she recalled the way his knuckles had gone white as he gripped his cane and told Crombie about how he'd found her. It only made sense that he'd want to steal a few minutes for himself. That wasn't the kind of memory you relived easily.

Nord held a hand out to her. "Ready?"

"God, yes."

He raised a brow at the vehemence of her words. "Night not what you hoped it would be?"

She gave him an incredulous look. "What part of the last hour and a half do you think I was hoping for when the whole point of tonight was to pretend I was still blissfully ignorant about my past?"

Nord laughed. "Fair point," he said, weaving his fingers through hers and giving her hand a little tug to close the space between them.

Her breath left her in a soft whoosh as he reached out and

brushed a piece of hair off of her face. His skin barely made contact with hers, but it was still enough to send goosebumps racing down her body.

His lips quirked up as he noted her reaction.

Leaning down so his lips were next to her ear, he whispered, "Let's see what we can do to get your night back on track."

CHAPTER ELEVEN
NORD

Seduction wasn't necessarily what Nord had meant when he'd made his suggestion. He'd been thinking more along the lines of a hot bath and a relaxing massage, actually. Things to help comfort and soothe.

But then, he picked up on the hitch in her breathing. The way her pulse fluttered rapidly along her neck. Drawing back, he easily made out the rosy flush staining her cheeks and the glassy, dilated cast of her eyes.

Arousal.

The proof of it was a siren's call stoking his own, stirring the beast within until he was rattling his cage and demanding to be released. The berserker wanted to claim Lina just as badly as Nord did.

It went beyond craving. It was deeper than hunger. It was pure, unmitigated need.

For her.

He needed to make her his in this final, most primitive way.

If not for his iron-clad control, he probably would have done so already. He'd been so close this morning, waking with the scent of her deep in his lungs, her lush curves pressed against him. It'd been impossible to resist the urge to taste her.

He wouldn't have stopped there if they hadn't been interrupted. Which had probably been for the best, hard as it was to admit. With as on edge as he'd been feeling these past weeks, there was no doubt the berserker would have taken over. And then, he'd be little more than a rutting beast. He didn't want that.

Not for their first time together.

Now, there was nothing stopping them. The penthouse was theirs alone, and there were hours yet before the dawn. They had the entire night to lose themselves in each other.

If he'd thought Lina was even remotely still under the influence of any substance, he'd reconsider. Resign himself to another night of cold showers and settle for holding her in his arms. But he'd been watching her, and she'd long lost her inebriated glow.

That was the downside of supernatural metabolisms, especially if one was trying to drink to forget. Magic burned through the alcohol, which made getting drunk difficult and staying drunk even harder. The more powerful the creature, the faster it wore off.

After Lina's influx of power, he was willing to bet she'd have to drink practically nonstop just to keep any sort of buzz going.

The unforeseen downside of her night's original plans was a definite boon for his current one.

Not stopping to overthink, Nord sent a command to Finley along their mental link.

"Don't come back tonight."

"Where am I—"

"Do. Not. Come. Home."

There was no response. He hadn't expected one.

Still holding Lina's hand, Nord took a backward step through the portal, pulling her with him. Between one step and the next, they left the glitzy chaos of The District behind. After closing the portal, he continued to guide her into the penthouse. She followed willingly, her eyes glued to him.

He waited for her to completely cross the threshold and then made sure she was paying attention as he raised his free hand and pressed it against the door just above her head. Crowding her body with his, he pushed the door shut with deliberate slowness. Each new inch brought them closer together so that by the time the door closed with a soft click, her back was flush against its wooden surface and his mouth was hovering just above hers.

Her eyes were wide, watching him with rapt fascination as she waited for his next move. He kept her waiting, drawing the moment out. The air grew charged between them as the moment stretched. All he had to do was dip his head, and their lips would be touching. From the way she tilted her chin up, he knew she was eager for him to do just that.

But still, he denied her.

When he claimed her mouth, he didn't just want her to be eager; he wanted her to be desperate.

Lifting the hand that still held hers, he pressed it back against the door over her head, locking her more firmly in place.

Lina's breathing grew shallow. They were standing so close that each rapid rise and fall caused her chest to brush against him. The brief friction sent tiny bolts of electricity racing down his skin.

Besides their hands, that brief contact was the only place they touched.

Lina held her breath as he leaned down that last inch. But instead of skimming her lips with his, he tilted his face to the side, bringing his mouth to her ear.

"Lina," he whispered.

"Hmm?"

"Tell me what you want," he breathed.

She made a strangled sound. "I think that's pretty obvious."

Nord grinned. "I want to hear you say it." He feathered a kiss over the velvety skin just behind her ear. "In detail."

Her throat bobbed as she swallowed. "I . . . I . . ."

"Yes?" he prompted.

"I want you."

"I want you, too." Nord shifted so that his hips were pressed against hers, allowing her to feel the truth of his admission. "But how do you want me?" he asked, his tongue darting out to trace the shell of her ear.

"Inside me," she managed, her voice a husky whisper.

"Do you want my tongue? My fingers? My cock?" He paused to enjoy Lina's sharp inhale. "Do you want me to take you hard? Fast? Dirty? Sweet? Gentle? Slow?" Each word was punctuated with another barely there kiss against her neck.

Nord wasn't sure which one of them he was turning on more with his questions, but Lina's breathless moan left no doubt about how they were making her feel.

"Yes."

"To which part?"

"All of it. Any of it."

He rocked his hips into her once more.

"Fuck," she groaned.

"Here? Against the door?"

"If that's what you want."

"Ah, but this is about what *you* want, my sweet Lina. Do you want me to peel that tiny scrap of a dress up over your hips, wrap your legs around my waist, and take you right here? Perhaps you'd prefer me to bend you over that table? Or would you rather I take you to bed?" He took the lobe of her ear between his teeth and let out a soft growl. "Tell me what you want, Lina, because if it's left up to me, no matter where we end up, I'll make you ride the edge until you beg me to let you come, and then I'll make you wait even longer."

He pulled back just far enough that he could see her face. Her lips were parted, eyes heavy-lidded, breath shallow. Her face and chest were flushed with desire.

Now, she was desperate.

"Last chance," he warned her.

Her tongue darted out to wet her lips. "Bedroom," she managed. "But I want the door thing."

One side of Nord's mouth lifted in a sexy smile. "Was that so hard?"

Fisting her free hand in his hair, Lina pulled his mouth down to hers. "I told you what I want. Keep up your end of the bargain."

"With pleasure."

His lips captured hers with the force of a conquering army. He laid siege to her mouth, claiming its silky softness as his own.

Releasing her hand, he pushed off the door so that he could slide his hands down the curve of her back and mold her body to his, fully closing the last sliver of distance between them. When his hands reached the bottom of her dress, he hooked a finger beneath each side and gave a sharp tug. The fabric put up little resistance, bunching up around her waist and leaving her ass bare for him to palm.

Still kissing her, he slightly bent his knees and adjusted his hold, easily lifting her up. Lina's legs wrapped around his hips of their own volition, anchoring her firmly against him. Turning so that his back was toward the wall, he ran his right hand along the bottom of her thigh, his fingers just barely grazing the damp heat between her legs. Even through the thin fabric of her thong, he could tell she was more than ready for him.

She moaned into his mouth and ground against him, seeking more than the ghost of a touch.

He chuckled against her lips, loving how responsive she was. He nipped at her bottom lip, pulling it into his mouth and sucking hard as his hand made its return journey from just above the underside of her knee back to her ass.

This time, there was no barely anything. His hand slowed when it reached her core, one finger hooking into the lacy fabric so that his knuckle parted her folds as it ran along her seam.

Lina gasped at the direct contact, her legs spasming as they squeezed him tighter.

"More," she demanded.

Pulling his mouth away from hers, he started a trail of kisses along her jaw.

"Your room or mine?" he asked, his index finger tracing a light circle around her opening.

"M-mine," she stuttered as he slid the tip of his finger inside of her. "It's closer."

Eyes focused on where he was going, Nord started walking in that direction, the shift in his gait causing Lina to bounce on the finger inside of her.

Her head fell back, her nails digging into his shoulders at the unexpected thrusting.

"More," she demanded again.

Nord tightened his grip on her and slid a second finger inside.

"Yes," she moaned, her inner muscles clamping down hard.

Reaching her closed door, Nord weighed his options. He either had to let go of her, or . . .

It wasn't really a choice. He wasn't letting her go for anything in this world or any other. Lifting up his foot, he kicked the door. It swung open with a crash.

Lina's eyes flew wide.

"Was that really necessary?" she asked with a breathless laugh.

"Yes."

"How are you supposed to take me against the door if the door is broken?"

"A wall works just as well."

Her answering smile was sin itself. "I like the way you think, Viking."

Before her lips could seal themselves over his, he noticed the new additions to her room.

"Lina?"

"Hmm?" she murmured, peppering kisses over his cheeks.

"What exactly did you and Quinn get up to this afternoon?"

She froze, confusion replacing the desire in her eyes as she pulled back. "What?"

He twisted so that she could see what he did.

Her face blanked and then turned an adorable shade of scarlet.

Unlit candles littered every available surface. In the corner, facing the mirror, a complicated-looking swing was hanging from the ceiling. Purple petals, so dark they were practically black, covered the bed. A bottle of champagne and two flutes along with a plate of chocolate-covered strawberries were arranged beside it on the nightstand.

On the other side of the room, arranged along the dresser, were a series of decidedly less sweet items. A black silk blindfold, handcuffs, a riding crop, something silver he assumed was a spreader bar, three bottles of lube, more condoms than he could count, vibrators and plugs of every possible shape and size, and two small feathered items he was fairly sure were some kind of clamp.

"I think it's Quinn's attempt to be helpful."

Reluctantly, Nord slid his fingers out and let her down. "Helpful?"

"It's a long story," she said distractedly, beelining for the pale scrap of paper in the middle of the bed.

"What's that?"

"Nothing," she said quickly, trying to hide it behind her back.

He raised a brow. "I could just take it from you."

Refusing to meet his eyes, she held it out for him to see. He skimmed the ivory surface, his lips lifting as he read the feminine scrawl.

A FEW THINGS TO HELP ENSURE A SUCCESSFUL MISSION.

"SUCCESSFUL MISSION?"

"Just a dumb joke," Lina said.

He spied a second ivory rectangle nestled against the items on the dresser. Lina followed his gaze and tried to beat him to it.

He plucked it up before she'd even made it over.

IN CASE YOU NEED SOME INSPIRATION.

NORD CHUCKLED AND SHOOK HIS HEAD, LETTING THE SCRAP OF PAPER FALL TO the floor.

"What'd it say?" Lina asked, trying to pluck it from the air.

He turned her away from the dresser and pulled her back into his arms, wanting all of her attention back on him. "Something about inspiration, but I think you and I have that taken care of."

Not wanting her to get any more distracted unless he was the reason, Nord started lifting up her dress, dragging it up her heated flesh and pausing only long enough to steal a kiss before he pulled it up over her head.

"Now, where were we?"

CHAPTER TWELVE
LINA

L ina bit her bottom lip as her dress fluttered to the floor. She couldn't remember a time she'd ever wanted anyone as badly as she wanted him.

The things he was doing to her body, there weren't words for it. And he was only just getting started.

With just a soft growl in her ear, he had her trembling with need.

Despite her jokes about being a born-again virgin, Lina was no stranger to sex. That said, the things she felt when Nord touched her were not even remotely in the realm of things she'd experienced before.

It would be like trying to compare a toddler just learning to walk with someone competing in the Olympics. To say she was outmatched was an understatement.

With over a millennium of experience at his disposal, Lina could have been all in her head about living up to his expectations, but when she saw the naked desire burning in his eyes, there was no room for doubt.

He wanted her every bit as much as she wanted him.

There was no room for anyone else.

The only thing that mattered was the two of them. Right here. In this moment.

The realization empowered her, making her feel like some kind of a sexual goddess.

Looking him straight in the eye, Lina reached back and unclasped her bra. She was deliberate in her movements, turning an everyday act into something straight out of a burlesque show. She drew out each move, never looking away from Nord's hungry gaze as she slowly dragged each strap down her arm.

He watched her with an intensity that bordered on mesmerized. She didn't think he could look away even if someone started shouting 'Fire!'

Breasts now free of the confining piece of silk and lace, she let him look his fill, dangling the bra off the tip of one finger before finally letting it fall on top of her dress.

Her body reacted to each pass of his eyes like a physical caress. Her breasts grew fuller; her nipples stiffened into tight peaks; goosebumps raced across her skin, and inside she felt a hollow ache that begged to be filled.

When his desire-heated eyes returned to hers, Lina started to work her thong over her hips.

"Wait," he said in his deep rasp. "Let me."

Liquid desire spiraled through her at the request. She nodded, letting her hands fall to her sides.

Nord held her gaze as he slowly dropped to a kneeling position before her. Still not looking away, he ran his tongue along the length of the fabric, kissing her throbbing center over the top of it.

Lina's moan broke off into a startled gasp as Nord's teeth clamped down lightly on the bundle of nerves between her legs. The fabric of her panties did little to dilute the carnal slide of his teeth against her sensitive flesh as he pulled away.

Her knees buckled, and she had to reach out to grasp his shoulders to keep from falling over because of the delicious friction that was equal parts too intense and nowhere near enough. She could already feel her climax hovering just out of reach.

One hand grasping her ankle, he tugged her legs slightly apart. "I've dreamt about doing this ever since I helped you put on your shoes," he admitted.

"Me too."

He grinned up at her, a wholly male smile that hinted at the things he had planned for her. Then, he took the scrap of black lace in his teeth once more and tugged. Hard.

There was a slight burn as the fabric roughly rubbed against her sensitive skin, but then it fell to the floor, joining its fallen brethren.

Lina had never felt as sexy in her life as she did right there, standing in only her heels while Nord kneeled before her.

His hands ran up her legs, starting at her ankles and roaming all the way up to her hips where his fingers dug into her skin.

Still holding her gaze, he repeated his early actions and pressed a kiss directly on top of the swollen bud at her center.

Lina moaned as heat surged through her.

"Do you trust me?" he asked.

"With everything in me."

The look he gave her then could have made even the holiest woman reconsider her vows. He moved his hand again, this time lifting her leg up by the knee and throwing it over his shoulder. Left leg done, he started to repeat the move on the other side.

"Nord," she protested as soon as the feeling of weightlessness hit her.

"I've got you, Kærasta. I'd never let you fall."

She swallowed back her nerves and gave him a little nod.

When he was certain she was ready, he picked up her other leg until he was fully supporting her weight. His hands were pressed against her back, providing a sense of stability as she straddled him.

"Try to stay still," he warned her seconds before he licked her straight up her exposed center.

Lina almost came right then.

Once he was certain she was stable, he devoured her with his tongue. She was squirming with need, riding his face as she chased release.

"I don't—I don't think," she panted, hands digging into his hair and thighs clamping around his head as she started to shake.

She could feel his smile against her exposed flesh. "Hold on," he warned her as he started to stand.

"Hold onto what?" she gasped, airborne not even a second later.

He was already climbing over her on the bed before she could fully understand what had just happened. Making short work of his clothes, he took a step forward, preparing to join her on the bed.

"Wait," she asked, pushing up to her elbows. "Just let me look at you for a second."

Nord, on a regular day, was enough to inspire a lifetime worth of fantasies. Nord, naked and hard for her, was not something she wanted to miss. He was all golden skin and black ink, chiseled planes, and lovely ridges. She was pretty sure he could put a sculpture to shame with the perfect symmetry of his body.

Pushing herself to a sitting position, she reached out, tracing the tattoo that covered his stomach with trembling fingers.

"Will you tell me what this means one day?" she asked.

He nodded, his arctic eyes glowing a brilliant azure.

Then she did something she'd wanted to do ever since she first saw the swirling lines traversing his skin. She began tracing them with her tongue. Following the pattern until it ended just beside the velvety length of him.

Grasping the base of him in one hand, she let her tongue continue its exploration. He jerked in her hold, one of his hands weaving in her hair as he thrust into her mouth.

"Lina," he groaned as she sucked him deep.

She loved that she was the one doing this to him. That she was the reason for that smoldering look in his eyes.

Never looking away, she watched his face as she moved up and down his length. The hand that held his shaft shadowing the path of her mouth.

"This is supposed to be about you," he ground out, pulling her hair slightly and sending electric tingles skittering down her neck and back.

There was a little pop as she released him. "Trust me, this is definitely about me."

His eyes burned even hotter as he put a palm to her chest and pushed her back flat onto the mattress before she could take him into her mouth again.

She pouted. "I wasn't done."

He kissed it away. "Neither was I."

There was no arguing with that. She was his to do with as he pleased.

He spread her open with one hand, running the length of his cock up and down, echoing what his fingers and tongue had already done.

Her eyes fluttered closed.

"Look at me," he demanded.

Her eyes flew back open. There was no denying *that* voice.

She was pretty sure she'd do whatever it demanded, no questions asked.

His fingers began running up and down her body. It was such a simple touch, but as aroused as she was, it was like throwing gasoline on a fire. She was so overwhelmed by sensation she wasn't sure how much more she could withstand.

Reaching back, he grasped one of her ankles in his hand and lifted her leg up, settling it over his shoulder.

"Okay?" he asked.

She nodded, well beyond speaking at this point.

Satisfied with her response, he took himself in one hand and positioned against her opening. The image seared itself into her brain. Nord, head bowed, eyes glued to her, hand on his thick cock, poised at her entrance. It was the most erotically beautiful thing she'd ever seen. He was every fantasy she'd ever had come to life.

Just as he'd done against the door, Nord drew the moment out. Rolling his hips so that his shaft drew tiny circles before pressing in ever so slightly.

A gasp was ripped from her throat at the delicious stretch. She'd known it would be a tight fit. Everything about the man was massive. But this . . .

Lina sucked in a breath.

Nord stilled. "Am I hurting you?"

"You'll be the one hurting if you try to stop now."

He laughed, but it was a pained sound like he was barely holding onto control.

Sliding her hands along his back, she pressed her hands into his taut ass. It was a request for him to slide deeper, not that he budged. She could have been tickling him for all he moved.

"Please," she begged. "Don't stop now."

"I could never deny you anything when you ask so sweetly," he murmured, a thumb on her chin as he leaned forward and claimed her mouth.

She would have laughed since all he'd done was deny her since they'd met, but then he pressed deeper, filling her with his length, and there were no words left at all. Only sensation.

A garbled sound that could have been his name left her lips, but still, he pressed, not stopping until he filled her completely.

Her lips formed a soundless 'o' as he rolled his hips, causing his cock to hit places inside her that she didn't know existed. Then, he did it a second time, making her light up like a firecracker after a parade.

Her orgasm hit her so hard and so fast that she was momentarily blind, the world falling to darkness with little lights exploding behind her eyes in time with the spasming of her inner muscles.

Nothing existed in that moment except the sea of sensation she floated in. She had no name. No body. She simply existed.

And what she was, was his.

Mind. Body. Soul. He owned it all.

She could not belong to him more completely if he inked his name on her heart.

Her eyes fluttered open to find him smiling down at her.

"Welcome back."

She gave him a cheeky grin. "So much for drawing it out until I begged."

"Sweetheart, you did beg." His smile took on a dangerously sexy edge. "The first one was free. The rest, you'll have to earn."

She swallowed, her desire peaking to dangerous levels at his taunt. "Uh oh."

He took her bottom lip between his teeth while his hips drew out and then slammed back into her.

"You have no idea."

Lina's eyes rolled back in her head as the tip of his cock rubbed over that newly discovered place inside of her once more.

"Look at me, Lina."

It was a struggle to fight through the fog of desire to obey.

"Every time those beautiful eyes close, I stop, and we start all over."

She spasmed around him.

He thrust into her, sending little sparks flickering at the edges of her periphery, but she kept her eyes open.

"Good girl," he breathed before thrusting in again.

She only made it three more thrusts before her eyes closed again.

Nord tsked, his body stilling completely.

Lina moaned in protest, nails digging into his skin as she silently urged him to keep going.

He refused to move until she forced her heavy eyes open. She was about to curse him for stopping, but the words were lost as she took in the sight of him. Muscles straining, jaw clenched, eyes burning with need. Delayed gratification was totally worth it if it meant she got to see that tortured expression on his face. He was waging a war against his own desire, fighting to stay in control so that he could ensure her needs were met.

Something shifted in her brain then, and it was no longer focused on what he was doing to her but on what her reaction was doing to *him*. Every moan had his eyes flaring brighter, the scrape of her nails down his back making him thrust harder. All of it only reinforced her own arousal and sent her spiraling higher until she was tittering just on the cusp of another mind-shattering climax.

"Nord," she panted, back arching up and pressing her body against him.

"Not yet."

"I'm so close."

"Just ride the edge for me a little longer."

She bit down on her lip, feeling a bit like she was trying to stave off a tidal wave with a piece of paper.

He shifted their bodies, the new angle allowing him to slide even deeper and hit all the right places. Her thighs started to shake, and she tossed her head to the side.

"Nord," she moaned. "Please."

He drew his teeth down the side of her neck, clamping down on the muscle between her neck and shoulder.

"Now," he whispered, slamming into her.

Lina shattered, clinging to him as her orgasm detonated with the force of an atomic bomb. Nord continued to thrust deep, the relentless drive of his hips extending her climax and sending her spiraling higher. Just when Lina thought she might pass out from the pleasure, Nord joined her, coming with a savage roar of her name that set off yet another aftershock within her.

She had no idea how much time had passed when the tickle of Nord's beard over her skin finally penetrated the post-orgasmic haze she'd been lost within.

She offered him a lopsided smile. "Totally worth the wait."

Nord's eyes flared with pleasure as he leaned down to kiss her tenderly.

"How do you feel?" he asked.

Lina pried an eye open to study him. "Like a piece of overcooked spaghetti."

He chuckled and kissed her again. "Is that a good thing?"

Lina nodded. "The best."

Nord brushed a few sweaty strands of hair off her face. "You aren't tired, are you?"

She looked at him more closely. "No. Why?"

"Good." He gave her one of his rare, full grins, devastating her with its sheer masculine beauty. "Because I'm nowhere near done with you."

Even sated as she was, her body thrummed with anticipation, already eager for another round—or ten.

"Me neither."

She let out a little whimper as he flexed his hips, the still hard length of him rubbing against her swollen, sensitive flesh.

"I should warn you, my sweet Lina. When it comes to you. I never will be."

His name was a moan as it left her lips, his thrusts torturously slow as he stoked the flames of desire and brought her back to the brink of climax once more.

As the night wore on, she lost count of the number of times she came, but Nord had been right about one thing.

She begged.

And he made her earn every single one of her orgasms.

CHAPTER THIRTEEN

LINA

Lina burrowed deeper into her cocoon of blankets, a contented smile touching her lips as images from the past few hours ran through her mind in a happy loop. Heat blossomed in her cheeks as she recalled a particularly pleasant one, and her smile morphed into a grin that would make the Cheshire cat proud.

"I hope that smile is for me."

Nord's voice reached her only seconds before his hand cracked down hard on her ass.

Lina jolted upright, her eyes flying open and her hand moving to belatedly shield the now stinging cheek. "It was," she grumbled, rubbing her tender flesh.

His lips twitched with laughter. "Come on. Time to get up."

Her brows lowered, and she glanced at the clock beside her bed. "No way. It's not even eight. We only fell asleep a few hours ago." Lina noted his sweat-damp hair and the way his navy tank clung to his chiseled body. "How long have you been awake?"

"Since six."

She would have been insulted he still had energy to burn off in the gym after the marathon sexcapade they'd been involved in, but he looked too damn sexy.

"Instead of me getting up, I think *you* should come back to bed," she said, lifting up a corner of the blanket and patting the mattress next to her.

He smirked. "Tempting as that is, I have other plans for the morning."

She was woman enough to admit that the pout she gave him was not for show. What could hold more sway than the two of them naked in bed? Especially after they'd proven—repeatedly—how mind-blowing it would be.

"Your reprieve is over. It's time to get back to your training."

"Doesn't last night count as a workout?" she asked with a hopeful smile.

His fingers wrapped around her ankle and gave a hard tug, pulling her down the bed. He planted his hands on either side of her head and leaned over until his lips were hovering just out of reach.

Her belly gave an excited flutter.

"No."

The flicker of hope his nearness ignited flickered out.

"Well, it should," she said with a huff. "I'm certainly sore enough."

He pushed up, speaking to her over his shoulder as he started heading toward the door. "Get dressed and meet me in the gym. I'll give you five minutes before I start adding extra reps."

Her frown deepened. "You and I have vastly different priorities."

He paused in the doorway, turning to look at her. "You are my priority. Your happiness. Your well-being. Your safety. Training you is another way of guaranteeing it."

Her heart turned to putty at the declaration.

Then, he ruined the entire moment by adding, "By my count, you've got four minutes."

Lina stuck her tongue out at his retreating back, but she wasted no time swinging her legs over the side of the bed and heading to the bathroom.

By the time she reached the gym, nearly twenty minutes had passed. Not because she was purposefully delaying her arrival but because she hadn't been lying when she said she was sore. Muscles she hadn't even known existed were aching with protest. Her poor body felt abused in the best possible way.

How the hell Nord thought she'd make it through a full training session, she had no idea.

She came to a dead stop when she finally stumbled through the doorway. While she'd been busy getting dressed and trying to walk without a limp, Nord had ditched his tank and continued with his workout.

She'd known he was a fierce warrior. He had the scars and muscles to prove it. But she'd never considered the other side of that persona. The grace and discipline that came with the kind of training required to keep himself in peak condition. There was no ignoring it now.

Nord was vertical, feet pointed above his head, body perfectly aligned. His hands gripped some kind of metal bars that rested about six inches off the floor. As she watched, he pushed his body down, arms flexing as his torso swung forward in a controlled dive, coming to rest mere inches off the ground between the bars. He held himself in that suspended plank position for a few seconds before reversing the move and returning to the handstand he started in.

Lina was transfixed. The sheer strength and control the move required was beyond impressive. The fact that he executed it effortlessly, no straining arms, no loss of breath, spoke of an athleticism and stamina no mere mortal could claim.

She watched him repeat this a few more times, blaming him and the creative ways he used her body the night before for the filthy direction of her thoughts.

Finished with his extreme push-ups, Nord placed a knee on the mat and picked up the towel he'd set to the side, wiping off his face before turning to look at her.

"You ready?"

Her brain short-circuited for a second as she conjured up potential meanings for the question. She was beyond ready to throw herself on the ground between those metal bars—sore muscles be damned if it meant she got a VIP pass to that party—when he stood and gestured toward the treadmill.

There was no hiding her disappointment as she trudged over to the machine. From the slight twitch of his lips, Nord must have known exactly where her mind had been. She would even go so far as to guess that he planned for her to find him in that pose, knowing exactly what images it would conjure when she did.

Asshole.

This whole morning was turning into one long punishment.

As soon as the thought hit her, she spun to face him, her eyes narrowed with accusation. "You're punishing me for last night, aren't you?"

"Maybe next time, you'll remember to let me know where you're going," he said with a smug smile.

Lina groaned. She should have known he wouldn't let that go.

"I hate you," she muttered without heat, stepping onto the machine.

"So you keep telling me." He moved in close to adjust the settings, dropping his voice low as he replied, "But if you recall, that's not what you were moaning last night." He paused to look straight into her eyes as he added, "Or this morning."

Lina bared her teeth at him in a snarl when the belt beneath her feet started moving. He huffed out a bemused laugh when she tipped forward, losing her balance with all the grace of a cartoon character. Even though she'd never admit it, she was thankful for his super-human reflexes since the palm he shot out and pressed to her chest was the only thing that kept her from falling completely. Tripping was bad enough, but actually sliding backward off the treadmill in a crumpled heap at his feet? She'd never live that down.

She shoved his hand away, causing his lips to twitch with amusement. Holding both handles in a death grip, she awkwardly managed to get her feet back under her and find her rhythm. It was more of an angry powerwalk than a jog, but it was something.

"Better get moving, Kærasta. You've already added twenty-seven minutes to your sentence. Clock doesn't stop ticking until you start actually running."

"Maybe if you stopped insisting on tormenting me, I wouldn't have to hate you," she shouted as he walked away.

He let out a bark of laughter, calling back, "I stand by what I said. That's not hate you feel. Twenty-eight and counting."

She cursed him as she ran, a dark smile tilting her lips as she started planning all the ways she'd make him pay for this.

Thirty minutes later, smile long gone and legs feeling like jelly, she was pretty sure she hated him.

After an hour, bruised, muscles shaking, and finding herself on the floor for the umpteenth time, there was no doubt in her mind that she absolutely hated him—at least in that moment.

"I told you, as soon as you show me you can do a takedown, we can be done for the day."

She glared up at him as she pushed herself back to her feet. "How can someone so beautiful on the outside be so evil on the inside?"

Having actually experienced true evil, Lina didn't really believe what she was saying. She was fully aware that in his own arguably sadistic way, he was on her side. But even knowing that he was only trying to help her get better, her pride refused to allow her to accept defeat with dignity.

With each failed attempt, her frustration grew. That combined with a lack of sleep, a night of drinking and debauchery, and a body protesting even the act of drawing in breath meant she was nursing a serious temper.

One she had every intention of taking out on the handsome Viking waiting patiently for her to get back in their starting position.

Lina knew she wasn't being rational. It wasn't his fault she couldn't seem to get the hang of this, but she didn't care. She just wanted to knock the smug smile off his perfect face. Okay, what she really wanted was to knock the cocky bastard on his ass.

If she could beat him, even once, it would prove that she wasn't useless. That would go a long way to soothing the sting of her perceived failures. Most of which stemmed from her newly returned memories and had nothing at all to do with what was taking place in this gym.

Lina wiped sweat off her face with her forearm, searching Nord's form for some weakness to exploit. It might have been the first time she looked at him without feeling even a remote pang of attraction.

He didn't even look out of breath. And why should he? He wasn't the one getting his ass kicked.

It was painfully clear she wasn't going to beat him in any feat of strength, not without handicapping him first.

Lina scowled, wishing there was a way to level the playing field. Something she could do to make him falter, just for a second. That was all she needed—an opening. Anything that would give her a fighting chance at besting him.

She started to picture, in vivid detail, the various ways she could make him lose his balance. If he was wearing shoes, she could untie one. But he wasn't, so that was out. There wasn't anything nearby that she could throw in front of him for him to trip over.

She sighed. Short of an impromptu earthquake or a totally implausible sinkhole ripping open the ground beneath him—

The floor swayed.

Lina's stomach dipped, and her arms flew out to keep her balance. For a second, she was uncertain if she'd just gotten lost in her grumpy plotting or if she'd really felt that. But Nord mirrored her movement, his expression one of concern as he scanned the floor.

There was another tremor, this one far worse than the last.

Weights clanked together, some even falling from the force of it. This time, the shaking didn't stop. It only grew in power as a snaking black line appeared in the ground.

Crack!

No, not a line. A fissure.

Right between Nord's feet—the exact place she'd imagined it.

His mouth fell open in shock as the fracture opened up, growing in every direction.

Lina remained frozen, stunned and horrified that she somehow manifested an actual sinkhole.

"Lina, run!" he roared, eyes wild with panic as the fissure raced toward her.

When she didn't move, he took matters into his own hands. He charged at her. She barely caught the flash of azure fire in his eyes before he crashed into her with the force of a runaway train and sent them both flying.

They landed several feet away in a painful tangle of limbs. Nord managed to land in a way that allowed him to mostly shield her with his body but did nothing to cushion her fall. She smacked the ground. Hard. There was an audible pop, and her vision swam as little stars exploded in her periphery. The metallic tang of blood filled her mouth from where her teeth had bitten through her cheek. She tried to move, to push herself up, but one arm was stuck between their bodies, the other trapped beneath her, twisted at an unnatural angle. Lucky for her, she was too focused on the fact that the ground had ceased its shaking to fully register the searing pain shooting up said arm.

He peered down at her, their breaths coming out in harsh gasps.

"Are you all right?" he asked, his voice rough with worry.

"I—I didn't mean . . ." she stuttered, mouth feeling like she'd tried to swallow a bag of cotton balls.

"Don't worry about that. Are *you* all right?"

She tried again to shift underneath him, the slight movement causing her to hiss. "My arm," she croaked.

Nord frowned and pushed off of her. "Let me take a look," he said, carefully helping her sit up.

Even that gentle jostling was too much. Lina's arm felt like it was on fire. It hung at her side with an unfamiliar heaviness that made her both more aware of it but also oddly detached. Like it wasn't really hers. She was lightheaded from the pain, and little spots danced in front of her eyes as she fought to stay conscious.

Instead of looking down to see her injury for herself, Lina focused on Nord. She could tell from the clench of his jaw that whatever he was looking at wasn't pretty. Although the amount of pain she was in had already been a pretty good indication of that.

His eyes flared bright with his power as he looked *through* her, using his Guardian abilities to see the extent of the damage.

"Fracture," he declared. "A pretty nasty one. I can fix it, but it's going to require me to touch you," he said apologetically.

Lina gritted her teeth. "Do it."

She whimpered at just the brush of his hand over her arm.

A vein in Nord's neck pulsed at the sound, and she knew it must be killing him to be adding to her discomfort even if it was a necessity.

"It's okay," she said.

After a deep breath, he nodded and started again. Lina barely managed to swallow back an agonized moan as he placed his hand flat against her broken skin. Pain shot through her body but rapidly dulled as Nord began repairing the damage to her bone.

"There, all done," he said, sitting back.

Lina was still breathing heavily, the chaos of the last few minutes leaving her with a bad case of emotional whiplash.

"Thank you."

He studied her, lips twitching as the power started to fade from his eyes. "You know, if you really wanted to be done, you could have just said something."

Her eyes narrowed, but she was fighting a small smile. "I don't know what happened. I was just so tired and so frustrated. I never meant to actually summon my magic. Hell, I didn't even know I *could*. One second, I was picturing ways to finally beat you, and the next, the world was attempting to split in two."

Nord glanced over his shoulder at the ugly gash roughly the size of two large sofas running through the center of the gym.

"Was this your first option?" he asked, but there was no judgment in his tone.

She rubbed a hand over her face and sighed. "I wanted to give myself an advantage, not topple the whole damn building."

"I guess it's safe to say your magic has made a full recovery." He stood and held out a hand to help her up as well. "And for what it's worth, you don't need an advantage. Just practice." He ran his thumb soothingly over her knuckles as they walked to the edge of the crater. "That said, I pushed you too hard this morning. This is as much on me as it is on you. Next time, we'll both be more careful."

For some reason, his understanding only made her feel more guilty. She squeezed his hand in a silent thank you and then turned her attention to the aftermath of her unintentional magic. Her stomach dropped as she peered down into the hole.

"Hi, Mrs. Montgomery," she said, giving her neighbor a half-hearted wave.

The woman gaped up at them from her living room, every inch of it covered in white dust and chunks of debris, including the coffee cup she held halfway to her mouth.

"We'll get this taken care of right away," Lina called down, tilting her chin toward Nord as she muttered, "Better call Quinn."

CHAPTER FOURTEEN
LINA

Alistair had just finished repairing the floor when Quinn breezed through, brushing her hands together like she was wiping off crumbs.

"All done," she said with a smile. "Now, care to tell us *why* you needed us to come to your rescue in the first place? Not that I mind, but a girl does get curious."

Lina wished she could have said that she hadn't needed to be rescued, but Quinn was the only person she knew who could make their poor neighbor forget that the sky had literally come falling down on her during breakfast. And, after a failed attempt at repairing the physical damage she'd caused—she'd been too on edge to focus and worried she might lose control and make matters worse —Lina had reluctantly called Alistair, requesting his help as well.

Now everyone, including a cranky Finley, was aware of her fuck-up. Except Mrs. Montgomery, of course.

Lina's eyes shifted to the newly mended floor. "What do you mean 'why'? Are you blind?"

"Oh, don't play stupid with me, Queen E. When I left you last night, you couldn't make a rabbit appear out of a hat, let alone rip a massive hole through a foot and a half of building materials. What happened between now and then?"

Nord chose that exact moment to make an entrance. Quinn's smile stretched knowingly as her gaze raked him over.

"I mean I've heard of windows shattering, but concrete . . ."

"Quinn," Alistair said warningly.

"What?" she asked innocently. "You know you're wondering too."

Her uncle's cheeks were tinged pink as he replied, "Extreme emotion is a well-known trigger for an animagus recovering from their Awakening. Our magic is unpredictable at best during the days and sometimes weeks following."

"You didn't think to mention that before now?" Finley asked dryly. "It's akin to letting us walk off with a bomb strapped to our back."

Alistair held out his hands and shrugged. "It wasn't exactly a secret. Lina certainly should have known it was a possibility."

Lina shrank further into the hoodie she'd commandeered from the floor, trying to escape the three sets of eyes that turned her way. Now that he mentioned it, that did sound familiar. Maybe if she hadn't been so busy metaphorically sticking her fingers in her ears and shouting 'la-la-la, I can't hear you' to her past, she might have remembered that little tidbit.

It was almost stupid, how badly she'd wanted her memories and then how quickly she tried to forget them again once they were back. She felt justified in her mental about-face though. It was some heavy shit to try and wrap her head around all at once.

What was it they said? Be careful what you wish for? Whoever 'they' were really deserved more credit. They were wise as fuck.

"I didn't even realize I had called on my power until after it happened. He was just pushing my buttons—"

"I bet he was," Quinn purred.

"Quinn!" all four of them snapped.

"Oh, come on," she said, rolling her eyes. "You were all thinking it."

"It's all right, Lina," Nord said, moving to stand at her side. "No one is blaming you. It was an accident."

"Be that as it may," Finley said, shooting her an apologetic glance, "we can't have you going around accidentally blowing shit up. What's to stop this from happening again?"

Her hands curled into fists inside her sweatshirt. "Me. Now that I know what I'm capable of, it won't happen again unless I want it to. Believe it or not, I was trained in how to control my magic. It's just been a while."

And it's a hell of a lot stronger than it used to be.

Sure, she'd been able to conjure things out of thin air—clothes, drinks, maybe something more elaborate like furniture if she really worked on it—but something of this scale? That was on a whole other level.

A part of her was a bit intimidated by the discovery. The other part gleefully wondered what else she could do now.

"Excuse me if I don't feel overly confident in your prowess just yet," Finley said.

Her eyes narrowed at him. What was his problem? It wasn't like she'd done any permanent damage to his beloved penthouse. This was the sort of thing he'd usually crack a joke about.

"Don't mind him," Quinn murmured. "His Prissiness didn't take well to sleeping on the floor last night."

Oh.

Well, that explained where he'd ended up. Not that she'd been concerned one way or the other. She'd had other things on her mind.

"Leave it, Fin," Nord interjected. "You know as well as I do that control comes with time and practice. The answer here is the same as it's always been."

"Is training your answer for everything?" she asked.

"Not everything," he said with a smile that sent her heart rate spiking.

Finley scrubbed a hand through his hair and let out a weary sigh. "You're right. Sorry, love." He flashed her a sheepish grin. "Didn't mean to take my mood out on you. Spent the better part of my morning trying to get the Director off my ass."

Nord's eyes sharpened at that. "About what?"

"Wanted to know why two of his men were spotted at The District without his authority. Tried to explain it was purely recreational. That went over about as well as you'd expect."

"Fuck," Nord swore. "That's not good."

"Yup," Finley agreed. "So much for flying under the radar."

"On a scale of one to Lina, how fucked are we?" Quinn asked.

"Seriously?" Lina asked, wishing Quinn wasn't halfway across the room so she could punch her in the tit.

"Sorry, last one. Promise," she said, miming locking her lips.

"If it's not, I'll go Picasso on your face."

Finley snorted.

Nord raised an eyebrow.

Alistair merely shook his head, a small smile playing about his mouth. He was no stranger to their sisterly bickering.

Quinn crossed her arms and lifted a single shoulder. "You need to get some new material. You've been using that since we were ten, and I've yet to end up with an ear on my forehead or a nipple for a nose."

"Must mean it's working," Lina said with a tight smile.

"Could she really do that?" Finley whispered to Alistair.

"And then some," he confirmed.

The Guardian whistled. "Keep going, Quinn. I need to see this."

Nord reached out and cuffed him on the back of the head.

Quinn tossed him a deceptively sweet smile, her wine-colored eyes glittering. "You just know that's the only way you'll ever see the goods."

Nord spoke before Finley could add more fuel to Quinn's ire.

"To answer your question, having the Director looking in our direction at all is troubling."

"Why?" Lina asked. "It's not like we're breaking the law trying to track down a murderer."

Nord's expression could have been carved from stone, and Finley purposely dropped his gaze to the floor.

"Are we?" Lina asked.

Finley cleared his throat and rubbed the back of his neck. "Strictly speaking, our actions the last few weeks would not be deemed completely legal according to the Brotherhood's bylaws. I guess you could say we've gone a bit rogue."

Nord crossed his arms and snorted at that. "Just a bit."

Finley flashed him a grin.

"I thought you Brotherhood boys were all about playing by the rules. Why break them now?" Quinn asked.

"When a mate asks for help, it's always better to beg forgiveness than wait and ask permission," Finley answered with an easy shrug.

Quinn's eyes seemed to hold a new measure of respect as they studied him. "I see."

Finley and Nord shared a look as Nord explained, "There were too many questions we couldn't answer, which would have tied our hands if we went through official channels from the start. It was just easier to keep them out of the loop and avoid all their unnecessary red tape."

"So you lied, and now the Director is popping up, which means he's not as easy to fool as you hoped," Quinn surmised.

"That would seem to be the case," Nord said.

"Well, you are part of a network built around gathering secret information. His finding out can't be much of a surprise," Quinn said.

"It's not, but we'd hoped to have this wrapped up before we had to worry about anyone looking over our shoulder," Nord said.

"Not to mention, if he is onto us, finding Mataius just got infinitely harder," Finley said, looking grim. "It's bad enough we're running our own op. But word gets back to him we're not only going after an heir; we're also working *with* members of the Mobius Council? We can all kiss our freedom goodbye."

Lina sucked in a breath. Nord and Finley had both made comments about not getting the Brotherhood involved, but they'd made it seem like no big deal. She'd never considered what it would mean for them if someone found out.

"Nord—"

He shook his head, causing the words to die on her lips.

"I already told you about my priorities, Lina."

They stared at each other, her trying to convey a thousand unspoken reasons he shouldn't risk himself for her and he projecting nothing but steely resolve.

"If the Director becomes a problem, I'll deal with him," Quinn said, shattering the moment with her matter-of-fact declaration.

Lina swallowed down a ball of emotion, feeling simultaneously thankful and undeserving of such unwavering loyalty from the people in this room.

"Way I see it," she continued, studying her nails, "you two are doing him a favor by keeping the Brotherhood out of this mess. I'll make sure he sees it that way, too."

Now, it was Finley's turn to give her a considering once-over. "You'd do that for us?"

She wrinkled her nose. "Not you. Lina. I just got her back; I'm not losing her again. Like it or not, the five of us are in this together until Mataius chokes on his still-beating heart."

Nord tossed her an approving smile before shifting his attention back to Finley. "You should probably fill me in on what the Director had to say."

Finley nodded his agreement.

"Do you mind if we leave you three alone for a little while?" Nord asked.

Quinn scoffed. "Why would she mind? We're her family. You need to work on your trust issues, big guy. In case you've forgotten, we're the ones who swooped in and saved the day."

He raised a brow at her. "Who said anything about trust? If I doubted your motives, heir, you'd never have set foot in this house. I don't care who you are to her."

Unlike Finley's threats, which inspired venom, Nord's only made Quinn beam at him.

"This is why we like you. So straightforward," she purred.

Lina was still shaking her head at her friend's antics when Nord crossed the room to stand beside her. Brushing a fallen piece of her hair off of her cheek, he asked in a low voice, "Want me to send them home?"

She gave him a tired smile. "I can entertain them for a little while. Go. Talk with Finley or whatever you guys need to do."

His eyes searched her face before he nodded once. Then, he dipped his chin and pressed a lingering kiss to her forehead. "We shouldn't be long."

After Nord and Finley left the room, Quinn let out a wistful sigh. "Tell me you at least tried the swing out."

Lina's eyes darted to Alistair.

"Pfft. Don't let the tweed fool you. Alistair gets more pussy than a whole university's worth of frat boys. Now spill."

Her uncle let out a quiet laugh, but Lina couldn't help but notice that he didn't deny Quinn's allegation.

"When did you even find the time to set all that up, by the way?" she asked instead, refusing to answer Quinn's question.

Quinn smiled. "While you were arranging for a ride."

"I only left you alone for, like, three minutes tops."

Quinn shrugged. "What can I say? I work fast."

"But where did you even find all that stuff?"

"I made some calls. It was delivered while you were shaving."

Lina shook her head. She might be the one who could modify reality, but when it came to getting shit done, Quinn had a special kind of magic all her own.

"So . . . about that swing."

"Quinn," Alistair smoothly interjected. "Would you mind making us some coffee?"

She canted her head to the side and studied him with narrowed eyes. "Is that your polite way of asking me to take a hike?"

An enigmatic smile was her only answer.

She rolled her eyes. "Fine. Get rid of me, but I'm not making anybody any coffee. If you need me, I'll be in Finley's room."

Lina's brows flew up. "Fin's room?"

Quinn's lips curled in a wicked smile. "I feel like doing some more redecorating."

"Are you sure that's a good idea? You haven't seen what the fallout from last time will be yet," Lina called after her, not that it did any good. She watched Quinn leave with a small shake of her head. "I guess we should be glad she's going after his room again and not the garage."

"Why's that?" Alistair asked.

"I'm not sure even I could save her if she ever does something to one of his precious cars."

They shared a laugh.

"Let's hope we never have to find out."

Alistair was still chuckling, looking oddly at home in the Guardians' gym as he leaned against one of the mirrors.

"Am I in trouble?" Lina blurted.

He blinked. "Trouble? Why would you think that?"

She gestured to the empty room. "Oh, I don't know. Maybe because you've always been kind enough not to tell me what a fuck-up I am in front of other people. Why else would you ask Quinn to leave if not to say that I should have known better than to let myself lose control so spectacularly?"

He peered at her over the top of his glasses. "Lina, you're a grown woman. I have no intention of lecturing you about anything. I only asked Quinn to leave because it seemed like you could use a break." He shrugged, hands resting on the cane in front of him. "Besides, it sounds like you're beating yourself up enough on your own."

Lina scrubbed her hands over her face and groaned. "I don't remember my magic being like this."

"Like what?" he asked.

"So responsive," she said, still speaking from behind her hands.

"Well, of course not. It was only a fraction of what it is now. To assume it would feel the same would be like expecting a firehose to act like a garden sprinkler."

A giggle escaped as she pictured that. Slowly, she lowered her hands. "So you don't think I'm going to be the biggest embarrassment the Cuska line has ever seen? Aren't heirs supposed to be naturals when it comes to using our power?"

Her uncle tilted his head. "Do you remember your father?"

They shared a smile, but it was tinged with sadness.

"I wish he hadn't hated me so much," she said in a quiet voice. "Maybe then, I would feel more prepared for all of this."

Alistair scoffed. "Even if he had taken the time to teach you, I don't think it would have changed anything. There's a difference between knowing about something and actually understanding it. Everything is mere theory until you experience it firsthand. For what it's worth, my brother rarely deigned to share anything about his power unless he was lording it over me. But what I can tell you is this. Never, in our hundred-plus years together, did I ever witness him do anything half as impressive as what you managed to do without even trying."

"Really?"

He dipped his chin in a nod, eyes twinkling with pride as he said, "Really."

Lina took her first easy breath since stepping foot on that blasted treadmill.

"Did I ever tell you about the day you were born?"

She shook her head. "I don't think so."

His eyes took on a far-off cast, his lips twisted in a wry grin. "It was not one of my best moments, I assure you. I was running around like a damn fool, but your mother . . ." His smile stretched. "You wouldn't have known Kat was in labor. She was the picture of calm and grace even then. I was in the middle of drafting a proposal for some magical sect or the other, and she walked into my study, hands cradling her belly with the most radiant smile I'd ever seen. 'She's coming,' she told me.

"Well,"—he chuckled—"I was up out of that seat so fast that I tipped the damn thing over. Your father was off on some errand for the Council, so it was up to me to get her to the hospital—he was going to meet us there.

"We'd gone over the plan a dozen different times, but in that moment, it was like I'd forgotten even the most basic things. I couldn't find the keys. I put my shoes on the wrong feet. It took me three tries to start the car because I kept dropping the keys. I was so nervous she was going to have you right there in the passenger seat, I don't think I let my foot off the gas once until we were actually in front of the building.

"The entire time, your mother just laughed at me and kept telling me to breathe. That everything would be all right. That we were about to meet the girl who would bring purpose and meaning to our lives. The true love of her life, she called you."

Lina hung on every word, feeling oddly sentimental as she listened to a story about a woman she'd never met but had always longed for.

Alistair's gaze refocused on Lina's face, and his smile softened. "She was right. But then, Kat was always right." He sighed, his eyes dropping to the floor. "I wasn't allowed in the room with her, so I didn't realize anything was wrong until much later. When the nurse popped out of the delivery room with you cradled in her arms, the world just fell away. Your father still wasn't there, so she asked if I wanted to hold you."

Her uncle's voice began to waver, and he paused to clear his throat.

"My hands were shaking when she placed you in my arms. I thought babies cried when they were born, but I was the one that was crying. You, on the other hand, were so peaceful and calm—just like your mother. Your eyes were wide open, staring straight up into mine. That was it. All it took for me to know that the course of my life had been irrevocably changed. I knew, in that single moment, there wasn't anything I wouldn't do for you."

Alistair broke off, lifting a trembling hand to brush a tear off his face.

"It wasn't until later that I learned she was gone. The nurse, the same one who placed you in my arms, told me that you still needed a name. Your father was beyond devastated, completely inconsolable. So they asked me. I told them it was Evalina—beautiful life."

He stopped speaking then, his eyes trained on the tips of his polished shoes.

"Uncle Alistair—" Lina said, moving toward him.

He flashed her a pained smile. "Your father always thought Kat named you. He never knew it was me. No one did. Until now."

Lina's lip trembled, and she fought hard against tears.

"Anyway, I didn't bring it up to tell you that but to remind you that it's not just your father's DNA you carry. You inherited his power, yes, but that's only part of who you are. And it's not even the most important part. You have so much of your mother in you. Her kindness, her indomitable will, her ability to laugh at herself when she made a mistake—which she did just as spectacularly as you. Everyone who knew her knew that telling her she *couldn't* do something was the fastest way to ensure she did."

He chuckled to himself.

"She may not have been born an animagi, but she was an exceptionally powerful witch in her own right. In fact, I'd be willing to bet that she could have bested your father if it came to a test of magical skill. There was nothing she couldn't do if she set her mind to it, but she never made anyone feel small just so she could feel important. She never took her ability for granted. She respected her magic, worked hard to master it. I used to ask her why she bothered when she was a natural. Do you know what she told me? She said that just because someone is born with a gift doesn't mean that they deserve it. She wanted to be worthy of what she was given. I'm sure, were she here, she would teach you to do the same."

Silence stretched between them as Lina reflected on her mother's wisdom, letting it take root inside of her.

"Thank you for telling me that," she whispered.

He nodded. "Of course."

"You loved her," she said, ignoring the tears trailing down her cheeks.

Alistair swallowed and was silent for so long that she'd started to think he wasn't going to answer. He still wasn't looking at her when he finally spoke.

"I did, but things were different then. With the animagi dying out, we had to marry to secure the bloodline, not for something as whimsical as love." The bitterness in his voice was unmistakable. "Katarina was a magnificent witch from a very prominent family. Anatoly was the Cuska heir simply because he had the foresight to be born first. Love her or not, she was never meant for me."

Lina's heart broke for the man who'd loved her mother from afar and then spent the rest of his life raising her child.

"I wish you could have been my father," she said, not for the first time.

He smiled at her, finally lifting his eyes back to hers. "I may not have sired you, but never doubt that you are mine. Even fate agrees. It ensured that I would be the first to hold you and be the one to give you your name."

Lina rushed to him then, throwing her arms around him and squeezing tight. "I love you."

He hugged her back, his voice gruff as he said, "And I you, my sweet girl."

When they pulled apart, he studied her for a few seconds before shaking his head.

"Anatoly wasn't always the cold, power-hungry man you knew, but he was a fool up until the day he died. He wasted so many years angry at you for stealing the one person he loved more than himself that he never realized the best parts of her lived on in you."

Alistair squeezed her shoulder, his expression a mix of pride and years-old heartache.

"I'm just so thankful I lived long enough to see you come back. Even if it was my short-sighted actions that got you killed in the first place."

Lina shook her head. "No. You didn't kill me. Mataius did that all on his own, and—"

Whatever else she was about to say was drowned out by the high-pitched wail of a siren.

"Oh, for fuck's sake, what now?" she growled.

CHAPTER FIFTEEN
NORD

Nord stared out of the window, unseeing, his mind a furious hive of activity.

Finley prattled on behind him, not really telling him anything he hadn't already surmised until he said, "The Director wants us to come in for a debriefing. Lina, too."

Nord spun around. "What?"

The word was softly spoken, but it cracked with the force of a whip.

To his credit, Finley didn't so much as flinch.

"I don't think he knows as much as he's letting on. He called her 'the blonde', but there's no mistaking who he was referring to."

Nord ground his teeth together. Anger pulsed through his veins as the berserker tried to claw its way to the surface.

A debriefing by the Director wasn't anything as straightforward as an interview. Oh, he'd ask questions, sure. But he wouldn't accept verbal answers. He'd chisel away inside their minds with all the delicacy of a jackhammer. Mentally peeling back layer after layer until every memory, every secret, every sin was exposed.

There would be no escape. No mercy. Nowhere to hide.

With Lina's connection to the Mobius Council and her current status as the Prism's vessel, it would be a death sentence.

"No."

Finley raised a brow. "Don't look at me like that. I'm not suggesting we actually bring her in. I'm just relaying the message."

Nord's protective instinct warred with his bloodlust, offering two vastly different solutions to the problem. One had him carting Lina off to the farthest world he could find—ideally one free from the Brotherhood's influence. The other had him storming castles and slaying dragons. Or the Brotherhood's main office and its Director, same difference, really.

Before he could settle on one, the wail of a breached ward pierced the air. Finley silenced the siren almost immediately, but it was too late.

Far too close to the edge already, Nord's last thread of control snapped.

The berserker let out a bloodthirsty growl, instinctively reaching for a weapon that wasn't there.

Finley took one look at his partner and stepped around the couch that separated them, trying to block his path. "It's probably just Quinn fucking around again. I'll handle it. You stay here and get your shit together."

Nord snarled, ignoring the order and elbowing past him. He barely registered Finley's hiss of pain or the low crunch of bone as he stalked out of the room and into the hall.

Spying an expensive-looking vase, Nord snatched it off its shelf, transforming it between one breath and the next until he was no longer holding a smoky-gray piece of crystal but a wickedly sharp battle ax.

His fury was potent but tempered by the familiar feel of the weapon in his hand. Whoever dared enter their home uninvited would not live to speak of the experience.

His grip tightened on the haft as he prowled forward, head slightly tilted as he listened for any hint of the intruder. He eased forward, a warrior's clarity taking hold as he prepared to step onto the killing field.

There was a rustle up ahead. It was too indistinct for him to parse its source, but it was coming from the direction of Finley's bedroom. The door gave a tentative twitch as if the person on the other side wasn't quite sure it was safe to come out.

It wasn't.

Everything in him went still, his focus homing in on the narrow strip of light spilling out into the hall. Grasping the knob with his free hand, he shoved the door inward, sending whoever was behind it flying backward with an unintelligible curse.

Not giving them a chance to right themselves, Nord sprang forward, ax already on a downward swing when a shadow shifted in his periphery.

There are two of them.

His rage burned white-hot. With a savage roar, he twisted to the left, his momentum easily altering the trajectory of his weapon.

"Nord!"

The sight of Lina's shocked face and frantic voice pierced through the bloodlust.

His muscles locked, trying in vain to prevent his ax from closing the gap, and a high-pitched squeak, like that of a child's toy, sounded under his grip as his weapon tapped—bounced off?—her neck.

Nord stood frozen, heart thundering in his chest as he stared at Lina with wide eyes.

She lifted a hand to where the ax had smacked her.

"You hit me," she said, stunned.

His hand spasmed. There was a hiss as air released.

Nord's gaze shifted to the source of the hiss. He blinked. His brain feeling like it was wading through tar as it tried to make sense of what he was seeing.

He no longer held an ax in his hand—well, he did, but one only a child would carry into imaginary battle. It was the same size as the one he'd created but inflatable. More carnival prize than lethal weapon, it was currently deflating, his vise-like grip squeezing the air out of it.

"You know, there are pills for that," Quinn's tart voice called from behind him.

Nord glanced over his shoulder to where she was pushing herself up from the floor then back to the limp toy in his hand.

He dropped it like it burned.

The trio watched the toy drift to the floor in silence before Nord managed to find his voice.

"I could have killed you," he said.

Lina raised a brow, her hand still curled around the side of her neck. "You almost did."

A shudder ran through him. He reached for her, crushing her against his body as he sent wordless thanks to whatever entity had been watching over them. He'd long since stopped believing in the gods, but divine intervention must have been at play here.

Divine intervention or Lina's magic.

It was too soon to say whether that particular wild card was a blessing or a curse just yet.

She hugged him back, a shaky laugh brushing against his throat. "I'm fine. You didn't hurt me."

His hand curled into her hair, and he squeezed her tighter, lips pressed against the crown of her head. "Just give me a second."

Quinn cleared her throat. "No, it's okay. I'm fine. Don't worry about me."

Nord stepped away from Lina, finally taking in the room, noticing the open drawers, scattered clothes, and unmade bed.

"What are you two doing in Finley's room?"

"I came to make sure Quinn was okay after the ward went off."

His eyes narrowed on Quinn. "And you?"

She shrugged. "Redecorating."

He closed his eyes and blew out a breath. "Of course, you were." He opened his eyes, refocusing on Lina. "And Alistair?"

"I told him to wait for me in the gym."

Nord nodded. "You should go wait with him. We still haven't determined the source of the breach."

Lina gave him a look, and he knew he'd lost before the fight even started.

"Just stay close," he said with a sigh.

Lina slipped her hand into his. "I intend to."

They moved back into the hall to find Alistair peeking his head out of the gym and a blood-spattered Finley heading their way from his office.

"See anything?" Lina asked her uncle.

He shook his head and joined them.

"What happened to you?" Quinn asked once Finley was only a few steps away.

He lowered the hand covering his broken nose and gave Nord a dark look. Bruises were already starting to form beneath his eyes.

"Next time you rage out, can you at least try not to take it out on me?" Finley asked, his voice thick.

Nord must have used a little more force than he realized when he'd shoved Finley out of the way. Not that he was about to apologize. Finley knew better than to provoke him once he made the shift. He'd been warned about what could happen more than once.

"Don't get in my way, and you should be fine," Nord said, moving to stand in front of him. "Here, let me."

Finley shot him one last glare but lifted his chin so Nord could heal the break.

The bruises faded almost instantly as the bones knitted themselves back together. He left the blood though. Just to make a point. Maybe Finley would think twice before trying anything that stupid again.

But probably not.

One look at the stubborn set of his friend's jaw confirmed it. He would never stop trying to save Nord from himself. His hero complex was just too firmly ingrained. The same was true for all Guardians and likely part of the reason why they joined the Brotherhood in the first place.

He clasped Finley's shoulder. "Better?"

Finley nodded. "Thanks."

"Don't mention it. You figure out what set off the ward?"

"Not yet."

"You and Alistair search the back half of the penthouse. Quinn, Lina, and I will take the front."

The group split without much fanfare, checking each room one at a time for any source of disturbance. Finding nothing, Nord opened the front door, half-expecting the elevator to be the culprit once again.

But the entryway and the elevator were empty.

"Well?" Lina asked.

"Nothing," he said, shutting the door with a soft click.

"Anyway, it could have been a false alarm? A fly or something setting it off?" she asked.

He shook his head. "Wards don't work that way. A fly wouldn't trigger it. They only respond to perceived threats. Unfamiliar magic, unwelcome guests, those kinds of things."

Quinn huffed, fingering the tail of her braid. "Then it seems to me you must have some faulty wards. How else do you explain them going off on Alistair and me the other day?"

"As I said. Unfamiliar magic and unwelcome guests." Nord leveled his eyes on her. "You never did explain how you managed to get around them, by the way."

Quinn wouldn't meet his gaze, but a smile was playing about her mouth as she shrugged. "I might have made the guard believe that we were already on your approved visitor list so he would let us up. Memories can be such fickle things."

"Quinn," Lina said with an admonishing laugh.

"What? You like the trick well enough when I'm using it to get your ass into places."

Lina rolled her eyes. "A VIP list and someone's home are hardly the same."

"Doormen are just skinnier bouncers. Where was the harm? Your boyfriend's precious wards tipped you guys off anyway, and even if they didn't, it's not like we would have just waltzed through the front door. At least, not without knocking first," she added with a grin.

Lina laughed, but Nord ignored their banter, still intent on finding the source of the breach. With each room they checked off, the women had grown more relaxed, but Nord knew better than to let his guard down. Despite Quinn's claims to the contrary, the wards weren't faulty. Something set them off, and the longer it took them to find the source, the greater his concern.

"Fin?" Nord called out once they'd finished with their half of the penthouse.

"In here," he shouted from the living room.

He and Alistair were already seated on the couch, both looking up expectantly as they came into the room.

"Anything?" Finley asked.

Nord gave a terse shake of his head.

Finley bit off a curse, his eyes flickering with power.

Quinn perched herself on the arm of the sofa, but Lina was staring at the mantle above the fireplace, her brows furrowed, and her lips tilted in a frown.

"Lina?" he asked, moving to her side.

She pointed to a black scrap of paper, nestled between Finley's antique cigar box and a set of runed silver knuckles that were gifted to him by his grandfather.

"Has that always been there?"

"No," Nord answered, checking the paper for signs of a magical trace. There was a beat of silence and then a snarled, "Crombie."

He snatched up the square of paper, turning it over in his hand. It was clearly expensive, the black cardstock thick and matte while the font was a dark metallic silver—almost impossible to read unless held at an angle under the light.

"What's it say?" Finley asked, peering over his shoulder.

"I don't know," Nord said, frustration making his voice rough.

The symbols on the paper glinted in the light, but he'd never seen them before. It could have been a meatloaf recipe for all he could tell.

"Really?" Lina asked. "It's perfectly clear to me."

Nord craned his neck to study her. "You can read this?"

Her voice was tentative when she asked, "Can't you?"

"No." Her eyes widened as he held the paper out to her. "What does the fae bastard have to say?"

Her tongue darted out to wet her lips as she accepted the note from him. Holding it up, she pointed to the symbols as she translated, "It's an address. 207 Delaney Court, Room 305." She paused, a slight tremor in her hand as she moved it to point at the next line. "Happy hunting. C."

Her eyes lifted to his, brimming with nameless emotion.

"He found him."

CHAPTER SIXTEEN
LINA

"Crombie found Mataius."

As soon as the words left her lips, the piece of paper began to burn—no, freeze—her fingers. The cold was so intense it merely felt like it was burning. The resulting pain was immediate, and she released Crombie's note with a startled cry.

Instead of fluttering to the floor, the stationary burst into dozens of silky black and silver butterflies that flitted around her playfully before disappearing up the chimney.

Nord muttered something under his breath that sounded like 'fae fuck', but she couldn't be sure.

Shaking out her stinging fingers, Lina turned to face the others. "Anyone recognize the address? Is it a warehouse or a club or something?"

Nord frowned and shook his head, Quinn looked thoughtful as if still trying to place it, and Alistair and Finley exchanged uneasy glances.

"What?" Lina asked.

Finley ran a hand down his face. "Delaney runs through a residential neighborhood, but I use the term loosely. You're as likely to find a row of boarded-up buildings filled with rotting bodies as you are anybody who actually lives there. It's not a place I'd want to be after dark."

Lina glanced out the window. "Good thing it's still midday."

Nord opened his mouth, but she was ready for him.

"You better not be about to suggest that I sit here with my thumb up my ass while you go looking for him."

He pressed his lips together, nostrils flaring as he huffed out a breath.

"I don't know," Quinn murmured, "could be a good time."

Lina closed her eyes and suppressed a smile with a slight shake of her head. *Fucking Quinn.*

"Well," Lina asked after a beat, "what are we waiting for? Let's go get the bastard."

"I don't think we should run over there half-cocked; we have no idea what'll be waiting for us. Something like this requires planning," Finley said.

Lina's eyes snapped to his. "And I think that twenty some odd years is long enough for a piece of shit like Mataius to get away with murder. I'm done waiting. We have the address. It's time to end this. Are you really trying to tell me that two Guardians and three animagi aren't a match for whatever's out there? Because if you are, then we might as well quit now. No amount of planning will ever be enough."

Just the thought of her gray-eyed ex sent a shiver down her spine, but it wasn't fear she felt.

It was soul-deep hatred.

Never, in either of her lives, had she loathed someone as much as she did the Drake heir. He'd betrayed her, used their relationship and her feelings for him to blind her to his true purpose.

While she'd been planning a wedding, he'd been plotting her murder.

It was an unforgivable sin. One that could only be repaid in blood.

A life for a life and all that.

Unfortunately for him, unlike her, he only had the one life to lose.

Finley sighed. "Lina—"

"Come or don't, Fin," she said, starting for the door. "I don't need your permission. I have the address; I'll go by myself if I have to."

Nord's hand caught her around the wrist, halting her mid-step. His voice was low, spoken only for her as he dipped his chin to look her in the eye.

"I understand better than most the need for vengeance, but trust me when I tell you there's no room for emotion in this. It will only cloud your judgment and see you or those you care for harmed. Sit, Kærasta. Let us discuss our options so that we are prepared for whatever waits for us."

It was almost absurd, a berserker arguing that emotion was a liability when they thrive on their rage. Then again, perhaps that was what made him uniquely suited to say exactly that.

When she didn't know where to find him, it had been easy to lock Mataius in a box in the back of her mind and pretend he didn't exist. But now that she knew where he was hiding, now that he was within her grasp, every fiber of her being urged her to act.

Immediately.

Her body quaked with the need to go and find him. To enact her revenge.

But instead, she pressed her trembling hands between her knees and forced herself to sit. To listen.

If anyone else had made the request, she probably would have dismissed it. But coming from Nord, there was an unspoken promise that she couldn't ignore. He knew how badly she needed this—to find Mataius and repay him for every vile thing he'd done to her— and he would do everything in his power to ensure that she did. Out of everyone gathered in this room, he, more than any of the others, was aligned with her in that purpose.

If he believed a conversation could mean the difference between success and failure, then she'd be a fool not to trust his assessment.

And Lina was many things—impulsive, driven by emotion, naïve even—but she was far from a fool.

One didn't grow up with Anatoly Cuska as a father without learning life's hardest lessons.

Two hours later, armed to the teeth with weapons of both magical and mortal origin, they were ready.

LINA STARED UP AT THE CRUMBLING BRICK APARTMENT COMPLEX, EYEING ONE of its boarded-up windows with no little apprehension. *How could graffiti look so ominous?*

Finley's assessment had been spot-on. The entire neighborhood was giving off serious uh-oh vibes. The kind that had the little hairs on the back of her neck standing on end and her sense of self-preservation screaming at her to get the fuck out of there. Stat.

Technically, it was still early afternoon, but you'd never know it by the anemic amount of sunlight. It was almost as if the sun had gone into hiding as soon as they'd stepped onto Delaney. Even it knew better than to linger here.

There was a sign with names and apartment numbers posted beside the door, but it was merely for show. If there was supposed to be some sort of buzzer security mechanism, it was a thing of the past. The intercom speaker had been ripped out, a tangle of stripped wires all that remained. Besides, Lina highly doubted the kind of people who lived here wanted the fact shared. That list had to be as outdated as the building's health and safety codes.

It was hard to believe pretty-boy Mataius would willingly hide out in such a rundown slag heap, but it was certainly the last place she'd ever expect to find him. So perhaps there was a little bit of ingenuity in the choice.

Beside her, Quinn lifted one foot and then the other, her nose wrinkled.

"You okay?" Lina asked.

"This place smells like a bag of ass. Old, dirty ass."

Finley snorted. "Intimately familiar with the scent, are you?"

Quinn glared at him and pointed to a nearby pile of garbage bags. "How much you want to bet there's a dead body in there?"

"Just one?" Finley drawled.

But Quinn wasn't wrong. The smell wafting around them was acrid and heavy. Tears were already burning Lina's eyes, and she was breathing through her mouth to try to avoid the pungent stench. Something that foul would likely cling to their clothes long after they'd been washed.

"Maybe it's better inside," Lina offered, pulling the barred door open.

Quinn rushed in and instantly put a gloved hand to her mouth, gagging as the others crowded into the dingy foyer.

So much for that.

If anything, the odor inside was worse.

Even Alistair discreetly covered his mouth with his handkerchief. Finley and Nord, however, seemed unaffected. As for Lina, she was trying not to vomit as she eyed the complex's shoddy interior.

The light from the lone bulb flickering above them was barely enough to illuminate the filthy rectangular space. An 'Out of Order' sign hung from the elevator to the left, the yellowed paper indicating it had been there for a while. Across from them and the entrance they'd just stepped through, a dark staircase loomed.

"You've got to be shitting me," Quinn muttered, eyeing the stairs with extreme distrust. "Of course, this place comes with its very own set of murder stairs."

Lina and the others stared at her.

"What?" she snapped. "Everyone knows the girl who goes up the stairs gets murdered. Thus"—she gestured to the stairwell—"murder stairs."

Finley rolled his eyes. "You watch too many movies."

Quinn crossed her arms. "Fine, tough guy. You take the lead. But when you get stabbed, I don't want to hear a peep. Not even a single man tear, you got it?"

Lina bit back a smile. It wasn't funny, not really, but the moment of levity helped soothe some of her nerves.

She moved past Nord and Alistair, resting her hand on Quinn's shoulder as she smiled. "Then I guess it's a good thing I wore my murder boots. I'll go first. Murder boots beat murder stairs every time."

Pride shone in Quinn's eyes as she returned Lina's grin. "I always knew my girl was a badass."

Lina winked and set her right foot on the first step.

"Nice try," Nord said, catching her jacket and tugging her back. "I'll go first and make sure it's clear."

He palmed his weapon, a small throwing ax with a hooked blade, and quickly made his way up the stairs. Lina went next, followed by Alistair then Quinn. Finley was the last up. She could clearly make out the metallic click of his gun as he cocked the hammer, ready to fire one of his spelled bullets at the first sign of trouble.

Lina's magic had never felt like a tangible entity prior to the Awakening, but she could most definitely feel it sparking through her now. Even though she hadn't consciously called on it, it was there, sending little bolts of electricity down her arms and into her fingers. It provided another layer of confidence, knowing that her power was ready and waiting for her to shape it to her will.

Thankfully, the awful reek dissipated as they made their way up the stairs. Lina noticed the windows at each of the landings. It was impossible not to. They'd been painted over in a deep, albeit flaking, crimson that only enhanced the sketch factor of the place. Even black would have been less creepy. At least then it would have only been dark. As it was, the subtle red hue made it seem like they were all coated in blood.

Lina suppressed a shudder, hoping that wasn't indicative of what was to come.

They reached the third floor, filing out into a narrow hallway. Room 300 was directly on their left, 301 straight across from it on the right. That meant that Mataius' room should be at the other end of the hall.

Nord motioned for them to stay put as he crept forward. He paused beside the door, pressing his ear to its surface as he listened for signs of activity. His posture relaxed slightly as he pulled back and shook his head.

Lina couldn't help feeling a bit of disappointment. What if they'd come all this way and he wasn't here? Or worse, he had been, but he'd somehow caught wind that they were onto him and he'd managed to escape.

Nord cocked his head, his eyes flashing with power as he stared down the hall at them.

"What's he doing?" Quinn whispered.

"I asked him to check for magical locks or traps," Finley answered, his voice pitched low.

"Good thinking," Alistair said.

Lina nodded her agreement, reminded once more just how convenient the Guardians' telepathic link could be.

For the second time in as many minutes, Nord stood back from the door and shook his head.

Lina worried her bottom lip between her teeth, her muscles tensing due to her mounting unease. Something about this wasn't adding up.

Surely, if Mataius was staying here, he'd rely on some sort of magic to keep him safe or hidden.

In addition to their ability to control and manipulate the weather, the Drake family was also notoriously lucky. Both of which were qualities believed to be passed down from their dragon ancestors.

While their luck was most often tied to wealth—all dragons loved a good hoard—it also extended to various other parts of their lives. Every member of the Drake family she'd met had at least one story of how they'd narrowly escaped capture or somehow defied death.

But there was being lucky, and then there was tempting fate.

Living somewhere like this without any kind of magical protection seemed like an unnecessary risk. Even for a Drake.

After all, luck always had a way of running out.

CHAPTER SEVENTEEN
LINA

"Could Crombie have gotten it wrong?" Lina whispered to Quinn.

She shrugged, replying in a hushed voice, "Anything's possible. His network is vast, and it's doubtful they'd knowingly pass on bad information. But, Mataius has covered his tracks for decades."

Lina turned back to Nord in time to watch him lift his foot, clearly preparing to kick down the door so that they could search the unit.

"Wait!" she hissed.

He paused with his leg in the air, looking at her expectantly.

"Maybe he's in there sleeping. Shouldn't we try something a bit quieter just in case? So he doesn't have a chance to flee?"

"Or so the neighbors don't call the cops," Alistair added.

"A neighborhood like this? No one's calling the cops," Finley said quietly.

"Still. Best not to give anyone a reason to notice us," Lina said. "Want me to take care of the lock?"

Even from this distance, Lina could tell Nord was less than enthused by her suggestion.

"Berserkers aren't well-known for stepping aside," Finley murmured.

"Or for their subtlety."

Finley grinned at her. "Goes a bit against their nature. Good thing being stealthy is taught by the Brotherhood."

"Somehow, I doubt he was at the top of his class for that particular lesson."

Finley's shoulders moved with silent laughter. Lina could tell by the pause in their conversation that he was relaying what she'd said to Nord, who merely rolled his glowing eyes and reached for the doorknob.

"Is he planning to just walk right in?" Quinn asked.

"Something like that," Finley said.

There was a soft glow around Nord's hands, and then the door pulled away from the frame without a sound.

"Ain't your mama ever teach you no manners?"

Lina jolted like she'd been stuck with a cattle prod.

She spun around, finding a rotund woman with faded red hair standing on the top step. There was a neon green leash in her gnarled hand, the other end of which was attached to the most miserable-looking cat Lina had ever laid eyes on. Assuming, of course, you could even call the hairless wonder a cat.

One of its ears was mostly chewed off, and there was a faded pink scar running across one of its watery eyes. As if it could sense Lina's assessment, it let out a pitiful howl.

She half-wondered if it was begging to be put out of its misery.

The woman stooped down and scooped the cat up in her arms, pressing its face into her ample cleavage. The poor beast looked resigned to its fate as it was forced to nestle against her. Although, Lina would have sworn it shot her an accusing glare on its way up.

She took a few shuffling steps forward, her eyes moving to the door still held in Nord's hands. Her painted-on eyebrows immediately lowered. "Hey now! What in Sandusky's name my poor door ever do t'you?"

Nord looked at the door then back to the woman. "This is your apartment?"

"Well, I've lived here goin' on thirty-seven years. I should hope so."

The others exchanged glances.

Quinn cleared her throat to ask, "Who's Sandusky?"

The woman clutched the cat cradled in her arms even tighter. "Why this handsome devil, o' course."

"Of course," Alistair said, somehow managing not to sound completely patronizing.

The woman's posture changed when she spotted Lina's uncle. She smoothed down her hair with one hand and gave him what Lina guessed was supposed to be a coy smile.

Out of the corner of her eye, Lina watched Finley holster his weapon. Apparently, the crazy cat lady wasn't deemed a threat.

Nord propped the woman's door back against its frame, and her smile vanished as if she'd just remembered that she'd walked in on their attempted B&E.

She cast a suspicious glance at all of them. "Ain't often Sandusky and I gets visitors. Burglars now, that's a bit more common. You all here to rob me?"

"No, ma'am," Lina instantly blurted. "We were here to visit our friend."

"How you not know your friend's address?" she demanded, surprising Lina with the shrewdness of the question.

"It's been a while," Finley interjected smoothly, offering the woman his most charming smile. "Please, forgive our error, Miss?"

"Celia Bell," she supplied, offering him her free hand.

Finley bowed low, pressing his lips to the back of her hand. "Pleasure to meet you, Ms. Bell."

Color bloomed high in Ms. Bell's cheeks, and she giggled like a schoolgirl. "Well, I suppose accidents do happen."

Lina would have laughed herself if not for the rapid hammering of her heart. Her brain was still struggling to catch up with the unexpected turn of events.

"Perhaps you might be able to help us find him?"

Celia batted her non-existent eyelashes at Finley. "I do know just 'bout everybody that lives here."

"He goes by the name Mataius," Lina said, moving into Celia's line of sight. Celia begrudgingly shifted her eyes away from Finley as Lina began to describe her ex-fiancé. "He's about 5'11, longish black hair, gray eyes, delicate features. Has a dragon tattoo covering most of his left arm."

Celia was still holding onto Finley's hand. She glared at Lina and then shot Finley another syrupy sweet smile. "Don't know 'im."

"Are you sure?" Alistair asked, offering her a picture he must have just conjured.

Lina could just make out the image on the photo from where she was standing. It was her first real look at her ex-fiancé in almost twenty-five years. He'd always been good-looking, in a pretty sort of way. His mixed heritage blended beautifully and was hinted at by his almond-shaped eyes, sharp cheekbones, and raven-colored hair. Looking at him now, however, all she could see was the monster lurking beneath the surface.

Celia briefly scanned the picture before handing it back to Alistair. He tucked the photo inside his jacket's breast pocket.

"Nope. Never seen't 'im. And even if I had, I ain't no snitch."

"Surely telling us which apartment our mate is in hardly counts as snitching," Finley cajoled.

Celia pulled her hand from his grasp. "You might be a pretty one, but Sandusky and I have lived here long enough t'know what happens ta people who open their mouths 'bout things they ain't got no right to speak on. If dis boy really's your friend like you say, give 'im a call and find out for yo' own self. Now, if you'll excuse me, it's time for my stories."

She started moving, leaving Finley and Lina no choice but to jump to the side to make space for her and her wretched cat.

Lina gulped back a wave of panic, feeling like she was watching their chance to find Mataius vanish before her eyes. They couldn't leave. Not before they figured out why Crombie had sent them here.

"Please, ma'am," Quinn said, stepping in front of her.

Yes! If anyone could salvage this venture, Quinn could. She'd find a way to get them inside and make the old woman think it had been her idea.

Lina could clearly see Quinn's face over the woman's shoulder. Her eyes looked like they were filled with swirling burgundy smoke, and her voice had taken on a hypnotic quality.

"We really appreciate you inviting us in to use your phone and urging us to make ourselves at home while we wait."

Lina's limbs were already loosening, preparing to move in anticipation of Celia's agreement.

But that's not what happened.

Celia stood frozen for a second and then shook off Quinn's hand. Lina could just make out the scowl on her face before she was moving once more.

"The hell are you talking about? Why would I go and do somethin' stupid like that? I don't know you from Eve. Now git 'fore I call my nephew and his friends to make ya."

Quinn stood dumbstruck, staring after the woman like she couldn't believe what just happened. Frankly, neither could Lina. No one had ever resisted one of Quinn's memory charms before.

"You mind?" she snapped, looking up at Nord, who was still standing in front of her door.

Lina could practically see the wheels spinning in his mind. Short of violence, there was no way they were getting inside, and berserker or not, Nord wouldn't beat up an old woman. With no other options left before him, he stepped aside.

While they'd been asking her about Mataius, he must have fixed whatever he'd done to the door, because Celia pulled it open with a huff and a high-pitched squeak.

"You should have someone look at those hinges," he murmured.

Celia ignored him, choosing instead to toss one last, lingering look over her shoulder. Apparently, she didn't like what she saw because she scooted inside, slamming the door closed behind her.

"What the fuck just happened?" Quinn asked, eyes darting to Alistair.

"You're asking us?" Finley said. "You're the memory weaver."

She narrowed her eyes on him. "You're right. I am. And you're about one more smart-ass remark away from forgetting how to orgasm. You ready to spend the rest of your immortal life without any kind of sexual satisfaction?"

Finley crossed his arms. "I might be more worried about it if I hadn't just watched you royally fuck up the only thing you're supposed to be good at."

Quinn's voice was laced with venom as she snapped, "You do not want to fuck with me right now." Dismissing him, she turned back to Alistair. "That," she said, pointing to Celia's door, "has never happened. Is it possible we just found a Null?"

Lina had heard of Nulls before, but they were incredibly rare. They were immune to all forms of magic even though they had magical bloodlines.

"Would a Null have been able to see Alistair's conjured photo?" Lina asked, not familiar enough with the species to know their limitations offhand.

"The photo was real," Alistair said, surprising her. "I've been carrying it in my pocket ever since I found out Mataius was responsible."

"Why?" Lina asked.

"In case we ran into a situation like today where we needed to see if someone recognized him," he replied.

Lina's heart sank.

If Celia Bell really was a Null, then the likelihood of Mataius being here had just dropped to less than zero. He'd never put himself at the mercy of someone he couldn't control. Even though other people's magic couldn't be used against them, his couldn't either.

This little scavenger hunt had turned out to be a complete waste. She didn't know where Crombie had gotten his information, but he'd been way off.

"Let's just go," she said, not even bothering to hide her disappointment.

She couldn't believe they came all this way just to end up empty-handed.

This time, as they made their way down the hall, they didn't bother trying to stay quiet. Alistair and Fin were discussing what they knew of Nulls while Quinn stomped along behind them, lost to her thoughts.

Lina fell behind, letting Nord catch up to her.

His hand was warm against her back. "You okay?"

"I really thought this was it. That he would be here and we'd settle this once and for all. But I guess we're just back to square one." She laughed bitterly. "I guess it was too much to hope that I'd finally be able to move on from that part of my past."

Nord's eyes were warm with understanding as he ran his knuckles down her cheek. "Don't lose hope. We're no worse off than we were this morning. We'll find him, and you'll still get your closure. Just not today."

Lina sighed. "I know."

Alistair and Finley were already at the second-floor landing by the time they'd reached the stairs. She was just about to start down herself when a familiar creak sounded behind them.

She glanced back to find Celia poking her head out of her apartment, a miserable-looking Sandusky peering out between her cankles.

"Did you need something, Ms. Bell?" Lina asked.

The woman flinched as if she'd been struck. "How'd you know my name?"

Lina blinked. "You just told us . . . remember? Not even ten minutes ago . . ."

Celia scowled. "I did no such thing. I've never met you in my life."

"But—"

Quinn stopped her with a hand on her forearm. "So sorry to disturb you, we were just leaving."

Celia gave them one last mistrustful look and eased back into her apartment.

Quinn beamed at her; her relief palpable. "Thank fuck."

"Am I missing something? Why are you suddenly so happy?"

"Don't you see? It wasn't my fault the weave didn't take. She's not a Null at all. She just has some kind of memory impairment. Alzheimer's if I had to guess."

"You can't work your magic on someone with Alzheimer's?" Finley asked from below them.

Quinn rolled her eyes and looked down at him. "No, asshole. I can't. The part of her brain responsible for memories is already impaired by the disease. Any attempt to modify what's stored there just gets canceled out. There's nothing for the magic to stick to."

Her best friend was practically giddy about it. She took the stairs two at a time until she was just behind Finley, her mouth right beside his ear although she didn't lower her voice at all.

"Besides, I deal with the memories themselves, not brain chemistry or anything remotely physical. For my magic to work, the disease would have to be dealt with first. That's not my territory and, as such, not my fault."

Then, she kissed his cheek with an obnoxious, drawn-out smacking sound and hurried past him to catch up to Alistair.

Lina shook her head, snorting in disbelief as they continued down the stairs.

What are the fucking odds?

Of everyone they could have run into, they came across a woman Quinn's magic was useless against but who still wouldn't remember they had ever been there.

That was some fucked-up luck.

Her steps slowed. Nord gave her a questioning look, but she was too deep in thought to acknowledge it.

But whose luck was it?

Had Mataius been hiding out here, after all, banking on his forgetful neighbor to keep his secret? There was no way of knowing, not without getting inside, and that definitely wasn't happening now.

Not while Celia was home.

Lina glanced back up even though she was no longer able to see unit 305 or the woman who lived there.

If she's already forgotten meeting them, what else has Celia Bell forgotten about?

CHAPTER EIGHTEEN
LINA

Lina shoveled ice cream into her mouth, barely tasting or appreciating its peanut butter and fudge flavor.

"Still sulking?" Quinn asked, sitting beside her on the sofa.

"I'm not sulking."

Quinn lifted a sculpted brow and gave the nearly empty half-gallon of ice cream a pointed look.

"I'm not," she insisted. "I'm self-soothing. There's a difference."

"If you say so."

"I do," she said, the words punctuated with another heaping spoonful.

"Well then, now that we've gotten that cleared up."

Knowing there'd be no peace until Quinn said whatever was on her mind, Lina dropped her spoon in the container with a long-suffering sigh. "Why are you still here?"

"Because we need to figure out what our next step is."

"Nord already sent Henry to The District with his message. What else can we do until we hear back from Crombie?"

"Do you really think it's the best idea to send a hired driver down there with a note? Crombie will eat the poor thing alive."

"No, but it's not exactly like I know how else to get ahold of him. You already said he blocked your number, and he kicked us out of the club. Sending a proxy is the only other option."

"Who knew the fae ass would hold such a grudge? He's no better than a child throwing a tantrum."

Lina shook her head, leave it to Quinn to conveniently forget the part where she instigated said tantrum.

"If Henry asks for Zilla or Kiko like I told him to, they'll keep him safe."

Quinn made a face. "I still can't believe the twins are actually going by your ridiculous nicknames."

"You say ridiculous; I say amazing."

"You know what I think is amazing? The fact that anyone tolerates you."

Lina gaped at Quinn, a shocked laugh escaping as she reached behind her to find a pillow, which she then proceeded to throw at Quinn's head. "Bitch. You love me."

"Very true, on both counts," Quinn said as she snatched the pillow out of the air. "But I made you laugh. See? Just a couple minutes in my company, and you're already feeling better. I win."

"Win? Win what?"

"The lifting Lina's spirits competition. Clearly, I kicked ice cream's ass."

"I'm not sure insulting me counts as lifting my spirits."

"Sure it does. You can't argue with the results just because you don't approve of the methods."

"I'm going to remember you said that."

They shared a look and laughed, feeling some of the lingering tension from the day starting to ebb.

Quinn reached over and squeezed her knee. "I'm sorry I couldn't get us inside."

"Don't apologize. It's not your fault. I'm not even sure there was anything for us to find," Lina said, even though the nagging voice insisting that Celia Bell was hiding something—knowingly or not—hadn't shut up since they'd gotten home.

"Still," she said, looking solemn for the first time, "I can't help but feel like I let you down. I never imagined my power would fail."

"None of us did. We accounted for so many possibilities—him being there, him not being there, having to fight, having to run, having to make people forget we were there—but none of us doubted you for a second. It's hard to plan for something you don't anticipate."

"True," she said, staring off into the corner of the room.

Lina knew nothing she said would get Quinn to stop beating herself up because, if their roles were reversed, she'd be the same way. Failure was not something either of them accepted easily. It was probably a side effect of being raised by parents with impossibly high standards.

The only remedy here was distraction.

"I've been thinking—"

Quinn perked up. "I knew you weren't just sitting here, trying to set a world record for most cartons of ice cream consumed in one sitting. What's that beautifully devious mind of yours come up with?"

Lina snorted. Quinn calling her the devious one . . . that was rich.

"Maybe it's time for the Mobius Council to meet the newest head of the Cuska family?"

"What?" Quinn's eyes grew comically wide. "Lina, you can't be serious."

Lina set the carton of ice cream onto the coffee table and turned to face her friend fully. "Think about it. When they learn what Mataius has done, they'll have no choice but to help us find him. Even if his father tries to protect him."

"Come on, Lina. There's no way the rest of the Drakes aren't in on it. They'd be more likely to help him finish the job than hand him over."

"It doesn't matter. I'll still have the other families on my side."

Quinn studied her, her eyes a tempest of emotion. "If you walk in there and accuse their heir of murder—"

"It's not an accusation when it's true."

"—you'd be declaring war."

Lina opened her mouth, but Quinn kept on talking, her voice growing more urgent.

"A war you might not be able to win. Things are a lot different since you . . . went away. The Cuskas don't hold as much sway as they used to. My mother said that Niko," she paused, weighing her words.

"Niko what?"

She grimaced. "That he's a glorified secretary for the Council. He's basically their errand boy. No one takes him seriously. In fact, the Drakes sort of assumed the controlling vote after your uncle disappeared."

Lina's jaw clenched. "Maybe the Council just needs to be reminded what a real heir can do. After all, there's a reason the Cuskas were originally granted the primary seat."

Quinn looked a little pale. "You know I have your back, always, but maybe we should see what that Viking of yours thinks."

"What I think about what?" Nord asked, a stein of ale in his hand and Finley and Alistair on his heels.

Quinn's relief at the sight of backup was tangible. "Your girlfriend has lost her damn mind."

Finley snickered. "Is this one of those situations where she's his girlfriend when she's in trouble and yours when she does something good?"

She ignored him and pointed an accusing finger in Lina's direction. "She just suggested handing herself over to Mataius tied with a fucking bow."

"Is that what I did?" Lina asked, hoping humor would keep Nord from latching on to Quinn's words.

His eyes flew to hers.

Lina sighed. *Too late.*

She held up both her hands before he could say anything. "For the record, I merely suggested trying to use the Council as a resource in drawing him out. There was no mention of my being bait anywhere in the conversation."

"It may as well have been," Quinn said.

"Not happening," Nord said in a voice that sounded like quiet thunder.

Low.

Angry.

Dangerous.

"I'm afraid I must also agree," Alistair said as the amber liquid in his high-ball glass sloshed slightly. "The Council cannot be trusted. The longer we keep your return secret, the safer you'll be."

Lina's eyes narrowed. "It's not exactly like we've been hiding the fact. If they don't know yet, word is bound to reach them soon."

"Yes, well," Alistair said, taking a seat, "let's not go borrowing trouble before we have to."

Lina frowned. What the hell had been going on since she'd been away? Her father murdered. The Drakes in control. The other three families just sitting back and letting it all happen. Shit was obviously spiraling out of control, and yet no one seemed willing to do anything about it.

This was not the revered group of animagi she remembered. They were infamous criminals known throughout the world for their dubious deeds and immeasurable power. But while the Mobius Council might act in the dark, they'd always stood for what's right, for the justice and the good of their people. When had they turned into a bunch of chickenshits?

What could they possibly be afraid of? Because fear was the only reason she could come up with as to why they'd refuse to act.

"Would it really be such a bad thing that they know?" Lina asked. "Surely, not everybody is on board with the Drakes taking over. I mean, Mikel has always been a bit of a dick, and that's putting it mildly. Maybe finding out I've returned could be the thing that sways everyone back to our side?"

Alistair shook his head. "It's possible but unlikely. Too many families are in debt to the Drakes. The risk is far too high if they were to align themselves against them."

Prior to the formation of the Mobius Council, when other animagi families were falling by the wayside and barely surviving, the Drakes prospered. They'd built an entire empire around their acquisition of wealth, helping create the mortal's stock market and running a number of the world's most successful casinos and gambling dens—not all of which were strictly legal. They were the obvious choice to be the Council's financial advisors since they excelled, not just at acquiring money but at retaining it. Just a single one of their family members was richer than most countries.

Lina's brows lowered. "You make it sound like they've been bankrolling everyone. I know I've been gone a while, but if things were as serious as you're making it out to be, I would have known about it."

"Lina, we're talking about the kind of debt that goes back for generations," her uncle said. "It's not the kind of thing people openly discuss."

Well, that answered her question about why the rest of the Council hadn't intervened.

Blackmail.

Mikel had them by the short and curlies. Until they could pay back whatever they owed his family, they'd be at his mercy. Judging by the severity of Alistair's expression, that wasn't likely to happen anytime soon, if ever.

A horrifying suspicion took root.

"And us? Are the Cuskas also in debt to the Drakes?" Lina asked, a sense of dread pooling in her stomach.

Her uncle looked uncomfortable. After taking a sip of his drink, he said, "There's a reason your marriage has been arranged since you were children."

Lina sat back in her seat, grappling with the ramifications of his confession.

Arranged marriages weren't uncommon in the animagi community, and hers had never been a secret. But to find out that she'd been sold off in repayment of a debt like some kind of prized broodmare . . . that was a tough pill to swallow. Even though the marriage was clearly off and her father was dead, she still felt the sting of his betrayal.

She'd been destined to be a queen, and he'd tried to turn her into a pawn.

Worse still, for all intents and purposes, Mikel Drake owned them. All of them. Which meant that he may as well *be* the Mobius Council.

From her corner of the couch, Lina silently fumed. If she tried to bring his son's crimes to light, it really would be a declaration of war.

While they'd been talking, Nord had moved around the room until he was standing just behind Lina. He rested his hands on her shoulders and squeezed. As usual, he'd found a way to offer both comfort and support without having to say a word. Reaching up, she placed one of her hands over his and released a breath she hadn't been aware of holding.

At least, if war was in her not-so-distant future, she'd have a berserker at her side.

A small smile touched her lips at the thought of Mikel facing off against Nord. She'd pay good money to watch that Drake shit his pants when he found himself on the business end of her Viking's blade.

But she was getting ahead of herself. Before she could worry about Mikel and the rest of the Council, she needed to deal with Mataius.

"Perhaps Lina is onto something though," Quinn said, her words slow and measured.

Four heads snapped in her direction.

"Talk about a change of heart," Finley murmured.

"No, not about going to the Council," she said with a roll of her eyes. "I was the first one to say that was a terrible idea, remember? But maybe there are some who would welcome a chance to break free of the Drakes' chokehold, regardless of the risks, so long as they knew others were willing to do the same." She drummed her fingers on her knees as she considered the possibility. "If so, it's not a stretch to assume they'd help us find Mataius."

"Wait, so you can go recruit them, but I can't?" Lina asked, finding it hard to summon the appropriate amount of exasperation as Nord began to massage the base of her neck.

Quinn shook her head. "I'm not suggesting going myself, but maybe my mother can do some digging for us. If anyone knows of potential dissenters, it would be her. She could make subtle inquiries without anyone suspecting anything because of her position."

"Weren't you planning to claim your seat on the Council?" Finley asked. "What changed?"

"After speaking with my mother at length, it no longer seemed like a wise course of action. Mostly for the reasons Alistair already mentioned."

"Are the Satori also in his pocket?" Finley asked.

Quinn's back went rigid, color flooding her cheeks at his question. "My family owes him money, yes, but we are no one's puppets."

Finley blinked, seeming surprised by her venom. "I didn't mean to imply—"

"Well, you did."

"I'm sorry, Quinn," he said, sounding truly repentant. "I was only asking if your family was in a similar position as Lina's. I meant no offense."

She stared at him for a moment before relaxing. "Don't worry about it." She sighed. "It was a fair question, considering our conversation. But no, it's not our debt that led me to reconsider. It was the thought of what Mikel would try to do with my power. With a memory weaver at his disposal, there'd be no end to his depravity. I couldn't give him the opportunity. Especially since he's the type of man who wouldn't hesitate to threaten my family in an attempt to control me."

Lina reached over and squeezed Quinn's hand. "First we take out the son, then we can deal with the father," she said, repeating the promise she'd just made to herself.

Quinn gave her a tight smile and nodded. "First the son, then the father."

They squeezed hands, sealing their vow.

"What do you think, Alistair?" Quinn asked, looking at Lina's uncle expectantly. "Should we ask my mom for help?"

The older man stared into his glass for a long moment and then gave a slow nod. "I think Cora is an excellent ally. Her instincts are rarely wrong. If she believes it is safe to approach someone, I trust her judgment. Besides, knowing who else is on our side may come in handy down the line."

Quinn jumped up. "I'll call her now."

Nord continued to knead the tight muscles in Lina's shoulders and neck, waiting until Quinn was out of the room before asking, "Are you sure it's wise to involve her mother?"

Alistair drained his glass and set it carefully beside him. "Truthfully?" he asked, lifting his head to lock eyes with Nord. "I don't."

Nord's hands stilled for a second, his fingers digging into Lina's skin. Just as it began to border on painful, he relaxed his grip. But there was nothing relaxed about his voice when he asked, "Then why place your niece's fate in her hands?"

"Because right now, we have to trust someone, and if there's anyone with access to the Council who can help us, it's her. But, more importantly, Cora has always thought of Lina like a daughter, and she'd never do anything that would put her or Quinn in harm's way."

Nord didn't press further. Lina interpreted that as his acceptance of her uncle's explanation, but she didn't think, for a second, he was pleased about it. His willingness to take risks when it came to her safety was practically zero. If anything, he was probably already plotting his retaliation so a plan would be in place if Cora betrayed them.

She heard a soft chirp, and Nord paused his ministrations once more to pull his phone out of his pocket. "It's from Henry," he informed them as he read the notification.

Lina held her breath as she waited to see what Crombie's reaction to the note was. "And?" she pressed.

Nord gave a little shake of his head and put his phone away. "He left our message, but Crombie wasn't there."

She'd known getting any answer, let alone an immediate one, was a long shot, but it was disappointing to have it confirmed.

With nothing else to do but wait, the room fell silent.

Lina could only assume the others' minds were as filled with thoughts of the days to come as hers. But somehow, seated all together as they were, the future didn't feel quite as bleak as it had even an hour ago.

Looking back, that sense of security should have been one massive red flag. What about her life had gone according to plan even before she'd returned to the land of the living?

Exactly. Not one fucking thing.

If she had known what the days ahead would bring, Lina would have barricaded the door to the penthouse with her body and refused to let any of them set foot outside.

But then, as she'd already told Quinn, there's no way to plan for something you never see coming.

CHAPTER NINETEEN
LINA

"Are you sure this is the right place?" Lina asked.

Quinn nudged her shoulder. "What? You mean you don't hold all your clandestine meetings on the rooftop of abandoned churches?"

"Not usually, no." She could not make out much of the roof from the sidewalk, but as far as Lina could tell, its iconic spire was all of the church that remained untouched.

Located just on the fringes of the city, St. Gerome's had seen better days. The gothic cathedral was covered in graffiti, its numerous stained-glass windows mostly shattered. Twisting vines crawled up the sides of the soot-colored stone from what was left of the award-winning rose garden that surrounded it.

There was something infinitely sad about finding a once-beloved sanctuary in such disrepair. At one time, it had been a place of peace and worship, but now it was little more than a testament to those that stumbled across its path. A warning that nothing—not even a god—was sacred.

And what hope was there for mortals if even their god could be forgotten?

Maybe it was the crumbling building looming over them, or perhaps it was the angry black clouds roiling on the horizon and obscuring the moon, but unease gnawed at her.

It was odd enough Deanne—Cora's contact—had requested a meeting just after midnight, but when she'd claimed she selected the location because it was neutral territory, this wasn't exactly what Lina had pictured. Not that the woman could be held responsible for the night's weather, but still, if there were such things as portents of doom, surely this combination counted.

"Come on," Quinn said, weaving her arm through Lina's, "it'll be fine."

Lina planted her feet and refused to budge. "Let's wait for the others first. She may be your mom's friend or whatever, but I don't feel comfortable going in without them."

She half-expected Quinn to roll her eyes and make a comment about unnecessary paranoia, but she only nodded.

Snap!

Lina jerked in Quinn's grasp and spun toward the sound with her hands protectively outstretched.

A familiar blond head appeared around the right corner of the building. Relieved, Lina blew out a breath although her heart continued its frantic drum solo in her chest.

Nord paused, taking in her defensive stance with something that looked like approval as Finley and Alistair rounded the corner.

"Area's clear," he said once he reached her. "No sign of any magical tampering."

Lina nodded, but even that news wasn't enough to help her relax.

"Fin and Alistair will stay down here," he continued. "Keep an eye on things and make sure no one tries to sneak in."

"You want us to split up?" Quinn asked.

Nord tapped his temple. "Finley and I will be in contact the whole time. And this way, we've got eyes in multiple places."

"There's also the added benefit of not having to reveal myself to someone on the Council," Alistair said.

Quinn raised a brow. "I highly doubt anyone would recognize you."

"Until he opened his mouth and started talking," Lina said.

"Good point," Quinn said after considering it for a moment. "Shall we head in? Deanne is probably already waiting for us."

"Why did she want to meet on the roof again?" Lina asked. "The church has clearly not been in use for years, and this far out of town, it's not likely someone's going to happen upon us."

"I don't know. Less chance of being snuck up on if we're out in the open? No one ever looks up? The chance of being seen a couple hundred feet in the air is unlikely even if they do?"

Quinn's guesses made about as much sense as anything else. With a final, nervous glance up at the roof, Lina nodded. "Let's get this over with."

Finley gave them a little salute before peeling away and heading back toward the shadows. Alistair hesitated a moment, surprising her when he moved in her direction instead of going after Finley. Her confusion evaporated when he gave her a quick kiss on the cheek.

"Be careful."

"You, too."

He smiled his agreement, but it looked forced like he wasn't confident it was a promise he could keep.

Once she could no longer see either of them, she turned her attention back to the church's arched double doors. Nord had already propped one open, gesturing for her and Quinn to duck inside.

Without the moon to illuminate their path, the interior was comprised of overlapping shadows. It was nearly impossible to distinguish between a pew and empty space.

Goosebumps broke out over her arms as Nord skimmed his fingers down her spine.

"Closest access point is through the left tower," he whispered in her ear. "Follow me."

Taking her hand, he led them to a hidden pocket door, which slid open after he twisted a seemingly random candelabra on the wall.

"How'd you know this was here?" she asked.

"I studied the blueprints before we left."

She bit back a smile. *Of course, he did.*

Stale air washed over them as they entered the revealed space. Lina peered into the darkness, wondering how long it had been since someone had stepped foot in here.

"I'd feel a lot less jumpy if we had a flashlight," Quinn grumbled. "This is starting to feel way too similar to one of those Halloween mazes where crazy shit jumps out and grabs you."

"I know what you mean, but we can't risk anyone noticing the light. Last thing we need is a well-meaning police officer or good Samaritan sneaking up on us," Lina said.

"I know, I know," Quinn said. "I was just saying."

"Stairs should be over here," he said. "I'll go first to test them out, make sure the wood isn't rotted. Be careful with the railing, too."

Letting go of her hand, Nord moved to the right. Her eyes were starting to adjust to the darkness, and she could just make out his tall frame as he started up the stairs.

"They seem sturdy enough. Let's go," he called down when he'd reached the first turn.

"I shouldn't have skipped so many leg days," Quinn whispered.

"You're about to make up for them now," Lina replied.

"If I don't pass out first."

Lina couldn't help but agree. Her stamina and strength had improved a lot since her daily workouts with Nord, but this had to be at least twenty stories up if not more. That was no cakewalk, no matter how fit you were.

It wasn't long before Lina was breathing hard, her legs shaking from exertion. At first, she'd ignored the wooden banister, not wanting to risk splinters or a piece of it giving way, but that didn't last for more than a dozen flights. The number of turns was dizzying, and the railing beneath her hand helped steady her.

"I think I'm going to puke," Quinn whimpered from behind her.

"Aim for the hole in the middle," Lina replied.

"Funny," she panted. Then after a beat, she asked, "Why is the center open anyway? You'd think whoever built this place would have been more concerned about falling."

"It was for the bell," Nord replied.

"This is a bell tower? I didn't see a bell," Quinn said.

"Was," Nord corrected. "It was replaced with a sound system in the sixties."

"Think it came with its own hunchback?" she asked.

"Definitely," Lina said.

The conversation dropped off again after that, leaving only the mingled sound of their breathing echoing throughout the tower.

Lina paused to wipe sweat from her brow when she caught Quinn's panicked inhale.

Her heart stuttered in her chest. "You okay?" she asked, spinning around.

Quinn was doubled over, her hand holding the railing in a death grip.

"Fine," she said, looking up. "My foot slipped; these fucking steps are so damn narrow."

The pressure in her chest eased. "Come on. It can't be much further."

"We're almost to the top," Nord confirmed. "I can feel a breeze."

A few more flights, and Lina could too. Dull moonlight seeped into the square chamber from a handful of badly shuttered windows, along with the howl of wind. While the bell was long gone, the wood and metal scaffolding that had held it in place remained. It looked oddly skeletal, and Lina couldn't quite suppress her shiver of apprehension. Her desire to get out of this tower and back out into open air was overwhelming.

Nord waited for her at the top of the stairs on a wooden loft that wrapped around the tower's interior. Lina couldn't help but notice that he didn't look remotely winded.

Ass.

"Watch your step here," he said once she was a few steps below him.

Lina nodded her agreement, unable to speak since her breath came in shallow pants that made forming words difficult.

The wood groaned in protest as Nord started for the door that was a few feet away.

He frowned back at her. "Let me open the door and step off before you get on. I'm not confident it can support both of us."

Lina nodded, her hands growing slick with sweat as she watched him make his way to the exit. She didn't draw a full breath until the door was open and he was peeking back in.

"All clear."

Lina placed her first foot on the platform without issue, but the wood creaked when she added the second. Heart in her throat, she didn't let go of the railing as she made her way to the door. As soon as she was within arm's distance, Nord grasped her forearm and yanked her out.

It was all she could do not to collapse in a puddle as she sucked in the fresh air, but her relief was short-lived. The wind had started to pick up while they'd been inside, and pieces of her hair tore free of her braid and whipped across her face.

Lina frowned up at the sky, not liking the way the clouds had gathered overhead. The distinct scent of ozone confirmed what she'd already suspected.

A storm was coming.

They needed to get this meeting over with. Fast. She didn't want to be caught out here once it broke.

Lina peered over Nord's shoulder back into the tower's dim interior, wondering how Quinn was managing. It was rare to see her friend nervous, but as she climbed up onto the loft, Lina could clearly make out the sheen of sweat on her forehead and the lines of tension bracketing her mouth.

The wooden planks gave another warning groan.

"Run," Nord commanded, his voice leaving no room for argument.

Quinn took one running step before the panel beneath her feet gave way.

Lina bit back a scream as Quinn dropped, her feet sinking through the rotten wood, but Nord was already there, one hand grasping onto the doorframe, the rest of his body leaning through the opening, bent nearly in half to reach her.

"Please, don't drop me," she breathed, her voice unnaturally shrill as she clung to his hand.

"I've got you," he promised as he started pulling back, lifting her up as he did.

She hadn't fallen far, just up to midcalf, but that didn't alleviate the sheer terror the almost-fall had wrought. The entire thing probably lasted a few seconds at most, but it felt like a lifetime before Quinn was standing safely beside them on the rooftop.

Lina launched herself at her best friend as soon as she was through, wrapping her in a bone-crushing hug.

"Lina, I can't breathe," she protested, but her grip was just as tight, and there was no hiding the tremor in her arms.

"Thank you," Lina mouthed to Nord, not quite ready to let go of her friend just yet.

He dipped his chin in a nod, the moonlight catching his pale eyes and making them shine.

Once her heart had returned to a somewhat normal rate, Lina released Quinn and started looking around.

It didn't take long to determine that there was no one else here.

Lina frowned. "Where's Deanne?"

Quinn shook her head. "She should have been here twenty minutes ago."

Frowning, they carefully made their way to the center of the flat, rectangular space that ran along the central part of the church below. Just ahead, jutting up into the sky was the main spire with its dozens of buttresses. From here, it was much easier to make out the intricate details, which any other time Lina would have appreciated. Right now, the only thing she could focus on was the fact that the woman they were supposed to meet was nowhere to be found.

"Do you think she stood us up?" Quinn asked.

"She confirmed the meet with us right before we left the house. It seems unlikely she'd change her mind between then and now," Lina said.

Quinn bit her bottom lip and cast her eyes around as if she could draw Deanne out of the shadows by will alone.

"Finley is doing another check to make sure he didn't miss her inside or on the grounds," Nord said.

Lina didn't bother saying what they all must have been thinking. There's no way the Guardians overlooked Deanne during their initial search. Not if she was really here.

What had started off as a general sense of foreboding transformed into full-blown dread.

Something wasn't right.

Before she could give voice to her concern, fat drops of rain started to fall from the sky. It went from a few icy droplets to sheets of rain within seconds. There weren't many options for shelter on the roof, but they darted toward the spire, hoping it would at least shield them from the worst of the wind.

Nord peeled off his jacket, holding the dark leather up over her and Quinn's heads like a makeshift umbrella as they huddled together.

If she hadn't been looking for it, she might have missed the subtle flare in Nord's eyes when he received Finley's update.

His gaze was wild when it met hers, and Lina's stomach dropped.

"We need to go. Now," he said, dropping his jacket and grabbing her arm in a punishing hold as he started to run.

"Why? What happened?" Quinn asked, sprinting after them.

Nord never slowed as he called over his shoulder, "They found a body. Alistair identified it. Deanne is dead."

Before they made it halfway back across the roof, lightning arced across the sky, one blinding bolt forking down and hitting the tower they were heading for. Then, two more. One landing in the exact place as the first bolt, the second striking the metal cross at its peak, sending sparks shooting into the sky.

Lina had never seen a lightning strike so deliberate. Or quite so accurate.

That's when she knew.

This was no natural storm.

"Mataius is here," she shouted over the gale.

Nord stopped dead, a shudder working its way down his back. Lina recognized it as a sign that he was fighting hard against his berserker.

His eyes burned with azure fire as he demanded, "Where?"

Lina wiped water from her face only to be near blinded by the rain again immediately after. "I don't know exactly, but somewhere close. The Drakes are weather shapers. Mataius is controlling the storm."

His grip on her arm tightened. "Let's go."

The rooftop was already starting to flood from the sheer amount of rainfall in such a short amount of time. The gutters, likely clogged with several years' worth of dirt and debris, were no match for it.

Lightning streaked across the sky once more, accompanied by a roar of thunder, which rattled the church with its force. With each step they took toward the tower—and the stairs that would lead them back to safety—there was a corresponding lightning strike. Given the amount of water pooling on this roof, they were in serious trouble.

When lightning blocked their escape for a third time in as many seconds, Quinn let out a frustrated scream.

"That shit-stain is playing with us," she shouted though her voice was nearly drowned out by the wind.

"We have to get off this roof," Lina shouted back. "We're sitting ducks up here."

Still being pelted by rain, wind ripping at their clothes, she searched for some other escape route. She could use magic to create her own ladder or stairs down the side of the church, but anything that required concentration and dexterity—not to mention time—for them to get down would only make them easier targets. They needed something faster. Something unexpected that would surprise Mataius long enough to give them an advantage.

As an idea began to take shape, Lina questioned her sanity. She wasn't even sure what she was contemplating was possible.

Rushing over to the edge, Lina squinted down, trying to make out the garden below. It was nearly impossible to see anything in the rain, but she knew in her bones that the blurred silhouette across the street was Mataius.

She bared her teeth in a snarl, knowing her words would be swallowed by the storm but saying them anyway. "You better start running, you son of a bitch. Because when I catch you, you're going to wish you'd never been born."

"Lina? What are you doing?" Quinn asked, rushing to her side.

She glanced over her shoulder. "I have an idea."

Fueled by her need for vengeance, Lina called on her power. It surged up in response, buzzing through her veins. Knowing what was at stake if she failed, she couldn't afford to second guess herself. Blocking out everything else, she began to visualize what she wanted her magic to do, holding each detail in her mind until the image was complete. She was so focused on her task; she didn't even flinch when lightning struck a bit of the stone ledge less than a foot to her right.

"Lina," Nord shouted, his voice thick with fear.

"I'm okay," she said, glancing back at them over her shoulder. "But we need to go."

There was no way to know if it worked. No way for her to see the results of her efforts through the fury of the storm, but she had never wanted something to *be* more than this in her entire life. After the way her magic had been responding to just her whims recently, she could only believe it had risen to the occasion when she needed it the most.

Releasing a shaky breath, Lina started to climb up onto the ledge.

"Lina," Quinn said, stretching her name out. "What the hell are you doing?"

"Do you trust me?" she asked, tilting her chin back to her shoulder but not taking her eyes off the ground.

"You know I do," Quinn said.

Her gaze lifted to Nord, who looked like he was mere seconds away from yanking her down. She could tell he was torn, his instinct to protect likely at war with his steadfast faith in her. This was no place for a lengthy debate, and she knew which side had won when his eyes pulsed with power, but he stayed put.

"Then I'm going to need you both to jump."

If they answered, their responses were consumed by the thunder.

As Lina bent her knees, preparing for what she hoped would be a graceful swan dive, lightning flashed directly above her. The bolt forked, one edge hitting the flat bit of stone she was standing on, the other disappearing somewhere behind her.

Her footing slipped as the block of stone gave way.

She tried to right herself, but she'd already started to lean forward, and without anything to support her weight, gravity pulled her down.

It was not a battle she could win.

It never had been. Mataius had seen to that.

But what he didn't know was that she just changed the rules.

CHAPTER TWENTY
NORD

Life is comprised of a series of moments. Many of which are easily forgotten, but others . . . others are burned so deeply into the brain that they define who a person becomes from that point forward.

Seeing Lina slip over the edge, her hair flying around her like a golden halo, was one such moment.

Quinn had already started to climb up after her, so she was kneeling on the ledge when the lightning struck. Nord was a bit farther away, still ankle-deep in the water when it forked and finally touched down on the flat surface of the cathedral's roof.

There was nothing he could do. No way to avoid the searing agony pumping its way into his body. He tasted blood as his jaw clamped tight, biting through his cheek and tongue. His nostrils filled with the unique scent of burnt flesh, and he knew it was his as the electricity held him captive in its conductive web.

For an endless second, he could not move, could not breathe. In fact, he was nearly certain his heart ceased beating entirely.

But he could see.

Thanks to his Guardian-enhanced vision, he could make out

every detail as if there wasn't an ocean's worth of water pouring down from the sky at all.

Being forced to watch as he and the woman he loved were robbed of their future should have been a curse, but to him, it was a blessing. At least this way, he got to see her whole one last time.

Quinn cried out Lina's name, but it sounded distant. It was hard to hear anything over his own internal screams.

As his eyes found Lina's, he expected to discover fear or regret in their depths, but he was met with a startling lack of both. All he saw there was conviction. Purpose.

Her lips moved, and while he could not hear the words, he could still read her lips.

"Jump."

The lightning holding him in its snare snuffed out, cloaking them all in darkness once more.

Nord dropped to his hands and knees, his body wracked with pain so acute that even breathing was agony. He didn't have to look to know that most of his body was badly burned. He wasn't going anywhere in his current state.

But staying put wasn't a choice. He had seconds—if that—before Mataius finished what he started.

The thought of that coward laying his traps and hiding in the shadows because he knew it was the only way he could win sent forth a tidal wave of fury that blunted the sharp edge of pain.

Yes.

With a battle cry that rivaled the thunder overhead, the berserker pushed to his feet. It was the first time in well over a century Nord consciously called on the transition.

Relief was instant.

Berserkers were made to fight through their injuries. To keep fighting until the last of their enemies had fallen or they died in battle, whichever came first. Never had that blessed numbness been so welcome. His body was still just as damaged, but now he could ignore it long enough to act.

His first step was uneven as his ravaged legs struggled to obey, but the second came easier. By the fifth, he'd vaulted up onto the ledge beside Quinn and gripped the back of her jacket in his fist.

She looked up at him, her face crumpled with grief and her tears mingling with the rain dripping down her face.

"She said jump."

They were airborne before he finished speaking although only one of them stepped off intentionally. He hadn't given Quinn a choice as he pulled her with him into freefall.

There wasn't much to do as they plunged to the ground but pray that whatever Lina had up her sleeve would make itself apparent before they collided with the pavement. He comforted himself with thoughts of her. She'd asked for his trust. That much he could still do for her. He wouldn't allow doubt to creep in.

But as the ground loomed closer and there was no sign of Lina anywhere, Nord's survival instincts kicked into overdrive. Pointless though they were. His magic and fighting skills were of little use against the laws of nature.

The best idea he could come up with was attempting to convert Quinn's jacket into a last-minute parachute, but they were already halfway to the ground when the thought occurred, which didn't leave enough time or space for it to make any difference.

When no other viable options presented themselves, Nord braced for impact.

His muscles tensed, and he curled himself into a protective ball as if that would do anything to keep his bones from shattering as soon as he hit the earth. Just as his eyes began to close, he saw Lina surging up from beneath the ground like she was some kind of land-dwelling mermaid.

He blinked, his brain trying to determine whether or not what he was seeing was real and how it could even be possible. He didn't have to wonder long. Everything made sense as soon as his body hit the dead leaves and vines littering the ground and kept going.

There was no pain. No jarring collision. Just the novelty of a completely new and unexpected experience. The further down he went, the less he could hear of the storm raging above, and the harder it was to make out anything around him.

The sensation of tumbling through the earth was a strange one. It was almost as if he'd fallen into a pool, but instead of liquid, it was filled with a spongy, gel-like substance. It cushioned him, drawing him deeper into its depths while also slowing his descent. When he finally came to a stop, the only comparison his mind could find to describe what had just happened was that of a bullet being fired into a block of ballistic gel.

Before he could worry about how he was supposed to get free, pressure began to build slowly beneath him, pushing him back up the way he'd come. It was a controlled rise but seemed to gather momentum as he neared the surface where he was spat back out onto firm ground.

Nord rolled onto his back, noting that the rain had stopped as he sucked in breath after breath.

The sound of running footsteps came from his left, and he tried to sit up. But exhaustion seeped through him, and not even the last of his rage was enough to stave it off entirely.

Lina's face came into view, blocking out what little he could make out of the moon. His relief at seeing her alive should have bolstered him, but instead, it leeched away the last of his bloodlust, leaving him without the buffer of his berserker strength.

"Nord. Oh my God, Nord."

She peppered his face with kisses that he tried to return, but his body was no longer responding to his demands.

"Finley!" she cried. "Over here."

It was growing harder to keep his eyes open. He blinked, fighting to retain consciousness, but everything immediately swam back out of focus. The only reason he recognized the blob above him as Finley was because of the voice in his mind.

"Rest, Brother. I've got it from here."

"Mataius?"

"Fled."

"If anything happens to her—"

"Don't worry. You have my word."

That was all Nord needed to give in to the sweet promise of oblivion.

CHAPTER TWENTY-ONE
NORD

Consciousness returned in pieces. First, there was the light warming his face. Next, there was the soft ache of overworked muscles. And then, finally, there was her.

The frantic cast of Lina's voice pulled him out of the depths almost instantly.

"What the hell do you think you're doing? The healer said he'd wake up once the healing was complete."

"Yeah, well, unfortunately, we don't have that luxury." There was an undercurrent of distress in Finley's voice that he hadn't heard before.

"What do you mean?"

"The Director heard about what happened at the church. He's called us in. You don't want to find out what happens if we fail to report."

Nord's eyes snapped open at that. He found Lina first, her eyes red-rimmed and her usually rosy complexion dulled with fatigue.

"You're awake," she said, her lips lifting in a smile that looked like it was seconds away from losing a battle against tears.

He lifted an arm and ran his knuckles along her cheek. "You say that like there was a doubt," he replied, his voice rusty with disuse.

She let out a watery chuckle. "Maybe just for a while there."

He shifted his attention to Finley whose always coifed hair looked like he'd run his hands through it a number of times. "When?"

"Immediately."

Nord gave a tight nod. "Give me a few minutes," he said, pushing himself up into a seated position. The sheet pooled at his hips, and he glanced at Lina. "Please, tell me you were the one who undressed me."

"The healer did," Lina corrected with a strained smile. "Your clothes disappeared along with your injuries. Although, to be fair, they weren't in that great of shape after . . ."

Knowing the memory must be far from pleasant, he reached out and squeezed her hand. He didn't care about the clothes. He just wanted to take the haunted look from her eyes.

"As long as it wasn't the handsy Brit."

Finley snorted. "Only in your dreams, wanker." He started making his way to the door, pausing just before stepping outside. "It's good to see you moving again, mate."

Nord raised his brow and shifted his gaze back to Lina. "From the way you two are acting, it sounds like I was knocking on death's door."

"You've been out for two days, Nord."

He took in the deep purple shadows beneath Lina's eyes and the rumpled state of her clothes, realizing she'd spent every second of those two days by his side. She hadn't even changed out of what she'd been wearing at the cathedral. While he'd been lost to the healing sleep, she'd been out of her mind with worry.

"Come here," he said, his words no less of a command despite the gentleness of his voice.

Lina complied immediately, rising from the chair she'd moved beside his bed and curling herself into his body. He wrapped his arms around her, running one of his hands down the tangled remnants of her braid. He kept his voice low, dipping his chin so he was speaking almost directly into her ear.

"Valhalla has never held much appeal to me. I'd prefer to enjoy heaven while still alive. And you, Kærasta, are my idea of heaven. Not even death could keep me from you."

Lina sniffled against his chest. "It didn't keep me from you either."

He smiled against her forehead. "See? We will always find our way back to each other. Never doubt it."

She took a deep breath, her ribs expanding and contracting beneath his arms. "You were in really bad shape. I've never seen anything like that."

He kissed the top of her head, sitting back just enough to look into her eyes. "Odin and His son are known for their tempers."

Lina blinked, confusion furrowing her brow. "What's Odin got to do with anything?"

"I do not believe in coincidence; I've lived far too long for that. For a berserker to be felled by lightning? That kind of irony is the work of a displeased god."

"The lightning was Mataius' doing," she protested.

Nord shrugged. "Perhaps he was just the vessel."

"I didn't think you believed in that kind of thing."

"Not for a long time perhaps, but at one time, I did."

"Okay, but if Odin created the berserkers, why would he want to hurt you?"

"Because I turned my back on Him and my people? I denied my heritage when I joined the Brotherhood and resisted the call of the bloodlust? He sees Mataius' continued existence as proof of my failure to uphold my vow to keep you safe?" Nord shrugged. "Who knows the mind of a god?"

"You haven't failed me. I'm sitting right here with you, aren't I?"

His arms tightened around her. "That you are. However, Mataius should never have been able to trick us as he did."

"His tricking us isn't a result of anything you did. We were betrayed by someone on the Council."

"Or, he got word of our visit to the Bell woman and has been tracking our movements since. That kind of sloppiness is unacceptable, Lina. I could have brought the danger we've been trying to avoid straight to your doorstep."

"You weren't the only one at that apartment, Nord. If you're going to blame yourself for that, you're going to have to blame all of us."

While she might absolve him of guilt, Nord couldn't bring himself to accept it. He was the one that made the vow and the one that was failing to live up to it.

Lina must have picked up on the direction of his thoughts because she pressed her lips together and gave him a considering look. "Think what you will. I still say it was just Mataius being a rat bastard."

Nord chuckled. "Fair enough. Speaking of tricks, doubt he was expecting you to pull off one of your own."

She flushed with pride. "To be honest, I was a little uncertain myself."

"But it worked, and it was truly incredible." He tucked a piece of her hair behind her ear, his fingers skimming her jaw and tilting her chin up. He hated the worry he found still clouding her eyes. "I'm sorry for scaring you."

"I'm sorry you got hurt."

His lips twitched up. "I've gone through worse."

She laughed outright. "Liar."

"For you," he whispered, "there is no end to what I would endure."

Their lips met in a hungry kiss, their bodies melding together in a desperate attempt to get as close as possible.

A series of loud knocks preceded Finley's shout through the door. "We've got to go."

Nord pulled away with a tortured groan. He rested his forehead against Lina's, his eyes still closed as he fought against the urge to finish what he started.

"To be continued."

"Count on it," she murmured.

He ran his thumb along her bottom lip, stealing a second to memorize the feel of her pressed against him and the way her hooded eyes burned with desire.

"I'll be back as soon as I can," he promised.

"You better be," she said, her voice a throaty purr as she wove her fingers through his hair and tugged his mouth back to hers.

Finley's insistent knocks came almost immediately.

"It's like he knows," Lina groaned.

Nord laughed, twisting away from her to swing his legs off the bed. He stood and started for the door.

"Aren't you going to put on some clothes?" Lina asked, her voice strained as her eyes traveled down his mostly naked body.

Nord glanced down and bit back a grin. Calling on his magic, he transformed the black boxer briefs into a full three-piece suit. "Better?" he asked with a wink.

"I think I preferred what you were wearing before," she muttered.

He chuckled. "I think you'd prefer it if I was wearing nothing at all."

Color flooded her cheeks. "True." She cleared her throat and blinked as if trying to focus. "Don't forget your shoes."

There was a pair of dressier boots he'd tossed by the door a few days ago that he snagged before reaching for the doorknob.

"Nord? Be safe, okay?"

He gave her what he hoped was a reassuring smile. "It's just a meeting. There's absolutely nothing to worry about. I'll be back before you know it."

Then, he stepped through the door and found Finley waiting for him with crossed arms and a pinched expression.

His smile dropped as soon as the door was shut behind him. "Ready?"

"For the Director to rip us a matching set of new arseholes?" Finley asked. "Fucking ecstatic, mate."

"Let's just get this over with."

CHAPTER TWENTY-TWO
NORD

Everything about the executive floor was plush and expensive-looking—except for the row of utilitarian chairs lining the wall of the reception area. Nord knew that wasn't an oversight but rather a less than subtle reminder of the power dynamics at play.

The chair's metal frame seemed to embed itself in Nord's ass. It probably had something to do with the fact that it wasn't made for a man his size. He shifted in one last futile attempt to get comfortable before grunting and giving up any pretense of respectability. Planting one of his booted feet onto the seat of his chair, he kicked the other out in front of him. Then, he rested his elbow on his raised knee and used his fist to prop his head up.

Much better.

The Director's assistant, Madame Bisset, scowled at him from behind her desk. He resisted the urge to blow her a kiss and really send her spiraling and, instead, settled deeper into his chair and resumed watching Finley pace and mutter to himself.

The one benefit about being forced to wait out here was the extra time it provided to prepare his mind. Once they were in the same room as the Director, not even his mind would be safe.

While the Brotherhood ensured each of its members received training in all aspects of their Guardian magic, it did not mean their skill level in each of those areas was equal. Some never made it beyond basic mastery while others had a natural affinity that no amount of time or experience could match.

And the man they were about to see? He was legendary.

His gift was telepathy, but reading thoughts was just the beginning of what he could accomplish using only his mind. There were maybe a handful of people at most who could consider themselves his equal. Talented though they were, Nord and Finley were not among them.

Faced with that knowledge, Nord knew this interrogation was going to be as difficult to navigate as a minefield.

There was no denying he had broken the rules, but that wasn't what the Director wanted to know. He would try to suss out just how far Nord had gone. The tricky part was that his questions could refer to his interactions with Crombie, Quinn, or Lina, and he would keep them intentionally vague, hoping that Nord would give himself away. If not in his words, then with his thoughts.

The Director was banking on the fact that the mind could simultaneously conjure a number of potential answers before someone was consciously able to filter through them and select the one they wanted to provide.

In short, Nord could fuck himself without ever saying a word.

The one thing Nord had going for him was that, while not limited to reading only surface thoughts, the Director tended not to dig unless he picked up on outright deception. So while Nord may not have any defenses if the man chose to tear through his mind like a subliminal hurricane, he could do his best to avoid giving him a reason to.

"How long is he going to make us wait?" Finley asked, coming to a stop in front of him.

"As long as he wants."

Finley braced his hands on his hips and blew out a breath. "I don't like it."

"I think that's the point."

"Ahem."

Nord and Finley's eyes darted over to the woman behind the desk though neither of them made any further attempt to move or acknowledge her.

She pursed her lips in disapproval as she stared at them. "The Director will see you now."

"Maybe you should let me do the talking," Finley said via their mental link as Nord pushed to his feet.

"You and I both know he's not taking anything we say at face value. He'll get the information he wants with or without our consent."

Finley's jaw clenched. *"That's what I'm worried about."*

Nord put his hands in his pockets to disguise the fact they were balled into fists. It's what he was worried about, too.

If the Director started digging around in Nord's head, there was no way he wouldn't find out about Lina and her connection to the Council. She was already on the Director's radar, but the last thing he wanted was to give the man a reason to look at her more closely. At best, he'd try to recruit her as some sort of double agent. At worst, he'd turn her into a lab rat in his attempt to retrieve the artifact she concealed.

Double agents and lab rats had one thing in common: they rarely stayed alive for long.

"Are you going to be able to . . . control yourself?" Finley asked as they approached the black lacquered door at the end of the hall.

"I guess we're about to find out."

In one of what Nord was sure to be many displays of the Director's psychic abilities, the door swung open without either of them touching it.

The Director stood with his back facing them and his hands

clasped behind him, looking every bit like a king surveying his kingdom as he stared out his window at the city below.

"*Sit,*" he commanded, his mental voice booming with authority.

The two chairs facing his desk swung out, leaving little doubt as to where he expected them to go.

Exchanging a look, Nord and Finley complied. There wasn't any other option if they wanted this meeting to end well. Although, it could already be too late for that.

"*Were the procedures we discussed when you rejoined us too complicated for you to follow?*"

Finley cleared his throat. "Director, if I may—"

"*I'm not speaking to you.*"

Finley sent Nord an apologetic look.

Nord tried hard to keep his mind clear, not wanting to supply the Director with any more ammo to use against him.

"No, sir," he replied.

He hated that the Director could speak to them telepathically while they were forced to resort to verbal responses. His telepathic prowess allowed him to shield his mind against them, but they had no such reprieve.

"*You've been back for how long? Two months now?*"

"Give or take," Nord confirmed.

"*And it took you, what, a week, a couple days, to decide that you were going to disregard the rules entirely?*"

A muscle pulsed in his jaw. "No, sir," Nord forced himself to reply.

"*So you didn't flagrantly disregard our policies when you began conducting an unauthorized investigation with a known enemy of the Brotherhood?*"

It was a struggle to hold onto his mental calm, but knowing what was at stake, he managed. Nord concentrated on drawing in a full breath, pushing everything from his mind as he released it.

"Not intentionally, no."

The Director spun around, his pale green eyes flashing a brilliant jade as he pinned Nord with his stare. *"Now that I find hard to believe."*

Nord lifted his palms, his rings glinting in the light. "It's the truth."

He tilted his head. *"How do you figure?"*

"I sought only to help the woman I vowed to protect. That required seeking answers the Brotherhood would require before I could request their official involvement."

The Director was quiet for a moment as he took several long strides into the center of the room. He looked much the same as he had the first time Nord had met him. Bald head, bushy red mustache that hid his upper lip, and a nose that had been broken so many times its natural shape had been forgotten. He may sit behind a desk now, but he still had the appearance of the Irish brawler he'd once been.

"You can't be stupid enough to think we wouldn't have found out about what you were doing, so why hide it?"

"I knew there was a chance you would not like the answers I found, but I needed to seek them anyway. She is my true purpose. The one that I was made to serve."

As he'd expected, the Director's eyes flared with interest. Not even he could argue with the sway such a person held over a Guardian. The bond was ancient and superseded any bullshit rules the Brotherhood might try to enforce. There was nothing he, or anyone else, could do to refute it.

"Do you know what it is the Brotherhood does, Nord?"

"We are the watchers. The ones who safeguard and protect the various realms and their inhabitants, magical or otherwise."

The Director nodded. *"And do you know how we've managed to do that successfully for so long?"*

He didn't quite manage to keep the sarcasm out of his voice as he answered, "By being good at our job?"

The Director's eyes flashed with jade. He was not amused. Unfortunately, neither was Nord. His patience for this game was waning fast, his berserker's rage steadily building the longer they remained.

"By not drawing unwanted attention to ourselves. You said it yourself, we are watchers, gatherers of information. We do not get involved unless the threat is such that to not act would negatively impact the greater good. And in the rare instances when our involvement is deemed necessary, we ensure that what needs to be done occurs in the shadows. Do you know why this is?"

Nord clenched his jaw, feeling more and more like he was being treated like an unruly child and less like a grown-ass man.

Finley managed to catch his eye and give him a warning look. Since they couldn't risk speaking to one another along their link, Nord took it to mean "Calm the fuck down."

He blew out another breath.

"Because if the things we did in the name of the greater good came to light, they'd be seen as acts of war by the very people we are trying to protect."

"Precisely. And we cannot protect them if they see us as the enemy. The reason the Brotherhood works is because we do not give anyone a reason to doubt us. So, I trust you can understand my concern when I hear two of my Guardians have been involved in a number of unsavory activities that call our reputation into question."

"But sir—"

"Do you understand?"

The wood beneath his hand creaked as his grip on it tightened. "I understand."

The Director moved so that he was standing directly over Nord, forcing him to tilt his chin up to look him in the eye.

"I am not without understanding myself. I know that you were part of an elite group that was required to make decisions outside of the Brother-hood's purview for centuries. It can be hard to break the habit after such an extended period of time; however, this will be your only warning. If I find out either of you threaten my organization with your selfish actions again, that will be the last time. Do I make myself clear?"

"Crystal."

"Yes, Director," Finley said.

"Excellent."

Nord began to relax, thinking they might just manage to get out of here with only a slap on the wrists after all.

The Director destroyed that illusion with his next words.

"Now, tell me about the woman."

Nord's vision started to turn red at the edges.

"You're going to have to be more specific."

"Do not push me. I am doing you a courtesy by allowing you to answer. I can always send a couple of agents to your penthouse and bring her here to answer my questions herself."

The threat was delivered with all the finesse of a mini-nuke.

It was one thing to come after him; it was another thing entirely to openly threaten Lina. Not only was it incredibly stupid for *anyone* to go after a Guardian's charge, but it was outright suicidal to provoke a berserker.

If the Director thought his position would protect him, he was about to learn a very painful lesson.

Nord's nails dug into the wooden arms of his chair, leaving little divots in their wake.

Finley's foot snaked out and stamped down hard on Nord's. He gave an infinitesimal shake of his head.

Don't.

The plea was clear.

Shit could go so very, very wrong if Nord lost control now. Provoked or not, if he attacked the Director—in the middle of their damn headquarters nonetheless—he'd be stripped of his power and executed inside of the hour. Finley, too.

There was no such thing as a trial or jury of your peers in the Brotherhood. Not for traitors.

It was almost impossible, but Nord managed to successfully suppress the urge to rip off the arms of his chair and start beating him with them. The only thing that kept the bloodlust at bay was the fact that if he gave in now, Lina would be alone. She needed him; Mataius was still out there. Getting back to her was the priority, not teaching this ass a lesson.

No matter how good it would feel to rip the bastard's head from his body.

He pried his fingers off of the chair and breathed deep, forcing the berserker within to recede. It obeyed, but only just.

"Good choice."

A growl built deep in his chest. "I think you'll find, Director, that in this matter, *you* don't want to push *me*."

"Tell me what I want to know, and I won't have to."

He ground his teeth together before biting out, "What do you want to know?"

"What is her involvement with the Mobius Council?"

This was the question he'd been waiting for. The one he'd been preparing himself to answer ever since Finley first mentioned the Director was sniffing around.

"One of its heirs attempted to murder her."

Nord allowed his hatred for Mataius to rise to the surface and stoke his anger. Hopefully, the genuine emotions would reinforce his words.

"Why?"

Letting Lina's description of the dark basement and the chanting she overheard fill his mind, Nord said, "Apparently, she was supposed to be the sacrifice for some kind of dark ritual."

The Director's eyes flared a blinding jade.

Nord focused hard on the image of a dagger being plunged into Lina's chest, allowing his hold on his berserker to slip just a little and fill him with its fury.

"And so this is who you've been hunting?"

"It is."

"In an attempt to avenge your charge?"

"Yes," Nord ground out.

"I see."

The Director pivoted and took two steps away before turning back and lifting a finger aimed at Nord.

"Then let me make myself very clear. You will cease your investigation immediately. You will have no further contact with any known associates of the Mobius Council. You will not," he thundered, his voice so loud Nord had to clench his jaw against the jackhammer sensation in his mind, *"harm the boy in any way. In fact, you will not interfere with the Council or its members in any capacity. The Mobius Council is completely, one hundred percent, off-limits to you. When the time comes, the Brotherhood will deal with them using the appropriate channels. But only I have the authority to decide when that time is. We cannot and will not risk decades of investigative work on petty revenge."*

"But sir—"

"I don't care who she is to you—"

Nord knew then that for all this man's power and status, he didn't actually understand a fucking thing about what happened when a Guardian found his true purpose. He recognized the term, but only in the way one recognizes a myth, he didn't understand what it meant. If he did, he wouldn't be speaking about Lina like she was a random girl.

"I am quite aware of your commitment to her, but the Brotherhood comes first. The needs of the Brotherhood must always come first."

Nord snorted with derision. "You only believe that because you've never discovered yours."

The Director's eyes flashed, and Nord knew that in the Director's mind, he had just treaded dangerously close to blasphemy.

"Let me explain what you do not seem to understand. My loyalty is to the Brotherhood. My purpose is *the Brotherhood. I have spent my life protecting its members and promoting its sacred mission. There is nothing I would not do to ensure it prospers, and that includes sacrificing the life of one to save thousands."*

Nord remained silent, knowing any attempt at further explanation was futile. The man was a fanatic. It would take nothing short of experiencing it himself to change his mind.

The Director continued speaking. *"So when I tell you that I do not care who she is, or what the heir did to her, it is because I am upholding my mission. The Mobius Council is too powerful. The ripple effect of an unwarranted attack—"*

"Unwarranted? Since when do we just look the other way when innocents are murdered?"

"Since our interfering now would lead to the kind of war this planet has never seen and may never recover from." The Director stalked back to him and leaned down until they were eye to eye. *"But more importantly, since I told you to."*

Nord's heart was pounding in his chest, his rage a caged beast that was seconds away from breaking free of its chains.

The Director's eyes pulsed with power. *"Is there anything about my order that you do not understand?"*

"No." The word was bitten off and angry. "Are we done here?"

"Not yet. I'll have your promise that you'll stand down first."

Shock jolted through him at the audacity of the Director's edict. There was a beat of silence and then Nord's ground out reply.

"Fine. You have it."

The Director smiled as he straightened, but it was a mockery of the real thing, devoid as it was of all warmth or sincerity. He gestured toward the door. *"Then you two are free to go. And Finley? That goes for you as well. I'm holding you personally responsible for his actions from here on out."*

Finley stood. "Understood, Director."

Nord seethed, his rage still on the brink of boiling over as they stormed out of the office.

Extorting a promise from a Guardian was a low blow, even from the Director. A true vow, once given, was unbreakable. The Director trying to force him into such a contract was a thinly veiled attempt to control him. He might be a mind reader, but once again, he'd demonstrated that he had absolutely no idea who he was dealing with.

A Guardian's vow could only be binding *if* it was genuine.

Even though he'd likely picked up on Nord's unwillingness to make the promise, he still thought he had Nord backed into a corner because, in the end, he'd gotten what he wanted.

But in all his smug superiority, there was one crucial detail he'd forgotten.

Nord's loyalty was no longer to the Brotherhood.

Ever since he'd made his vow to Lina, the only person he served was her.

CHAPTER TWENTY-THREE
LINA

Lina chewed on her bottom lip and stared at the window, not seeing anything beyond the rain-splattered pane.

"I'm sure everything's fine," Quinn said for what had to be the fifth time.

And as she had every time Quinn tried to reassure her, Lina gave a little non-committal murmur in response.

No one was believing anyone here.

Shit was definitely not fine.

Even the weather was seeing fit to fuck with her. Each drop that smacked the glass made her flinch. Lina had always loved the chaos of a good storm . . . until now. Mataius had robbed her of that, too.

Perhaps it wasn't the rain itself that was setting her on edge so much as that it was a reminder of Mataius and the fact that he was still out there. Running free.

"Come. Sit down," her uncle called. "I want to talk to you about something while we wait."

Lina tucked her chin to her shoulder and glanced at him seated behind her on the couch. "I'm not really up for it."

"I wasn't really asking."

Sighing heavily, she turned and woodenly marched herself to the couch. "What do you want to talk about?" she asked, her voice taking on an acerbic bite.

He raised a brow at her tone.

"Sorry," she muttered.

"Since it's just the three of us, I figured it was as good a time as any to let you in on a family secret."

Lina's attention sharpened at that. "What do you mean 'family secret'?"

His lips twitched. "I thought that might get your attention."

Not in the mood for games, she snapped, "Well?"

He pressed his lips together, his eyes still shining with his amusement. She may not be in the mood, but he was clearly entertained by her antics.

And then it came to her. A memory of a time when she barely stood above his knees and was begging him to give her her birthday present. He'd pretended he'd forgotten and was patting down his pockets in a mock attempt to search for something. Then, he'd given an exaggerated sigh of relief and produced a gift-wrapped box—much too large to have actually been in his pocket—and held it out to her. It was just one of a dozen times he'd used his magic to entertain her.

She could tell her impatience with him now must have called to mind a similar memory for him.

Her lips tilted up against their will. "Some things never change." Temper diffused, at least for the moment, she tried again. "What did you want to tell me?"

He settled back in his seat, hands resting on his knees. "Have you ever heard of the Codex?"

"You know I haven't."

His grin stretched. "Quite right."

"Are you sure I should be here for this?" Quinn asked.

Alistair nodded. "This applies to you, too, in a way. The Codex itself is not a secret so much as what it contains. Each of the animagi families had one. Many were lost to the ages, all but forgotten except for cryptic references to their existence. From those, I've been able to discern that they were history books, for lack of a better word, created by our ancestors to pass down the secrets of our kind. They are rumored to list the various shapes our powers can take and track the most common to the rarest and how often they appear, and . . ." he trailed off, his smile stretched as she leaned forward with unabashed interest, "how an heir may access them."

Lina's mouth dropped open. "If something like that existed, my father would have been all over it."

"You assume he knew about it."

Her eyes widened. "You mean . . ."

Her uncle's eyes twinkled behind his spectacles. "He'd heard the whispers, of course, but never made much headway in uncovering ours."

She rubbed the Prism inked onto her forearm. *No wonder he grew obsessed with other ways of obtaining power.*

"So if they're still all lost, why bring it up now?" she asked.

"Just because he failed doesn't mean that I did."

Lina smiled, secretly loving that her uncle had managed to one-up her father. She had to admit, the Codex sounded promising. There was a fight coming; it was simply a matter of when. Access to a document like that could be a game-changer, and she wasn't exactly in a position where she could afford to turn away help.

"So what's it say?"

Her uncle's excitement dimmed slightly. "Well, I didn't get a chance to translate much of it before I had to hide it. Just a reference to something called the transfer."

"Hide it? Why?" Lina asked.

But Quinn was talking over her. "You mean the Transference?"

They looked at each other with embarrassed smiles. Lina because Quinn clearly knew about something she didn't—as usual. And Quinn for interrupting their conversation.

Alistair's eyes were trained on Quinn's face. "You've heard of it?"

"I mean, in theory. My grandmother mentioned it. She said it could only happen between true mates. I thought it was an animagi version of a fairytale."

Lina's eyes ping-ponged between them. "What am I missing?"

Her uncle gestured for Quinn to share.

"You know how animagi genes are always dominant? It's why we can have children outside of our species and ensure the line doesn't die out."

Lina nodded; she was a child of such a union. "Obviously."

Quinn's lips pursed with suppressed laughter for a second before she continued with her explanation. "Apparently, this is a way that an animagi can share their power with their mate. So, for example, if their mate is not from a long-lived race, they would not have to watch them die after a mortal lifetime."

Lina could see the appeal; it would be impossible to watch the love of your life grow old and die while you barely aged. Thankfully, Nord was already immortal, so she wouldn't have to worry about that . . . although come to think of it, he might.

"But it's not just one-sided," Quinn continued, interrupting Lina's runaway thoughts, "the power transference goes both ways. So any magical ability one mate has, they share it with the other."

"Well, that's just convenient," Lina murmured.

Quinn couldn't have realized she'd just provided Lina with a potential solution to a problem she'd never verbalized. But perhaps it was one she'd thought of on her own because she smiled and said, "I thought you might like that part."

It wouldn't be the first time Quinn provided key information necessary to solve a puzzle. She was kin to the sphinx after all; conundrums were sort of their playground.

Then she remembered the caveat.

"But it's limited to true mates?"

Quinn shrugged. "Apparently."

"How do you find or know if someone's your true mate?" Lina asked.

Quinn gave her a pointed look. "Honey, if I knew the answer to that, I wouldn't still be single."

"Uncle Alistair?"

He shook his head. "Lifelong bachelor, remember?"

Lina's heart twisted in her chest at the reminder of the torch he'd carried for her mom. She couldn't help but wonder if they might have been destined for one another and how different things may have been if they'd ended up together.

She drummed her fingers on her knees. "Well, as romantic and interesting as all that is, I still think finding Mataius should be our priority."

"Lina," Alistair said, "you shouldn't dismiss the Codex's usefulness. It extends far beyond Mataius. It's an invaluable tool. One you'd be a fool not to use. Think of all you could stand to gain by revealing its secrets."

Lina shrugged, finding it hard to pin her hopes on a book that wasn't even currently in their possession. "I mean, it *sounds* great in theory. And I'm sure you're right that Quinn and I would gain a lot, learning from its pages, but you just said it had to be translated *and* you had to hide it again. I just don't see how that can be our priority while Mataius is still roaming free."

Quinn reached out and squeezed her hand.

Alistair leaned forward. "Lina, I appreciate your focus, but I think you're missing the bigger picture here. The Codex may be hidden, but that's easily remedied, and I can handle the translation. Mataius is only going to be the first of many adversaries you will have to face. You may not need its secrets to defeat him, but that doesn't mean you won't benefit from having access to them."

Lina couldn't really argue the wisdom of that. "True, but how do you even know it's where you left it?"

"I hid it back where I found it. It had survived there for ages prior to my discovery. It's unlikely anyone else would stumble across it in the meantime."

"But what if—"

Before she could finish voicing her next question, they all looked to the hall as the front door opened and slammed shut.

Her uncle waved away her concerns, knowing they needed to switch focus as soon as Nord and Finley reached them. "I've already started making arrangements to retrieve it. Things have been so hectic since your memory returned; I haven't wanted to leave you. But so long as you don't mind being without me for a couple of days—"

"If you truly believe it's that important, then we'll manage without you," she said.

Her uncle looked relieved. "I'll leave tonight."

The words had barely left his lips before Nord and Finley spilled into the room. It might be raining outside, but the real storm had just walked in.

There was no masking the thunderous fury burning in Nord's eyes. Finley's expression better hid his anger, but the crackling energy pouring off him in waves left little doubt as to his mood.

"What happened?" Lina asked, jumping to her feet and rushing over to them.

Finley removed his suit jacket in a series of jerky movements before flinging it at the back of a nearby chair. "The fucking Director, that's what happened."

Quinn and Alistair exchanged worried looks.

Lina's eyes never left Nord. "What did he say?"

"He told me to stand down. He didn't care who you were to me; he told me I wasn't to get involved any further."

She stiffened, blood roaring in her ears at the mere thought of Nord being ordered away from her. "He can't do that, can he?" she whispered, her lips feeling numb.

"He made Nord promise. Fucking idiot," Finley snarled, shaking his head. "Doesn't he realize how ridiculous that is?"

Lina's heart stuttered. "And did you? Did you promise to stay away from me?"

The look Nord threw her immediately thawed the ice that had started to fill her veins.

"Never."

She sagged and pressed a hand to her chest. "Fuck, don't scare me like that."

Nord silently summoned her by opening his arms. She accepted the invitation and curled into his warmth.

"It wasn't you, specifically, Lina," Finley went on to say. "It's Mataius and the other Council members. He doesn't want us causing waves and drawing attention. The fucker tried to tie our hands and make it so that we *couldn't*."

Lina's brows snapped together, and she tilted her head back. "What does he mean?"

Nord didn't answer. He just continued to stare at her with that icy fire burning in his eyes.

"Let's just say, if Nord gets caught anywhere near anything having to do with the Council, we're both fucked. In the permanent no longer breathing sense of the word."

"Is that even possible?" Quinn asked.

"What's given can be taken away," Finley muttered darkly.

Her arms spasmed around Nord. "Is that true? Will he really kill you if you get caught helping me?"

Nord shrugged, looking every inch the bloodthirsty berserker he was born to be. "So we won't get caught."

Nord's words continued to echo in her mind as she rinsed the last of the honey-and-almond conditioner out of her hair.

"So we won't get caught."

She hadn't bothered to remind him that hadn't exactly worked out for them the last time. The Brotherhood—or more accurately, the Director—had eyes everywhere. But she stayed silent because she knew any protest would have fallen on deaf ears.

Nord had already made up his mind. Regardless of the conse-quences, he wouldn't leave her to face Mataius alone. What he'd done to her the first time was reason enough, but after what happened at the cathedral? There was no way in hell.

They'd just have to do their best to keep the blowback from the Council at a minimum. That meant no epic showdowns. No big, flashy magic or battles on the roof. They couldn't engage in any activity that could be traced back to them.

When she finally meted out her revenge, it would have to be done in the shadows, her battle cries comprised of whispers instead of shouts. Just because it had to be handled discreetly didn't mean it wouldn't be effective.

She let out a breath and turned the spray of hot water off.

Stepping out of the shower, she blindly reached for one of the towels hanging on a rod beside it. She bent over and started ringing out her hair and wrapping it in the forest green terry cloth. Once it was in place, she straightened and started to reach for a second towel when the shriek of the ward pierced the air and she went airborne.

Still slick with water, her feet slid when they reconnected with the tile floor. Her arms flailed out in an attempt to grab purchase and keep her body from hitting the floor.

"Motherfucker!"

With the number of times the ward had gone off this week alone, she should have been used to that shrill wail by now, but suffice it to say, butt-ass naked, still dripping from her shower, she. Was. Not.

Heart lodged in her throat, Lina scurried over to the vanity intending to tug on the pajama bottoms she'd left on its counter so she could at least be dressed when she faced whatever fresh hell was waiting for her. Her hands touched the soft flannel, but that's as far as she'd gotten when words started to form in the fogged glass of her bathroom mirror.

The information is accurate.

Lines of condensation were already dripping down from the first couple of words when the sentence was erased by an invisible hand and replaced with another.

Don't blame me because YOU don't know how to use your eyes.

Nord burst through the door, his wild eyes landing on her before moving over her shoulder to the words in the mirror. She wouldn't have believed it possible, but his scowl darkened even further.

"That fae fuck," he growled.

The siren stopped. Either on its own because Crombie's message vanished and took the threat of foreign magic with it or because Nord looped Finley in and he disarmed it.

"Guess he wanted to make a point," she muttered, still shaky from the surge of adrenaline.

"Next time I'll be the one making a point, but it will involve me shoving my blade into his throat."

Lina couldn't help the bubble of laughter that rose up in response.

It had been a long day, for both of them, and if the look in his eyes was any indication, it was about to get longer.

If she was reading it right, they were going hunting.

And this time, they weren't coming home without their prey.

CHAPTER TWENTY-FOUR
LINA

The afternoon's rainfall had turned into a light drizzle, and the night air was just wet enough to sink into her clothes and settle. Lifting her hands to her mouth, Lina breathed into her palms and rubbed them together to generate some warmth while also stomping her feet.

"Come on, come on," she chanted under her breath, staring up at the awning to Quinn's building while she waited for Finley and Quinn to join her and Nord outside.

Originally, Quinn was supposed to meet them downstairs, but when they arrived and she wasn't there, Finley volunteered to go up and make sure everything was all right. Since he was unarguably better equipped to deal with any number of scenarios, Lina agreed. She opted to stay outside with Nord and keep watch, knowing that the men would keep each other informed if there was a problem.

Nord's low rumble sounded beside her, "We could have waited inside."

Her eyes started to dart to the left where she knew he was standing, but she checked the instinct. He was glamoured, and she was supposed to be pretending she was waiting outside alone so as not to give anyone a reason to look too closely. If she started carrying on a conversation that she appeared to be holding by her lonesome, that would certainly raise some eyebrows.

She dipped her chin so the movement of her lips would be hidden. "Easier for you to avoid having to maneuver around people out here, not to mention carry on a conversation without being overheard."

This was true mainly because the sidewalk they were standing on was deserted and there were still one or two residents mingling in the building's lounge—a series of deep-seated chairs arranged in a ring just off to the side of the elevator bank.

Nord had shown her his illusion skills before, but tonight was the first time she realized just how extensive they were. This time, he wasn't just disguised as someone else; he'd made himself practically invisible. Practically, because she wasn't actually looking through him. He'd just taken on the details of whatever he wanted her to see. Right now, if she squinted, she'd just be able to make out his shape against the brick wall he was both leaning against and appearing to be. However, if they were inside and someone accidentally ran into him because they thought there was empty space where he was standing, that would be a much bigger headache than getting a little damp.

"How come tonight's the first time I'm learning about your epic camouflage skills?"

"Because it's a pain in the ass," he replied.

Her lips twitched, but she schooled her expression when her eyes peered through Quinn's door once more.

"How's it any worse than your usual illusions?" she asked with her back to him—or where she thought he was still standing.

"It's much easier to hold a static image than be in near-constant flux. If I'm moving versus standing still, it requires continuous effort and attention to tweak the weave and keep it realistic. So while it's effective, it's rarely ideal."

Lina pressed her lips together, debating the merits of asking the question that popped into her mind and then deciding to go for it anyway. "And you really think our best play tonight is to complicate things further by using it, not just on yourself, but all of us?"

"There's a reason I haven't volunteered to do it before."

The warmth of his breath tickled the back of her neck. She shivered, but he'd already moved away by the time she turned around.

"Because it's hard?" she guessed.

"Because if all my attention is focused on the weave, that means I lose valuable seconds if I need to react."

"React?"

"To a threat or attack."

"Oh."

"It's a vulnerability I hate to have, especially stepping into enemy territory. But," he sighed heavily, "Finley and I agree it's the only way to ensure we're unseen. We can't take the risk of anyone spotting us, at least not until we've made it into the apartment. And you can bet your ass the Brotherhood will be on the lookout."

"I thought they see through illusions?"

"They can, but only if they have a reason to summon their power and look beneath them. If there aren't any people for them to see going in and out of the building, they won't."

"Which is why we're not just changing our appearance."

"Right."

Lina nodded, piecing together that information with the rest of their plan. Picking up Quinn was step one—Alistair was already on his way to wherever it was he'd hidden the Codex, so they were going ahead without him. Since they knew the lay of the land after visiting a few days ago, Finley was going to portal them into the complex's third-floor hallway. From there, under the veil of Nord's camouflage, they would break into Celia Bell's apartment.

Thankfully, they didn't have to worry about her coming home and interrupting this time.

Before everything had gone down with the Director, Finley had done a little digging into Ms. Bell. Apparently, she had family in

Kentucky, who had no idea just how badly she'd deteriorated since their last visit. Finley—her concerned health care provider—placed a call to her niece and emergency contact, one Amelia Bell, explaining the state of things. Upon receiving said call, Amelia—near beside herself with worry over her favorite auntie—immediately made plans to have her picked up and placed into a twenty-four-hour care facility until she could drive up and make arrangements to bring Aunt Celia home to Kentucky.

Which meant the apartment was empty as of two hours ago.

Well, hopefully not completely empty. They were banking on Mataius being there or, at the very least, finding something that would lead them straight to him.

Lina stomped her feet a few more times, sensing the promise of winter in the brisk November air. She was suddenly grateful they only had to deal with a little rain and not snow. In another week or two, that wouldn't be the case. Snow meant footprints, and she wasn't sure even Nord's gifts could help them avoid that.

"Hurry up, Quinn," she muttered. "We don't fucking have all night."

Nord pressed closer to her. She could feel his heat against her back. The desire to lean into him was strong.

"Thank you," she murmured.

The flash of the elevator panel caught her eye, followed by Finley's head and then Quinn's as they stepped through the metallic doors.

"Finally."

Quinn caught her gaze and gave her an apologetic grimace. She pointed to her gloves and mouthed, "Sorry."

"If she kept us waiting because she was accessorizing—"

Nord's chuckle interrupted her flow of words.

Lina pressed her lips together and shook her head. "You laugh, but it wouldn't be the first time."

Quinn and Finley joined them on the sidewalk less than a minute later.

"Sorry, sorry," Quinn said, giving Lina a hug. "When you called, I was already in bed. It took a bit longer to get myself together than I thought."

Lina returned Quinn's squeeze. "It's all good. Thanks for coming with."

"Pfft. As if there was any doubt. We're in the home stretch now, babe."

"We ready?" Finley asked.

The girls stepped away from each other and nodded.

"Okay, follow me."

He led them around the side of the building to the place where the garbage bins were kept.

"Lovely," Quinn said.

Finley tossed her a look. "Don't worry, princess. We won't be here long."

He was already at work on summoning the portal.

Lina watched it stretch into being, its undulating surface reminding her of those wavy bits of heat coming up off the ground on a hot day. Invisible but somehow still noticeable.

"Everyone clear on the plan?" Finley asked in a low, tense voice. "Once we step through, it's radio silence until we're inside. Even then, probably best we don't speak unless we have to."

Nord dropped his illusion just enough to show his face as he nodded. Quinn also agreed, and Lina was about to when a thought sent panic spiraling through her.

"Wait," she said. "I just thought of something. How are we going to be able to see each other if we're all camouflaged?"

"Think of the glamour like a blanket," Nord said. "It covers all of us. Anyone outside of it sees what we want them to see, but those of us beneath it can still see the world as it is."

Lina nodded, relieved there was one less thing for her to worry about going wrong. She couldn't help but feel that everything rode on what happened tonight. One wrong move could very well mean the difference in how things went down. The knowledge of that meant that she was wound up tighter than a turkey on Thanksgiving day.

"Ready?" Finley asked, his hazel eyes trained on her.

"Yeah," she said.

"Do it," Finley said to Nord.

She wasn't sure what she was expecting, but there was no discernable difference between being glamoured and not. One second, she was Lina, and the next she was apparently half of a trash can.

"Follow me," Finley said as he stepped through the portal.

They had to stay close for Nord's magic to work, so Quinn wasted no time obeying. Filled with nervous energy, Lina paused only long enough to fill her lungs with air and shake out her limbs as she released it. With the sensation of Nord's fingertips drifting down her spine, Lina shoved the last of her jitters away and took the step that led her out of the alley and deposited her beside Quinn a few doors down from their target.

She was careful not to make a sound as she shuffled forward to make room for Nord. Now that they were here, there were no more nerves, just an overwhelming sense of anticipation.

Her lips curled up in a dark smile.

I told you to run while you still could, motherfucker. Now, we're coming for you.

FINLEY MADE QUICK WORK OF THE DOOR, USING HIS MAGIC TO DEAL WITH the locks and usher them inside. Nord dropped their glamour as soon as they confirmed that the apartment was empty.

The place was what she'd expected. Outdated floral patterns, wicker furniture with plastic coverings on all the cushions, the stale smell of cigarette smoke, and tiny cat figurines littering almost every available surface.

A sweep of the bathroom and bedroom revealed that Ms. Bell

only had time to gather some clothes and toiletries. Most of her belongings had stayed behind.

Lina felt a pang of sympathy for the old woman. Hopefully, whoever helped her pack encouraged her to bring some sentimental things as well. She couldn't imagine that a woman in her condition would react well to being displaced.

But the alternative—her being the casualty of a magical showdown—was far worse.

Reminding herself to stay focused, Lina crept into the guest bedroom just a few steps behind Nord.

He reached for the closet door, pulling it open.

Lina about jumped out of her skin when a flesh-colored blur leapt out with a yowl of feline rage.

"Sandusky," she breathed.

The cat streaked by, darting out of the room and squeezing itself between the couch and the wall where it peered out at them with distrustful, albeit watery, eyes.

Finley stepped out of Celia's bedroom with his gun drawn. Quinn darted out of the kitchen and into the living room, a steak knife gripped in her hand.

Since there was no imminent threat, Lina couldn't quite contain her bubble of laughter at Quinn's choice of weapon.

"It was the biggest one she had," Quinn snapped in a whispered hiss.

Realizing the scuffle had been the result of an angry cat and not a rogue animagi, Finley re-holstered his weapon.

"There's nothing here," he declared.

No! Her internal wail was filled with heartfelt denial. This couldn't be another dead end. *It couldn't.* Crombie sent them back here for a reason. They were missing something.

Beside her, Nord let out a deep growl, his frustration a twin to her own. He started to pace, having completed two circuits when he stopped and gave the wall a considering look.

"Does something about this room feel off to you?"

Lina wasn't sure who the question was directed to. It seemed like a run-of-the-mill, albeit small, guest room to her. What was already a tight fit was made even tighter with Nord and Lina crammed in.

The furniture was cramped. A twin bed, woven rug that was half-hidden beneath it, slender bookcase that came up to just under the ceiling, and desk with a sewing machine set atop it were all the room could contain. The desk didn't even have a chair. Celia must have to drag one in from the kitchen when she wanted to sew.

"What do you mean? Magical?" Finley asked, popping his head and giving the room another once-over.

Nord's lips were pressed together, and he gave a slow shake. "The dimensions."

There wasn't space for Finley to join them inside, but his brows dipped low, and he shifted to the side so that he was looking more fully into the room. "Now that you mention it . . ."

"What is it?" Lina asked, still not seeing anything out of the normal.

Nord's eyes flared with power as he scanned the wall with the desk and bookcase. The visible part was covered in peeling wallpaper. Its pattern was mostly faded, but Lina could still make out swirls of green ivy and pastel pink flowers. The rest of the wall was covered by dozens of picture frames hung without any rhyme or reason, each one containing a different painting of a cat.

Upon closer inspection, Lina found these were no drugstore purchases. Each one was painted, in great detail, with textured acrylic paints and done in the manner of a Victorian portrait. There were some cats with top hats and monocles, others depicted in elaborate dresses or naval uniforms.

"Do you think she painted these?" Lina asked.

"Given the number of them, I'd say it's likely," Finley answered.

Nord, Lina discovered, was still staring at the wall like he was trying to see through it.

She brushed his arm to get his attention.

He dragged his eyes away from the painting with the naval officer to look at her.

"What are you thinking?" she asked once she had his attention.

"The room should be bigger."

"I mean, it's pretty tight—"

"No," he shook his head and vaguely gestured to the rest of the apartment with his left hand. "This wall sits in a different place than the walls in the other rooms that run along this side of the apartment. This room *should* be bigger."

It took a second for what he was saying to click.

"You think there's a hidden room?"

He dipped his chin. "Something is definitely hidden."

Lina started studying the wall in earnest. She wasn't looking for anything specific, just something that stood out.

"If the bookcase swung out, wouldn't there be marks on the floor?" Finley offered.

They all glanced down.

"Rug's in the way," Lina said.

Nord tugged it, but the hardwood underneath didn't reveal anything unusual.

"Is any of the dust on the shelves disturbed?" Quinn called from behind Finley.

Nord started pulling books off as he checked, likely in an attempt to spring a secret door.

Lina bit her lip and looked back over the pictures. There was something about them that niggled at her. She just couldn't put her finger on it.

"See something?" Finley asked.

She was squinting, tilting her head this way and that as she studied them.

"I don't—" She broke off because what she'd unconsciously noticed finally became apparent.

They were all hanging askew. All of them, that is, except for one.

Only one picture was hanging perfectly straight.

Lina stepped forward, gently pushing Nord out of the way with her hip. Reaching out, she cocked her head and gave the frame a gentle shove.

It moved easily.

She held her breath, wondering if perhaps she'd been wrong, but then she heard the sharp intake of breath and felt the subtle vibration beneath her feet.

The bookcase slid to its right, into what should have been the closet.

"That's why the floor wasn't marked. It doesn't swing out; it slides to the side," Finley said.

Nord was the first to peer into the dark space the bookcase revealed, hands braced on either side of the opening, torso leaning in.

Just as fast, he pushed himself back out, eyes finding hers.

His voice was the barest of whispers as he said, "Someone's up there."

Before she finished drawing breath, Nord was already rushing up the hidden staircase. Lina bolted after him. He moved quickly but silently. His eyes were burning with power when he glanced over his shoulder.

For a second, she wondered if he'd spoken to her telepathically because she could have sworn she heard the low rumble of his voice in her mind say, "This ends tonight."

Then, his eyes were gone, and the door in front of him crashed open with a loud bang.

Lina wished she had Crombie's ability to freeze time. She would have lived in this second for as long as she could because when she rushed through the door, Finley hot on her heels and splinters still raining down, they finally found the devil they'd been searching for.

Mataius.

Eyes blown wide, mouth hanging open, body frozen in shock.

"Hi, honey. Miss me?" she crooned.

CHAPTER TWENTY-FIVE
LINA

Mataius lurched to his feet. The table tilted, sending chips, bills, and cards falling to the floor. The four people sitting at the poker table with him, supernaturals, given the size of two of them, stared at him in shock.

Nord's body practically blurred with speed as he hauled ass across the rectangular loft. Mataius jumped, one of his feet hitting the raised edge of the table—which was now leaning on its side—and using the connection to propel him into the air away from the charging berserker.

Quinn, Finley, and Lina rushed forward at the same time Mataius' four companions surged to their feet.

The two over-muscled men jumped in front of Mataius, cutting off Nord as Mataius landed and sprinted toward the couches. One picked up the chair Mataius vacated and hurled it at Nord in an attempt to slow him down.

While Lina split her attention, stalking around the fight to get to Mataius, she also watched Nord's back as he caught the chair by one of its legs, used its momentum to spin around like some kind of Olympian discus thrower, and sent it flying back at Tweedledum and

Tweedledee. It crashed into the first of the brutes, who toppled backward into the second, and they both landed on the ground like a couple of bowling pins.

Mataius peeked around a couch, tracking the fight's progress with panicked eyes. Quinn and Finley fought back-to-back as they faced off with the other two. The female poker player had a wicked-looking dagger she wielded with lightning-fast swipes that slowed the moment she met Quinn's gaze. Finley unloaded half his clip into the now-shifted werewolf's stomach in rapid succession.

Lina inched closer, the movement drawing Mataius' attention. She smiled, the curl of her lips filled with promised retribution. Without the weather as a weapon, Mataius was pretty pathetic.

His gaze darted to Nord, who had lifted both of the brutes up by their hair and used his grip to smash their heads together and toss them away from him back onto the ground. The men were out. Given the amount of blood pouring out of their heads from the impact, Lina was pretty sure they weren't waking up. Ever.

Nord lifted his attention from the men on the ground and looked up directly at the spot where Mataius was cowering behind his couch. He did this slowly, looking up first with his eyes and then following with the rest of his head. The effect was terrifying. His face and torso were splattered with the blood of his first two victims. The veins in his arms and neck stood out in sharp relief, and his eyes glowed with an unholy light.

The berserker had taken over.

Even Lina wasn't completely immune when he bared his teeth and let out a savage growl.

Mataius wasn't a fool. He knew if Nord got his hands on him, he'd be well and truly fucked. Determining Lina was the lesser threat, he popped up from his crouch and came barreling at her.

She had no weapon save her magic, and she was still far from a great fighter, but one thing she had that Mataius didn't was a complete lack of fear. Nord and Finley had knocked her on her ass daily. She knew she could take a hit and get back up.

Hell, even death hadn't kept her down.

No matter what, she would never stop coming.

Bracing her legs and lifting her arms, she prepared herself for impact.

Mataius crashed into her, sending them both to the floor.

"Sorry, sweetheart. No time to kiss and make up," he said in her ear before pushing himself up and making for the wall of windows.

Lina twisted her body and pushed to her knees. It was like she could see what was about to happen in slow motion. Mataius was planning on breaking the window—most likely to escape, but on the off chance he grew a pair of balls and planned to fight, the rain would be the key to him turning the tide. Either way, she could not let that happen.

Summoning her power, Lina threw her hands out to the windows, feeling the surge of magic rip through her body as it obeyed her will.

Mataius made it to the windows less than a second after Lina's new reality took hold.

He slammed face-first into a brand-new brick wall.

Crunch!

He twisted around with a groan, his hand cupping his nose, blood dripping between his fingers.

"Fucking bitch!"

At least, that's what she thought he said. It was hard to make out the words, muffled as they were.

There was a loud snap to her right. Lina craned her neck in time to watch Nord lift what had once been the table leg and hurl it like a javelin straight at Mataius.

It moved so fast it was almost impossible for her eyes to track the movement before it was sinking straight through Mataius' flesh and pinning him to the solid brick wall behind him.

"Holy shit," she breathed.

The force required for that to even be physically possible was too much for her to wrap her head around. Just went to show that in the hands of a berserker, literally anything could be a weapon.

Mataius was sucking in pained breaths, his left arm sliding along the wood jutting out from his other side. It was probably instinct that had him trying to pull it out, but he couldn't even reach the end of it, skewered as he was.

He wasn't going anywhere.

Lina spared a glance to her left, noting that Finley and Quinn had made short work of the female as well—although Quinn hadn't gotten away entirely unscathed. Blood dripped down her cheek from a deep gash. As for the woman, she'd been stabbed through the eye by her own dagger. As Lina started to look away, her hand twitched once, and then her entire body went still.

Four for four.

The only one left to deal with was Mataius.

Nord reached her first, holding out a bloodstained hand to help her back to her feet. She accepted it gratefully. Side by side, they walked to where Mataius struggled against the thick piece of wood pinning him in place.

He lifted his head and spat a mouthful of blood at her face. The metallic tang of it hit her nose before the warm spray. She closed her eyes and gritted her teeth. After exhaling sharply through her nose, she opened her eyes and forced herself to stare Mataius down and grinned.

"Thanks for that. I love when my Viking and I match. Makes us look like a real couple, don't you think?"

"Kill me, and get it over with," he snarled though it lacked any true heat. Mataius was clearly in pain, and his voice was thready because of it.

Lina tsked. "What would your daddy say if he knew his heir was begging for death? Is that any way for a Drake to act?"

Mataius flinched, confirming something Lina had already started to suspect. He hadn't undergone the Awakening yet. His father still retained the bulk of their family's power.

"Fuck you," he said, but his eyes had lowered to her chin.

"I'll pass on that." She dropped her voice. "From what I remember, it wasn't all that great anyway. And now that I have something to compare it to, I'm definitely *not* interested in a repeat performance."

Mataius squirmed, anger blazing briefly in his eyes at her taunt. "If you aren't planning on killing me, what do you want?"

Lina made her eyes go wide. "Why, answers, of course."

"Like I'd tell you anything, bitch."

"You've already used that one," she said.

"Cunt," he spat.

Lina lifted her elbow and drove it into his already broken nose.

Mataius' head slammed back into the wall as he cried out in pain.

"I always did hate that word," she said conversationally.

Mataius glared at her. "That the best you've got? 'Cause we'll be here all night. I'm not telling you shit."

Lina stared at him, the silence stretching between them until he shifted uncomfortably.

"Maybe not. But I'm willing to bet you'll tell him," she said, tilting her head to the side to indicate Nord.

Mataius winced as Nord crackled his knuckles.

"I'm sure we'll find a way to help him remember," Finley offered from behind her.

Lina's smile stretched. "Last chance, Matty. You can talk to me, or you can talk to them. Either way, you'll talk."

"Fuck. You."

"Right then," she said, crossing her arms. "Can't say I'm too disappointed you went with door number two. After what you did to me, I didn't want you to get off *too* easy."

With that, Lina turned away and went to stand by Quinn. Nord and Finley moved into place.

"Take your best shot," Mataius hissed.

"Oh, we will," Finley assured him. "But not here."

What little color Mataius had left fled at that. He must have been banking on someone showing up to save him or to see what happened and spread the word. If they took him somewhere else, the chance of rescue just disappeared.

Nord broke off the end of the makeshift spear, and then Finley helped him pull Mataius off of what was left of it.

He screamed in pain as they did, his eyes rolling back in his head as he passed out.

Finley shook his head in disgust.

"Where are you taking him?" Lina asked quietly.

"To the penthouse," Finley answered as he began to summon a portal.

"The penthouse?"

"Well, the Berserker Bunker," he corrected with a tight smile.

Understanding dawned, and her eyes shifted to Nord. "I'm not invited, am I?"

"It would be easier for me to do what needs to be done without you there."

Lina studied him, feeling torn. A part of her wanted—needed—to be there, to see Mataius get what he deserved and hear his confession firsthand. To be the one looking him in the eye as she forced it out of him. Another part knew that there would be no coming back from participating in that kind of violence. In the end, she decided Mataius didn't deserve to have a piece of her soul.

"We can't kill him," she whispered.

Nord's eyes shuttered.

"Nord," she said more firmly. "It's not worth it. We can't risk what happens if the Director finds out."

"Let me worry about that."

"Nord."

"Lina."

She pressed her lips together. Knowing there wasn't time for her to say all that was on her mind but needing to try. She opted for what she hoped would be the most convincing argument.

Looking him straight in the eye, she dropped her voice so that it felt like it was just the two of them. Not them in a room filled with dead bodies, with their best friends eavesdropping, and an unconscious Mataius slumped in Nord's arms.

"Nothing is more important to me than you. Not even revenge. He did a lot of awful things to me, but I don't care, not anymore. Everything he did brought me here, to you. So do what you need to do to get the information we need, and then let him go. I don't need his life. I need you."

Nord's eyes flared a blinding azure and he held her gaze for a long time before dipping his chin.

Then he stepped through the first portal Finley had created.

"This one's for you two," he said, pointing to another portal just to the left of the first. "I'm going to take care of cleanup here and then join him. I'll let you know once it's done."

Lina glanced around the loft, noting the destruction they'd wrought in only a few minutes. The fight may have been short, but it had been effective. Between the broken furniture, pools of blood, and the four dead bodies, Finley would have his hands full.

"Sure you don't need some help?" she asked, forcing herself to look away from the dead woman and the dagger she'd driven into her own eye.

He nodded. "I'm sure. You two get out of here."

She touched her lips to Finley's cheek. "Thanks, Fin. Make sure he doesn't do anything stupid, okay?"

Finley's lips twitched. "I've been trying for months and haven't been successful yet."

She squeezed his forearm. "Just try, okay?"

"Of course."

Finley's assurance would have to be good enough. But somehow, as she stepped through the portal and back to the penthouse's entryway, she knew it wouldn't be.

She could already sense the next storm gathering on the horizon.

CHAPTER TWENTY-SIX
NORD

Mataius lifted his head up slowly, spitting another mouthful of blood on the ground. There was no small amount of hatred shining out of his eyes as he glared up at Nord. Well, from the one eye Mataius could open anyway, the other had swollen shut after the first of many backhands.

They'd been in the bunker for almost an hour. Half of that was spent waiting for Mataius to come to. Despite his broken nose and a series of blows to the face and kidneys, Mataius wasn't feeling any chattier, and Nord was losing patience. So far, he had managed to keep the violence to a minimum, but it wasn't getting them anywhere. It was time for a strategy change, one that would guarantee results.

"Tell me what you were after, and this ends," Nord said.

"Like I've told you every time you've asked, conjure yourself a cock and go fuck yourself."

Nord sighed, hating the muffled, pathetic sound of Mataius' nasally voice, and called on his magic.

Noticing the glow of power in his eyes, Mataius jerked in his chains. "What are you doing?"

Nord didn't answer, focusing instead on repairing the damaged cartilage.

Mataius' eyes narrowed suspiciously. "Why'd you fix my nose?"

Nord allowed some of his barely checked fury to leak into his voice. "Maybe because I want to break it again."

No need for the sorry excuse of a man to know the small mercy had nothing to do with alleviating pain and everything to do with not wanting to decipher what the fuck he was saying.

Mataius tilted his head and gave Nord a shrewd once-over. "She put you up to torturing me, didn't she? Bitch has got you by the balls."

Nord returned his stare, giving nothing away.

"Gotta say, man to man, I've had a taste, and I just don't get the appeal. I mean, she's a hot piece, sure, but I've had better pussy—"

Nord drove his fist into Mataius' jaw with enough force to snap his head to the side. "Enough."

Mataius spit out two of his teeth and then looked back up with a gap-toothed grin. "I was wondering if you were ever going to nut up."

Mataius blanched at the sight of Nord's malicious smile.

"Maybe you haven't noticed, but I prefer it when things get bloody. The only thing keeping me from breaking your jaw is the fact I need you to speak. But you insult her again, I'll rip it off and cram it down your throat. Then, just before you choke to death, I'll heal you, and we'll start all over again. Think I'm bluffing? Test me. I fucking dare you."

Mataius paled even further, and silence was his only answer.

"Pity," Nord murmured. "I was really hoping you'd take me up on my offer. Now, since you only seem to understand how serious I am when pain is involved, we're going to try something different. I'm going to ask you a question, and you're going to give me an answer. If you don't, I snap one of your ribs. Sounds fun, right?"

Mataius' throat bobbed.

"I don't hear an answer."

"Silence is all you're going to get from me."

"Ah, Mataius. Thank you. I was hoping I'd get to show you what happens when you don't follow the rules, and you already know how I feel about getting bloody."

Nord picked up the silver dagger Finley had set out for him and walked back to Mataius, who was now squirming in earnest.

"Do you like it?" Nord asked, holding the weapon up so it glinted in the light. "I was inspired by you. You're a fan of daggers, right?"

"If you think your little show—"

Nord sliced through his shirt, allowing the tip of the blade to cut through the skin as he ran it up over his rib cage.

"What was that?" Nord asked.

Mataius tried to jerk away, but Nord only pressed the tip of the dagger in deeper, causing him to cry out in pain.

"Sorry, I can't hear you. You were saying?" When the only response he got was the ragged sound of Mataius' breath, he leaned back to peer into his face. "What, no more smart-ass remarks?"

Nord shoved the rest of the blade in to the hilt.

A ragged cry was ripped from Mataius' throat.

Nord pulled the dagger out and studied the dripping blade before letting it drop to the floor with a clatter.

"That all you've got?" Mataius panted.

Nord laughed. "I'm just getting started."

Then he drove his hand into the wound he'd created with the dagger, slid his fingers around the first rib he touched, and jerked, snapping it clean in two.

Mataius screamed, a long high-pitched wail. His knees buckled, and he sagged against his restraints. Nord gripped him by the hair and lifted. Mataius' feet slid against the floor, which had grown slippery with his blood.

"I told you what would happen if you didn't answer my question. I'm nothing if not a man of my word. Now you know. How much pain you endure before we're done is up to you. Shall we try again?"

Tears were streaking down Mataius' face. He was trying hard to maintain his haughty stare, but true fear had taken hold.

"I see you're finally starting to understand your position. Good. Now we're getting somewhere."

Beads of sweat started to drip down Mataius' face.

"What were you after the night you killed Lina?"

"D-didn't . . . k-kill."

"But you meant to, didn't you?"

"Yes," Mataius hissed.

Still gripping Mataius' hair, Nord jerked his head back. "Why?"

"T-take b-back," Mataius sucked in a breath, his stutter growing more pronounced as he fought against the pain, "w-what sh-she st-st-stole."

"What do you think she stole?"

"P-p-prism."

Nord's eyes narrowed. "Why do you think she stole it?"

Mataius pressed his lips together and shook his head.

Nord slid his hand back into the wound at Mataius' side, taking not one but three of the thin bones in his hand and, yanking back, snapped them with the force.

Mataius screamed, his body spasming from the intensity of the pain.

"Let's try that again. Why do you think she stole it?"

It took a second for Mataius to focus his gaze back on Nord's face. "Told . . . me."

"Who did?"

Mataius' tongue darted out to lick his lips. Despite his obvious discomfort, he looked almost excited as he answered.

"Never guess."

Nord reached for Mataius' rib cage. "Do you want me to snap the rest?"

Mataius' eyes were clenched, but he shocked Nord by starting to laugh. The sound was a low wet rasp, but there was no mistaking it.

"Hates her more than I do."

"Who?" he demanded, sliding his hand in deeper.

"F-father," Mataius spat, sounding victorious.

"Yours?" Nord asked, already devising a plan to take down Mikel Drake.

"No," Mataius said, voice sounding firmer than it had in a while. Then he grinned. "Hers."

Nord stepped back, disbelief momentarily overriding his anger. "Are you telling me it was Lina's father who sent you to kill her?"

The one eye Mataius could open was shining with an unnatural light. "Yes."

"He'd kill his own daughter for a trinket?"

Mataius cleared his throat and spoke in a surprisingly clear voice, given all his earlier panting. "If you knew what it could do, you'd never call it a trinket. Besides, it wasn't his. He promised it to *us*. He *owed* us. He thought his daughter would help lessen the debt, but she was always meant to be disposable. I was taking back what was ours."

Nord forcefully shoved his hand back into Mataius' side, fingers searching for their next victim.

Mataius screamed, but it wasn't in pain. It was the adrenaline-fueled cry of someone who had completely lost his mind. When the scream subsided, he broke into a bout of maniacal laughter.

That's when Nord realized Mataius was purposefully provoking him, egging him on with his confession so that he would hurry up and kill him rather than draw it out. Little did Mataius know he wasn't about to give the bastard the reprieve of a quick death.

Despite the bruises on his face, the psychopath looked downright gleeful as his face split into a wide grin. "I'll tell you a secret."

Nord remained silent, refusing to play into his hand.

"Anatoly's request was just a boon. Good fortune, you might say."

Then Mataius sealed his fate.

His voice dropped, and his smile turned cruel. "Evalina was never going to live. I had it all planned out. Was just waiting for our wedding night to make it official. Her death was going to be my wedding present. A gift for putting up with her bullshit for twenty years. And, the best part? I'd tested out my plan on other girls to ensure when the time came, her suffering would be absolute."

The berserker slipped from his leash.

By the time Finley found him, the room was a sea of red, and what was left of the body was unrecognizable.

CHAPTER TWENTY-SEVEN
LINA

Lina bit the side of her thumb and stared at the front door of the penthouse like she could summon Nord back by will alone. It had been hours since she'd returned from Mataius', and now she regretted sending Quinn home. The wait was unbearable.

As time continued to crawl by, the pit in Lina's stomach grew. She couldn't come up with a single reason why it was taking this long. She wasn't an idiot; she knew exactly how Nord planned on procuring Mataius' answers—it was the entire reason Nord hadn't let her come with him in the first place—but surely, Mataius' pain threshold wasn't that high.

Just as thoughts of all the various terrible ways things could have gone wrong started to parade themselves through her mind, the door opened.

Her heart lifted and then immediately stuttered as Nord came into view. Every last inch of him was painted red.

So much for not killing Mataius.

But even as she thought it, she knew that whatever he'd confessed must have been truly awful if Nord couldn't keep his promise to her. Then again, a large part of her had always known it could end that way, no matter what the consequences may be. Nord was, and would always be, a berserker. There was only one way they dealt with their enemies.

Nord's eyes found hers, and Lina's breath caught in her chest. He looked absolutely feral and not remotely human. That's when she realized that he was still fully consumed by his bloodlust.

He started walking toward her, and she braced herself, but he never reached her. Instead, he turned and walked into his room without a word.

Lina hesitated only for a second before rushing after him.

Both Nord and Finley had warned her more than once never to get in his way when he was like this, but Lina knew that no matter what state he was in, Nord would never harm her.

The sound of falling water met her ears as she reached his room, so Lina made her way to his bathroom, pausing in the door to drink in the sight of him.

He stood under the spray of water, his hands pressed against the tile on either side of the showerhead, muscles bunched and tensed as rivers of red ran down his inked back.

"You should go," he said, his voice coming out in a deep growl.

"Tell me what happened."

Nord's hands spasmed and the tile beneath them cracked and fissured. "I cannot be trusted right now."

"You know there's nothing you could say or do that would scare me away," she said softly.

He visibly shuddered. "You only say that because you do not yet know the horrors I am capable of."

Lina started to strip, recognizing the only way she was going to get them through this was to force it. She joined him, allowing her fingertips to trace the lines of the tree that spanned his entire back. His muscles were hard as brick, but as she continued her careful strokes, he began to relax under her touch.

"I killed him," he whispered.

"I figured."

"I tried to restrain myself because you asked, but when he'd admitted that he'd always planned to kill you and that he'd murdered countless others in prep—"

Lina cut him off, realizing she didn't need or want the details. She'd already lived through the end result of Mataius' depravity. Once was enough.

"I don't care about Mataius. It turns out he wasn't just a piece of shit. He was a sociopathic serial killer. He deserved what he got. But I do care about what happens to *you*. I only asked you not to kill him to avoid painting a target on yourself." She wrapped her arms around him and pressed herself against his back. "Then again, if our roles were reversed, I probably would have done the same."

As she said the words, the truth of them reverberated through her. She was disgusted to learn she'd once been intimate with a man who turned out to be so evil, but she was more worried about the man in her arms than the one he'd killed.

Nord dropped one of his hands, his fingers trailing down her arm until reaching her hand and weaving his fingers through hers. "That's not all."

Lina closed her eyes and listened to the steady beat of his heart under her ear. "I'm not a priest; you don't need to confess your sins to me."

"No, I mean, that's not all Mataius told me."

"Oh?"

"Lina, I don't know how to tell you this—"

"Whatever you're about to say, I'm sure I've already dealt with worse."

Nord bit off a curse and started to turn in her arms. She squeezed tighter, trying to keep him in place. If he was that worried about what he had to tell her, it might be easier to hear it if they weren't looking at each other.

"Your father put him up to it. He was the one behind your murder."

Lina waited for the sting of betrayal or burn of anger to spiral up inside of her, but all she felt was a pang of bitter acceptance. There was no love lost between her and her father. Perhaps she should have been more surprised by the news, but he had never been her father in anything but name and, of course, biology. It actually made more sense finding out he was behind it versus Mataius acting on his own.

She let go of him and reached for the soap, focusing on getting Nord clean rather than the words coming out of her mouth.

"He made no secret of the fact that he loved power more than me. Can't say it's a shock he wanted me dead so he could keep it all to himself. Or that he'd double down and go after the Prism. He probably thought killing me would take care of two birds with one stone. We're just lucky Uncle Alistair had the foresight to protect it. Now, the Prism's safe. I'm standing here with you with my magic intact, and he's rotting in the ground with no one to mourn him. All said and done, I think I came out on top."

Nord took the soap out of her hands and turned to face her. Then he tilted her chin up until their eyes met. "Still, he was your father."

"No," she said firmly. "He wasn't. Not in any way that mattered."

His eyes searched hers, and she could see in the icy depths that he was still riding the edge of his rage. Apparently, not even killing Mataius had been enough to assuage it.

"Are you okay?" she asked.

Nord considered the question. He seemed to be choosing his words carefully when he finally answered, "It's like this sometimes when my emotions are deeply entangled with the rage. The blood-lust abates only to flare back up seconds later without warning."

"Like a wildfire," Lina murmured.

Nord nodded. "A bit."

"So what do you do to put it out?"

His lips twisted. "Generally, I kill."

"And when you run out of things to kill?"

"I fuck."

Arousal hit her like a tidal wave, sweeping away everything except for him in its wake. Nothing else existed in that moment.

"Is that an invitation?"

His eyes burned with hunger, but he made no move to touch her. "I can be . . . intense when I'm like this. I may not be able to control myself."

Lina grinned. "If you're trying to warn me off, you're going about it all wrong."

"I just want to make sure you know what you're getting yourself into," he said, his lips hovering just above hers.

She tilted her head. "It won't hurt will it?"

His smile was pure sin. "Only if you want it to."

"Well then, berserker, do your worst."

CHAPTER TWENTY-EIGHT
NORD

Nord paced through the Brotherhood's lobby and checked his watch for the sixth time in as many minutes.

"What the fuck is taking you so long?"

Finley responded almost immediately. *"I wanted to stop by the Archive before we head home. I think I remember which book referenced the Codex. I knew it sounded familiar when Lina mentioned it, and I figured any information we have on it could help her when Alistair returns."*

Nord blew out an impatient breath. *"Just hurry up."*

Finley's mental laughter floated through his mind from their link. *"Should only take ten more minutes."*

Despite Finley's reassurances, Nord's sense of urgency didn't abate. He wanted to get home to Lina and didn't want to spend a second longer in the Brotherhood's HQ than necessary. They'd reported to work as usual the last two days to keep up appearances, but that didn't mean he felt comfortable leaving Lina alone.

Nord's eyes dropped to his newest ring as his thumb brushed over its uneven surface. The metallic band still held some of the intricate details from its previous form although Nord couldn't recall whether the dagger had always held a faintly reddish sheen or if that was a result of the animagus' blood mixing with the metal during forging.

So far, there'd been no sign that anyone, outside of the four of them, knew Mataius was dead. And yet, unease continued to gnaw at him. Instinct warned that the danger was still out there. Only now it no longer had a face. Nord hated that he couldn't sense which direction the threat was coming from because it made it almost impossible to protect against.

As they had every time Nord found himself without a specific task to focus on, his thoughts turned to Lina. She'd taken the news of her father's betrayal better than he'd expected. But then, she was always surprising him with her boundless strength. In the end, she'd been more concerned about taking care of him than anything he had to say.

They'd spent hours working off the last of his bloodlust. She'd been nearly as insatiable as him, her need spurring his own until they were both little more than a tangle of sweaty limbs. He should have known she would be more than a match for the lust. She was made for him; of course, she would be able to handle the worst his beast had to offer.

Even so, it had taken a long time to fall asleep that night. Usually, after a battle, he slept like a babe. Knowing that the enemy was vanquished—this one especially—and that the people he cared about were safe in bed, should have been enough to bring peaceful dreams.

And yet, he'd lain with Lina curled in his arms, his fingers running through her hair until the dawn's early light trickled into the room. He carried no guilt over his actions. A berserker learned early on to deal with the taking of a life. Even if that hadn't been the case, it was hard to summon remorse when ending Mataius didn't just avenge Lina but ensured that his depravity would never touch another living creature.

No, it wasn't guilt that kept him awake. It was the overwhelming sense that this wasn't over. The only reason he found sleep at all was because sheer exhaustion forced the issue. Even so, he was far from rested when Finley woke him for work mere hours later.

Unfortunately, that lingering feeling hadn't eased in the days since. He was more on edge now than he'd been in the days leading up to Mataius' capture. As much as he hoped he was wrong, Nord knew he wasn't. His instinct was too finely honed for that.

Which meant all he could do was wait and pray he was ready when the next shot was fired.

"Ahem."

The obnoxiously loud, falsely polite attempt to get his attention snapped him from his thoughts.

"Camille," he said, snapping his eyes up to the woman's pinched face.

"I've asked you repeatedly to refer to me as Madame Bisset," she snapped.

Being on edge meant that his temper was close to the surface. Usually, he would at least try to mask his irritation. Today, he didn't bother.

"I'm aware, *Camille.*"

She flushed scarlet with anger. "Your lack of respect has not gone unnoticed. I'll be adding this incident to your file."

Nord raised a brow. "You do that."

She lifted up the clipboard she was holding like its presence somehow granted her authority. "The Director would like to speak with you before you leave."

The sense of foreboding swelled.

Nord didn't waste time. The Director had told him what would happen if he disobeyed. On the chance the Director had found out and this was the threat Nord had been anticipating, better to be prepared than caught with his dick out.

"Finley. You need to get out of here."

"Nord? What's going on? Has something happened?"

"I've been summoned."

"Shit."

"Get to Lina."

"Nord—"

"Make sure she knows . . ." He wasn't sure how to finish that sentence, so he didn't.

The ravaged quality of Finley's voice when he replied told Nord it didn't matter. He understood.

"Brother—"

"Now. Before it's too late."

"If you'd follow me, Mr. Andersson. I'm to take you to him straightaway."

Nord didn't know why she bothered phrasing it like a suggestion. If he tried to leave, there'd be four guards on him before he reached the door.

He gestured for her to precede him, fighting hard to keep his expression placid and his fury in check. All he could do now was buy Finley time. On the off-chance the Director wasn't already aware of what transpired, he'd know soon enough.

And it was no mystery what would happen then.

Nord had known going after Mataius was a risk, but it was one he hadn't hesitated to take. They'd taken every precaution to keep what happened under wraps, but when a supernatural intelligence agency was involved, nothing stayed secret forever. Now, he simply had to deal with the consequences.

Camille led Nord through a series of hallways and then to an elevator he hadn't noticed before. After hitting the bottom button, they stepped out into a fairly non-descript room with three hallways branching off, one in each direction. There were no furniture or people, which was odd for the headquarters because there were almost always a couple of people milling around.

She took him down the right hallway. Doors lined either side, but she didn't stop until she reached the end. She gestured to the closed door.

"Just through there."

He spared her a glare, not liking her haughty expression, and then pushed the door open.

The Director was waiting for him in much the same position as the last time. Back to the door, hands clasped behind him. This time, however, there were no windows. Instead, he was gazing down at the counter that ran along the wall.

Besides the Director and the counter, the only other object in the room was a single chair in the center of the room with wrist and ankle straps attached to the arms.

"Have a seat."

His berserker roared in protest, not wanting to willingly put himself in a vulnerable position. Nord fought against his instinct as he obeyed the order.

The only way to buy Finley time was to play along. He had no choice.

As he expected, the straps snapped closed as soon as he was seated, tightening until they were digging into his skin.

"How many days ago was it that you were seated in my office, promising to leave the Drake heir alone?"

"Three."

"Then perhaps you can explain to me how it is that less than twenty-four hours after you left my office, he's reported missing."

The question confirmed Nord's suspicions. The Director must have put people on Mataius as soon as he'd learned who he was. Would have been easy enough to do once he had a name.

"Of course, we tracked him down. It's in our best interest to keep tabs on everyone connected to the Mobius Council. Now, tell me where he is."

Nord didn't bother replying. Anything he said would be a lie, and the only way the Director was getting the truth was by stealing it from his mind.

The Director glanced at Nord over his shoulder.

Nord met his stare.

"It is no coincidence that he went missing. You will tell me where he is."

"I cannot."

"Cannot or will not?"

Both. Finley dealt with the remains. Nord had no idea what he'd done with them, nor did he care.

Once again, Nord let silence be his answer. It was not lost on him that he had now switched roles with Mataius.

"Answer me."

"I don't know."

The Director turned to face him fully. *"Lies will not protect you."*

"I'm not lying."

His eyes narrowed, and his head canted to the side as he studied Nord. *"If you don't know where he is, you know what happened to him. Tell me."*

Silence.

"I will not ask again."

"I'm sorry, was there a question in there? All I heard was more bullshit."

The Director's eyes glowed a blinding jade as white-hot pain lanced Nord's skull. His body arched in the chair, the magic-infused bindings straining to contain him. Memories rapidly flickered through his mind, some so old he'd all but forgotten them. The sound of his father's voice as he taught him the correct way to hold his weapon. The feeling of his mother's lips pressed against his cheek. The day his father was killed. The first time his berserker took over. The day he joined the Brotherhood.

Each one there and then gone as the Director riffled through his mind like it was a history book. The memories continued to flow through him faster than he could process until a familiar blonde rose to the surface.

Lina.

The flood of images slowed somewhat as if the Director sensed he was getting closer to what he wanted to know.

No. Not these. These are not for you. She's mine.

He tried to force the Director out of his mind, but it was futile.

It was all there. Their entire time together. Him giving her his Guardian's vow. Her asking him to hold her shoes so she could dance. And then glaring up at him during training. Then again, with water sluicing down her body as she slowly rose from her bath. Gasping his name as she came. Telling him she loved him.

Nord roared.

The Director continued to take what he wanted, scrolling through each and every memory while forcing Nord to simultaneously relive them.

Lina regaining her memories. Her connection to the Council. Discovering that Mataius killed her. Hunting him. The storm on top of the cathedral. Discovering his hideout . . . and the bloody aftermath.

Finally, the Director stopped.

Nord slumped in his chair, sweat soaking through his shirt, chest rising and falling in giant heaves. Never had he felt more violated than he did sitting there staring up at the man who had stolen every private moment he'd ever had. Memories that belonged to no one but him.

The Director's voice flooded his mind once more.

"The Brotherhood's pristine reputation cannot be sullied. We must remain above reproach in order to protect those we serve; you've said this yourself. Furthermore, you've disobeyed a direct order and, in doing so, have betrayed our esteemed order. Gunnar Bloodaxe, I declare you a traitor to the Brotherhood. You are hereby stripped of your power and will be executed for your crimes."

As the rage boiled over, there was another sensation like his skin was slowly being peeled away. The pain was excruciating. He fought against the binding, trying to call up the bloodlust, but the unending waves of pain overshadowed the rage, and he couldn't make the transition.

Once it was done, Nord's chin fell to his chest, and blood dripped out of his eyes and down his cheeks. His limbs felt heavy, his chest oddly empty like something vital had been ripped out. The agony of it only underscored the truth.

He'd been unmade. Nord was a Guardian no more.

CHAPTER TWENTY-NINE
LINA

"I'm going to go make myself another. Do you want one?" Quinn asked, gesturing to Lina's empty glass.

"You know I can make another round appear, right?"

"As much as I love watching you use your magic to play bartender, getting up gives me a reason to sneak off to the bathroom."

Lina laughed. "So why don't you just say you need to pee, and I'll take care of the drinks?"

Quinn scrunched her nose. "There's something about announcing the fact that makes me feel like a child. I'd much rather you believe I'm being super generous by offering to get up and do the dirty work than having you know I'm off to break the seal."

Lina snorted and started to make a shooing motion with her hands. "Just go. I'll do my best Jon Snow impression when you return."

Quinn canted her head. "If you're Snow because you know nothing, that makes me Tyrion because I drink *and* I know things."

Lina laughed harder as Quinn turned and danced out of the room. What had started off as a celebration of Mataius' defeat had devolved into a *Game of Thrones* marathon and drinking game. Now that the threat of imminent danger had passed, Quinn was on a mission to properly introduce Lina to the best of the last decade's pop culture. Lina suspected she was just tired of having to correct her outdated and generally butchered attempts at using colloquialisms.

The front door opened and slammed.

Lina pushed to her feet, chuckling as she shouted, "Where are you going? You could have used one of our bathrooms."

Her laughter died off as Finley rushed into the room. One look at his face sobered her instantly.

"What's wrong?" She looked over his shoulder for Nord. A pit opened up inside her stomach when she realized he wasn't there. "Where is he?"

"Lina—"

She flinched at Finley's tone. He'd just confirmed her worst fears with a single word. There was a reason that voice was only used when imparting terrible news. It warned whoever was being spoken to that the sky was about to come crashing down.

Finley reached out a hand, his eyes brimming with unwanted sympathy.

"No," she said, the word firm and unyielding as she jerked away from him.

"Please—"

"Tell me where he is," she demanded.

"The Director—"

Lina squeezed her eyes shut. *Please, no. I only just found him. Please, don't take him away from me. After everything we've been through, don't we deserve a little happiness?*

"Lina, look at me."

She obeyed, focusing hard on Finley's face.

"I'm not going to lie to you. This is bad, the worst actually."

Lina's heart felt like it had just been tossed in a blender. She had to force herself to breathe as he continued.

"But . . ." Finley trailed off, looking pained.

"But what?" she asked, snatching up the small flicker of hope like it was a lifeline.

"There's a chance, albeit a small one, that it may not be too late."

"So what the fuck are we still doing standing here?"

Finley grabbed her arm as she prepared to storm off half-cocked.

"I'm not sure he'd want us to risk it. He seemed pretty set on keeping us—you specifically—away."

"You know he'd never stay away if I was in trouble and there was even the smallest chance he could save me. There's no way I'd do that to him."

"That's about how I thought you'd react."

Urgency and panic were combining inside of her to create a potent mix of energy that left her feeling like she'd been supercharged. It was hard to stand still as the need to go find him screamed at her to get a move on.

"I'm assuming the Director found out about Mataius?"

"That's my working theory."

"But you don't know for sure? Can't you ask him through your link?"

Finley gave an apologetic shake of his head. "It's not safe for us to communicate telepathically while he's with the Director. For one thing, the chance of our messages being intercepted is high, but even more than that, I don't want to risk interfering with Nord's concentration while they are together."

Lina pressed her lips together. She couldn't argue the logic of that, but the lack of communication meant they were operating in the dark and on assumption. That rarely ended well.

"So what do you know for sure?" she asked.

"Only what he told me. The last we spoke, Nord told me he'd been summoned. He warned me so that I could leave and come to you before the Director got to me, too. Otherwise, I'd end up right there with him, and you'd be totally defenseless. Especially once he found out the truth about what we did."

"What does that mean for Nord?"

"First, he'll be interrogated, which is a kind way of saying the Director will forcefully delve into Nord's memories and steal whatever information he wants. Once he learns about Mataius, he'll react one of two ways. One, he will imprison Nord for failure to obey direct orders and acting without proper authority. It's a harsh punishment, but not permanent. It's generally used in cases of extreme disobedience but in situations that are not considered outright treason."

Lina gulped. "And option two?"

"If the Director decides Nord's actions directly put the Brotherhood and its sacred duty at risk, he will declare Nord a traitor."

"And then?"

"They'll strip him of his powers and execute him."

The floor felt like it dropped out from beneath her, and she reached out to the wall to brace herself.

"Which way do you think it's going to go?"

The truth was written on Finley's face—he didn't think Nord stood a chance.

"The odds are against us because of who Mataius is and what retaliation from his family would mean if it gets out the murder was committed by a Guardian. But, there is some good news."

Lina let out a humorless laugh. "I find it hard to believe that anything about Nord's execution will fall under the realm of good news."

Finley grabbed her shoulders and forced her to look into his eyes. "Even if the Director calls for his execution, it will not proceed until two of the Director's peers arrive to bear witness."

"So we might still have time to save him?"

Finley nodded.

"How long?"

"Hours at best."

Lina's thoughts raced as she tried to formulate a plan. She rejected ideas as swiftly as she thought of them, realizing the sheer impossibility of their situation. They needed to break in and out of the Brotherhood's headquarters without detection. It would be easier to walk into the White House and assassinate the president without capture than successfully do what they were contemplating attempting.

A feeling of hopelessness surged up, but she forced it back. Nord would never give up, no matter how dire the odds, so neither would she.

Quinn's voice broke through their strained silence. "Finley, when did you get back? Where's the big guy?" Her eyes found Lina, and her expression fell. Setting the two drinks she was holding down, she asked, "What happened?"

Finley filled her in while Lina tried to come up with something that didn't get them all killed. It was safe to say strategy was not Lina's strong suit. Nord was always the one coming up with the brilliant plans. She was an 'act first, think later' kind of gal. That really wasn't going to work here. She couldn't even figure out how they were going to get inside let alone the rest of it. And it wasn't like they could just walk through the front door.

Could they?

"Fin, do you think you can get us in? Like with glamour or something?" Lina asked.

Finley considered the question and then gave a slight shake of his head. "Not without help. My illusion magic is nowhere near what Nord can do, and trying to fool a building full of Guardians is going to require expert-level skill. Plus, the wards will notify them of any attempt to sneak in with magic."

"So what we really need is a way around the wards," Lina said. "Any ideas?"

Finley blinked. "There isn't one. Not that I know of anyway. Ward magic is ancient. I'm not even wholly certain it comes from this world."

"Quinn?"

She shook her head. "You saw what happened the last time I

tried to trick my way through a ward. I got access, but the alarm was still tripped."

Shit.

It wasn't exactly like she had a phone full of contacts she could call for help either. The only other person she could even think of who managed to breach a ward was Crombie.

At the thought, Lina's head snapped up, and her eyes narrowed.

On two different occasions, the fae prince had found a way to work magic through the penthouse's wards. True, the alarm still went off, but the wards were supposed to prevent anything like that from happening at all, and yet he somehow got through.

"Finley, we're going to need a portal."

"Lina, you know we can't just portal into the—"

"No," she said, shaking her head quickly. "Not there. To The District."

"The District?" he repeated.

"Lina, that's brilliant!" Quinn said at the same time. "If anyone knows how to get around the wards, Crombie will. He's always getting into places he shouldn't."

"Not to mention his little time trick," Finley added somewhat begrudgingly. "That could come in handy while we search for Nord."

Lina nodded, having just thought the same. His ability to freeze time would definitely be an asset. Especially when there was no way to know how long it would take to find out where Nord was being kept or how much time they had to begin with.

"There's only one problem," Finley continued, drawing her attention. "He banned us, remember? How are we supposed to convince him to help us if we can't get to him?"

Lina's excitement momentarily faltered, but she recovered quickly. They had far bigger hurdles to deal with tonight than Crombie and his wounded pride. Whatever the cost to get him to help them, she'd pay it.

'No' simply wasn't an option.

"Leave that to me," Lina said.

"You're proving harder to get rid of than a dried cum-stain on fine silk," Crombie drawled.

He stood beneath The District's awning with his arms folded across his chest, flanked by Kiko and Zilla. The way they angled their bodies made it appear like they were actively blocking the stairs up to the club and were thus physically keeping Crombie from heading back inside. Lina wasn't sure what the twins said to get him down here in the first place, but as soon as they heard what she needed, they didn't waste a second going to locate their boss.

"Have a lot of experience with that, do you?" Quinn snapped.

His gray eyes flashed. "As much as I enjoy trading insults with you, Weaver, I'm not really in the mood. Tell me whatever it is you came here to say, and then kindly fuck off."

Lina took a step forward, drawing Crombie's attention back to her and effectively cutting off Quinn from whatever barb she'd toss out next.

"We need your help," she blurted.

He raised a brow. "This seems to be a bit of a pattern with you. I give you what you want, and then you come back and demand more. When, exactly, am I going to start getting anything out of this arrangement?"

"Last time we came to you, you said you would have helped if we'd just asked. So this is me asking. Please."

"Yes, but that was because I'd thought we were becoming friends. You made it clear, during that same meeting, that we are not."

The words cut because they were true. She'd asked a lot of a man who didn't owe her anything, and here she was, asking for more.

"I know that you've already done a lot, helping us find Mataius and all, and I appreciate it so much. I swear, if it wasn't quite literally a matter of life and death, I wouldn't have intruded on you again after you asked us to stay away."

"Yes, clearly, boundaries are something you accept without question."

"Crombie, he's got Nord. We might already be too late, but if there's a chance we can get there in time . . . I have to take it. Please."

His eyes sharpened. "Who has him?"

"The Director. He found out about Mataius, and he . . ." Lina trailed off, unable to say the rest out loud.

"I see." He stared at her, the intensity of his gaze making her feel like he was evaluating her worth. "And what role do you see me playing in this rescue attempt?"

"We need you to help us get through the Brotherhood's wards undetected. And, since we aren't exactly sure what we're going to be up against once we get inside, we were hoping that you might, um . . ." she trailed off, instinct warning her she'd already asked too much but desperation pushing her to keep going.

Crombie remained silent as he waited for her to finish her thought. His expression was hard to read. At this point, Lina wasn't sure whether he was offended, amused, or bored.

"Be willing to come with us and do your time-freezing thing . . ." she finished lamely.

She fought the urge to rephrase her explanation as the silence stretched. Time was ticking, and she'd already spent more of it than they could probably afford, trying to come up with a plan.

"There are a lot of assumptions in that request."

Lina inwardly cringed. The way he'd said *request* was clearly mocking. Afraid he was about to refuse, she reached out and gripped his arm.

"Please, Crombie. I'm not sure we can do this without you. I can't leave him there to die. I can't."

Crombie appeared unmoved by her plea.

"Frankly, sweetheart, I couldn't care less whether the berserker lives or dies. He's been nothing but a pain in my ass. So, if you want me to do this, then you will have to pay for the privilege just like everyone else."

Lina blinked. For all her internal bravado about not taking no for an answer, she really hadn't expected him to agree.

"Of course. Anything."

"Lina," Quinn hissed.

Crombie's eyes glinted at that, and one side of his mouth curled up. "Careful, sweetheart. You don't know what I'm going to ask for yet."

She already knew, no matter what cost Crombie demanded, that she would pay it. When it came to Nord's life, there was no price 'too high'.

"What do you want?" she asked.

"There's an object I've been trying to acquire for quite some time. It would be quite the pièce de résistance in my personal collection."

Lina's brows furrowed. "All right."

"The issue is the current owners are rather unwilling to part with it."

"And you want me to convince them?" she guessed.

Crombie laughed. "No. You're going to walk in and steal it from right under their noses."

"If it's that easy to steal, why haven't you already done it?" Finley asked.

Crombie's eyes flicked to him over her shoulder. "Because only an ascended heir of the Mobius Council has access."

"It's in the vault," Quinn breathed. Then her gaze turned furious. "So that's what this little charade of yours has been all about. I couldn't figure out why you were so interested in her, but now it's obvious. You've been planning this all along. All your claims of friendship are complete bullshit. You've been trying to lure her into believing you were friends so you could turn around and use her."

"I guess we'll never know now, will we? As memory serves, Weaver, *you* were the one who defined the terms of any future relationships when you decided to blackmail me. You're lucky I'm deigning to speak with you at all after the shit you pulled." Then he turned his attention back to Lina. "So, I will help you reacquire your berserker, and in exchange, you will bring my treasure to me. Are we agreed?"

The exchange left a tendril of unease unfurling within her, but Lina decided that ultimately Crombie's motives didn't matter. As far as she was concerned, if he helped her save Nord, she owed him whatever the fuck he wanted.

Still, caution made her ask, "Do I get to know what the object is first?"

Crombie waved his hand. "Does it really matter? Didn't you already say you'd give *anything*?"

The only item tied to the Mobius Council that she knew that she could never hand over to Crombie was currently concealed as a tattoo on her arm. Whatever Crombie wanted he believed was in the vault. That didn't mean there weren't other, powerfully dangerous items hidden away in there that should never be placed in the wrong hands. But, so long as he didn't request the Prism, she didn't care.

Since the fae were notorious for their loopholes, Lina decided to word her agreement carefully. Just to be safe.

She held out her hand. "You help us get Nord out—alive—and I will retrieve the object of your choosing from the Council's vault."

"Lina—" Quinn tried again.

"Are you sure that's wise?" Finley asked in a low voice.

"Well?" Lina asked, ignoring them both.

Crombie slid his hand over hers, lifting it to his lips like he was about to kiss it. He peered at her from over their joined hands.

"The fae don't deal in handshakes, sweetheart. We deal in blood."

"No!" Finley shouted.

Even Zilla and Kiko jerked like they were about to pull Crombie away from her, but it was too late.

Before she could blink, Crombie flipped her hand over and sliced through her wrist with a surprisingly sharp canine. He maintained eye contact as he ran his tongue over the line of blood, magically sealing the wound as he did. Then, he straightened and licked his lips.

"Mmm," he murmured.

Crombie's pupils were blown wide, likely from the potent dose of Lina's power that small taste had caused.

Lina yanked her hand out of his hold, cradling it to her chest. It hadn't hurt—it'd actually felt shockingly good—but the fucker already knew that. The fae could taste emotion in blood. He knew exactly what she'd been feeling when he'd licked her.

Unlike vampires, who drank blood to survive, a fae's consumption of blood was far more nefarious. They drank it for one of two reasons. To get high or to ensure a deal was blood sworn. This was the first time Lina had experienced either firsthand.

His smile turned mean. "Yes, I see you know what that means. Consider it my insurance. Now, there's nowhere you can hide from me until you uphold your end of the bargain."

Knowing exactly where she was wasn't the only thing being blood sworn entailed, but she'd worry about the specifics later. She could only deal with one crisis at a time, and compared to Nord's life, Crombie's bargain didn't register.

"You have your insurance," Quinn gritted out. "Now it's time for you to keep up your end of the deal. Can you get us through the wards or not?"

"Wouldn't that have been a more prudent question before she agreed to my terms?"

"If you tricked us . . ." Finley started.

Crombie rolled his eyes. "Oh, relax. I was just making an observation. I can get you in. The spell works best if I have a sense of the ward's specific magic. The only way to trick the ward into not sensing your presence is to make it believe you're one and the same."

"That's why you kept setting ours off when you sent your messages," Lina realized.

Crombie smiled. He'd seemed almost giddy since they'd struck their deal. She wasn't sure if that was because he was looking forward to his prize or if it was simply a lingering effect her power had on him.

"Yes, that was fun, wasn't it? I got a good laugh out of picturing you all running around like a bunch of frightened rabbits. Nice towel, by the way."

Lina flushed as she realized he'd seen her in—or at the very least stepping out of—the shower.

He glanced back at Finley. "So, can you get me close enough?"

Finley glowered at Crombie but jerked his chin in a nod.

"Well, then. I do believe you said this was a matter of some urgency. What are we waiting for?"

CHAPTER THIRTY
LINA

"Why did you have to turn me into Grandpa Myrtle?" Quinn asked, plucking at the ill-fitting suit Finley had glamoured for her disguise.

Finley sighed. "For the last time, Jonah does not look like a grandpa."

Quinn raised a bushy salt and pepper eyebrow. "Then how come you three are beefcakes, and I'm a withered old man?"

Finley threw up his hands. "I don't know? Because Jonah and his sons were the first group of four Guardians I could think of who wouldn't raise eyebrows being seen together? Does it matter what you look like if it gets us in without suspicion?"

"If it doesn't matter, why don't you be the old man, and I can be part of the sex-on-a-stick threesome?"

Crombie, who along with Lina and Finley looked like they could be a group of Greco-Roman wrestlers, studiously ignored their bickering as he wove the magical cloaking device that would help them pass through the doors without setting off the alarm.

Lina, however, was losing patience with their bullshit. Just under an hour had passed since Finley came home and sent her world in a tailspin, and she felt every passing minute like a blow to the kidney.

Logically, she knew that they'd rallied as fast as they could, but she also knew that they were running out of time. The Director's peers could have already arrived. He could be on his way to execute Nord right now, and they were standing out here like a bunch of braying jackasses.

"Almost done?" she asked.

Crombie nodded, never ceasing his whispered chant. Thankfully, there were no hand motions or other physical requirements for his spell. If there were, someone would have definitely cottoned onto them. It was easier to hide in plain sight when they merely appeared to be a group of men chatting on the street corner after work.

Once Crombie was finished, they'd cross the street and enter the building. Then, the real test would begin.

Finley was pretty confident he knew what floor Nord would be on and that he could get them there without anyone batting an eye. Once there, they'd have to search each room until they found him. That's where the rest of them came in.

Not knowing what they might encounter, Fin warned them to prepare for anything. Crombie would help by opening one of his pocket dimensions. It would only freeze part of the floor at a time, but it should allow them to search fairly unhindered. If someone did stumble across them, Quinn would be ready to modify their memory. Fin would stand watch and act as muscle if needed, and Lina, well, it would be up to her to counter any and everything else they came up against.

"Remind me again of what the containment cells are like," Lina said, interrupting Quinn before she could start her next bout of griping.

"They look like a basic jail cell but without any windows. The doors are a combination of iron, silver, and eternium. The rooms were made to neutralize powerful supernaturals, so don't get caught in one."

Lina pressed her lips together and nodded. "And the floor's layout?"

"That's harder to say. I was only down there the one time, but from what I remember, there's a bunch of branching hallways. Given what I've seen, it's a bit of a labyrinth. We'll have to keep track of our route so we don't get lost when it's time to get back out."

She couldn't help but notice that he didn't say 'Once we get Nord.'

"Right," she said.

"Maybe we should Hansel and Gretel it," Quinn said.

Lina turned to her. "What?"

"You know, leave a trail of breadcrumbs?"

"And give the other Guardians a direct path to us while we're at it," Finley replied. "Great idea."

"I don't see you coming up with anything," she said. "Is there some kind of camouflaged equivalent we can use? Something only we would notice?"

"Like a handprint on the wall glamoured to look like paint maybe?" Lina offered.

Finley considered it. "If it's something I can see with my Guardian sight, so can the others," he pointed out.

Lina frowned. Thinking of ways to best the Guardians was proving tricky. They had almost all of the same skills at their disposal, not to mention they easily outnumbered their small group.

"It's done," Crombie said.

"Then I guess we'll just have to wing the rest once we're in there. Let's go," Lina said.

Finley took the lead, but Lina was close on his heels. It felt like she couldn't walk fast enough.

Nord was in there somewhere, waiting to die.

Even though he couldn't hear her, a part of her hoped he'd, at least, sense she was near.

We're coming. Just hold on.

On the heels of that thought came another, this one causing a fissure of anger to open up inside of her.

How dare the Director treat one of his own this way? All because Nord had chosen to defend her and countless others instead of stand-down and let a self-admitted murderer roam free. Some protector of the realm the Director was. What happened to leading by example? What kind of Guardian chose to do nothing because he was afraid of upsetting the status quo? One who didn't deserve the title, clearly.

Well, fuck him and his rules.

Lina was done playing by any but her own.

As they reached the front doors, Lina held her breath, but as Crombie promised, they passed through without detection.

"I'm not sure how I feel about the fact that you just breached some of the most powerful defensive magic I've ever encountered," Finley muttered.

"Child's play," he replied, offering him a smile that was lacking its usual dangerous edge. She assumed that was due to the very un-Crombie like glamour he was currently sporting.

Finley shook his head. "Come on, this way."

He led them past the receptionist and down a hallway on the left. They walked past a few people but no one who took any real notice of them.

"Elevator's just up there."

They reached the end of the hall, and Finley pressed the call button. Lina's anxiety ratcheted up several notches as they waited for it to arrive. It was one thing to be actively moving through the building, but she felt far more vulnerable standing still. Maybe because it provided more opportunities for someone to try to interact with them.

When the soft metallic chime announced its arrival, Lina felt like an eon had passed. She blew out a relieved breath as they all crowded inside.

Then a voice called out, "Hold the elevator!" and her anxiety returned ten-fold.

A short, plump woman pushed her way into the elevator.

"Thanks," she panted, her ample chest rising and falling dramatically. "Can't be late for this meeting or I'll be sacked for sure." She threw Quinn-as-Jonah a grateful smile. "Be a dear and push six for me, would ya, love?"

Quinn's finger was still hovering over the button panel where she'd been frantically pressing the door close button to no avail.

"Sure," she replied, her voice that of a gruff older gentleman.

She did as asked, and then she randomly pressed button number three instead of the one labeled with a 'B'. Lina assumed it was just in case the woman was paying attention to where they were going since it's what she would have done as well.

"I must say, Jonah, you and your wife made pretty sons, God rest her soul. But I didn't realize Brutus was already back from assignment in the Amazon. You were taking care of a nest of naga that were attacking human villages, right?"

She looked expectantly at Crombie.

Fuck. Lina was already looking at Quinn, trying to telegraph with her eyes it was time to work her mojo when Crombie shocked the hell out of her by playing along.

"Afraid I can't answer that. Classified." Then he winked at the woman, who blushed furiously.

"Of course, of course. Oh, this is me," she said as the elevator came to a stop. "Well, good day to you."

She rushed out after a final, flirtatious glance back at Crombie.

Lina didn't breathe again until the doors slid shut and they were moving.

"That was close," she said, slumping against the elevator wall.

"We're just lucky it was Gina," Finley muttered, rubbing his temples. "She's chatty but harmless. Could have been worse."

They fell silent as the elevator stopped on the third floor and then finally made its descent to the correct level.

She could feel it as soon as the doors slid back open. The palpable energy. The electric charge that fills the air in those seconds before the first drop of rain falls and announces the impending chaos of a storm.

Nord was here. Somewhere.

Lina's eyes roamed over the bare walls and located three potential paths for them to start their search.

"Which way?" Quinn asked.

For a second, Lina was paralyzed with the choice. What if Nord died because she chose wrong? Then she closed her eyes and forced the doubt away. Instead, she focused on Nord, recounted every detail of his chiseled face. She drew on the feelings he ignited within her. The sense of belonging to each other she'd felt ever since he found her at the ball.

With those thoughts in mind, she opened her eyes.

"This way."

There was nothing logical about how she arrived at her decision. She was running on sheer instinct. All she knew was that it *felt* right.

They veered to the left. Doors lined the hall, but Lina moved without stopping. They wouldn't keep him that close to an exit. He'd be further back. When they reached the next fork, she stopped and again listened for that inner voice to guide her.

This time, they went right, and when they came across a door, they tested to see if it was unlocked and then stopped to peer inside after Crombie worked his magic to ensure they weren't surprised by occupants within.

And on it went, picking a direction and checking the rooms down that corridor.

Left.

Right.

Right.

Straight.

With each new hall and row after row of empty rooms, Lina's

desperation grew. She was all too aware of the minutes draining away like sand in an hourglass, but there was no rushing.

They were just about to go left when a hand in her shirt tugged her back.

"Someone's coming," Finley whispered in her ear.

At first, all she heard was the pounding of her heart, but then there was the low murmur of voices. A few more seconds, and she could make out three distinct timbres.

"They're coming this way," Finley warned.

"Should we go back?" Quinn asked.

"No," Lina decided. "These are the first people we've come across. There's gotta be a reason."

"They could be checking on prisoners or preparing something for the Director," Finley confirmed.

"Are there many prisoners of the Brotherhood kept here?" Crombie asked.

Finley shrugged. "Nord is the only one that I know of. But that doesn't mean there aren't others."

Crombie snorted. "Why is it righteous men never see the hypocrisy of their actions? Preserving freedom by stripping others of their own, killing in the name of peace." He shook his head. "I'd much rather deal with someone who recognizes their capacity for darkness and embraces it than anyone who claims their actions serve the 'greater good'."

"Quiet," Finley hissed.

"Should we follow them?" Quinn asked.

"No. I want to see what's down there," Lina said.

"Are we fighting, or am I up?" Quinn asked.

"You're up. Fighting may draw out others. We've made it this far without getting caught. I'd rather not give ourselves away if we can avoid it."

Quinn stepped out into the hall and greeted whoever was coming.

"Hey, guys, can you come here for a sec?"

The swell of angry replies was immediate.

"Hey!"

"What are you doing here?"

"You're not supposed to be here!"

"Crombie, I think she could use a little help," Lina whispered.

Crombie sighed, appearing put out, but when the shouts fell silent, she knew he'd done as she asked. Lina took that as her cue to step out into the hall behind Quinn, who had her hand on a burly Guardian's shoulder and was talking to him in a low, soothing tone. The dazed look in his eye confirmed that Quinn's magic had already taken hold.

They waited until she dealt with the other two and then squeezed past, which was trickier than she'd thought, given how much of the hall they filled. Finley had to physically move one of them just to make space.

Once they'd regrouped at the end of the hall, Lina glanced left and right and then realized the path on the right didn't branch off like the others. They'd finally reached a dead-end. There was also something about the doors that looked different. It took a second for her brain to register what her eyes had already noticed.

There were no door handles. The slightly metallic sheen of the gray rectangles was all that distinguished the doors from the similarly colored walls.

Finley spoke behind her. "The doors are coded to only open for the Director or whoever else has permission to enter the cells."

"So then, we don't go in through the door," Lina decided, her eyes already roaming the walls and imagining various ways to pass through or otherwise remove them.

Before they could worry about that, though, they needed to figure out which room Nord was in. There were no windows in the doors, and if the doors couldn't be opened, they'd have to see within another way.

Lina's eyes narrowed as she summoned her power and tried to assert her will. Despite the crystal-clear mental image of the wall's becoming transparent to reveal what was within, nothing happened.

Frustrated, she tried again, this time imagining that the walls lining the hallway faded entirely, leaving it one long open room.

Still nothing.

Panic gripped her. "It's not working. My magic isn't working," she said, spinning around to look at her friends.

Finley frowned. "I was afraid of that. These rooms neutralize magic. Its why the locks are controlled with biodata. Whatever prevents magic from being used within must also be keeping your magic from taking effect."

"You didn't think to mention that earlier?"

Finley shrugged apologetically. "Your reality shaping is unlike anything I've ever seen. I wasn't sure the spells would affect you the same way."

Lina wanted to scream. She didn't come this far just to fail at the finish line.

"Then I will summon some fucking dynamite, and we will blow up these goddamned walls because there is no way I am leaving here without him."

"Wait, I have an idea," Quinn said.

Lina looked at her expectantly as she started to unbutton her shirt and then reached in and pulled a compact out of her bra.

"What?" she snapped at Finley and Crombie's dubious expressions. "I never go anywhere without some emergency makeup. You never know when you'll need a touch-up or who you're going to need to flirt with. Plus, the mirror comes in handy when you need to spy on someone."

Lina's shoulders sagged. "Quinn, we aren't flirting our way into that room."

Quinn made a face. "Who said we were?"

She moved to the nearest door and started sliding the little powder puff across its surface around chest level.

"I saw this on a documentary once. We can use powder to reveal the fingerprints of whoever last touched the panel or whatever. Then we just cover our hand with a sleeve or something and place it over the prints to apply pressure, which will make the scanner read the correct fingerprints."

She kept dabbing at the door, but no fingerprints revealed themselves. Quinn frowned. "This one must not have been used recently."

She turned and tried the door behind her. It took her another minute, but this time, she found some prints. Tugging down the suit sleeve to cover her hand, she pressed, and shockingly, the door slid open.

"Voila!" she said, turning around with a grin.

"I can't believe that actually worked," Finley muttered.

Lina couldn't either, but she wasn't about to argue with results.

"The Guardians aren't worried about people getting in. They're worried about prisoners getting out. Besides, they assume, like so many supernaturals, that the only true threats are magical. I bet the thought never crossed their minds someone would use mortal technology against them," Quinn said with a shrug.

Lina shook her head, not about to waste time arguing either way.

"Using your compact will take forever," she said, using her magic to conjure four bags of flour. "Everyone, take one of these and work your way down the hall."

Crombie lifted one and raised an eyebrow. "What exactly am I supposed to do with this?"

Lina handed him one of the three makeup brushes she'd just created. He eyed the rainbow and glitter-covered handle with distaste.

"Do you seriously expect me to use this?" he asked.

She narrowed her eyes at him. "We had a deal, remember? You help me, I help you. Get to work."

They spent the next several minutes in silence, working their way down the hallway. Each time one of them discovered a set of handprints, there was always an excited inhale followed by a deep sigh of disappointment.

So far, they'd opened three of the ten doors they'd tested. There were only four more doors left to try.

Taking a deep breath, Lina loaded up her brush and started dusting the door. The fingerprints showed up almost immediately. She couldn't quite quell the rush of excitement even though she'd been disappointed every other time.

Please.

Once the final print had been defined with the white powder, she covered her hand and pressed against the smooth metal.

A choked sob pushed its way out of her throat as Nord's head shot up. The first things she noticed were the trails of dried blood staining his cheeks and the unnatural pallor of his skin. Then she focused on his bloodshot eyes. Eyes which were no longer flecked around the pupils. At first, they burned with icy hatred, but then he blinked, his face going slack.

Finley must have dropped her glamour because Nord jumped to his feet. "Lina?"

For a second, she was surprised that he wasn't bound, but on the heels of that thought came the realization that the Brotherhood didn't consider him a threat now that they'd stripped him of his Guardian power.

She rushed forward into his arms, Finley's warning about not going in the cell long forgotten. Nothing, not even the threat of imprisonment, would keep her from touching him.

Nord held her so tightly she could hardly breathe. She couldn't stop kissing every inch of his face she could reach. Technically, that meant she was kissing more beard than skin, but she didn't care.

He was in her arms and he was alive.

"We've got to go," she said, pulling away.

Nord, pragmatic as ever, didn't bother asking unnecessary questions. Holding her hand in a death grip, he followed her out of the cell and back into the hall. He eyed the flour-covered doors with interest.

"Clever."

"When magic didn't work, we had to rely on mortal tricks. It was Quinn's idea."

Nord's gaze drifted over the others, his eyes landing on the old man as Quinn transformed back into her true self.

"My thanks."

She shrugged. "I'm not much of a fighter, so I have to bring other skills to the table."

Nice as the moment was, Lina couldn't shake the feeling of urgency that consumed her.

"We can talk later. Let's just get out of here," she said.

They made it halfway down the hall when the rumble of running footsteps started. It wasn't close yet, but it was unmistakable.

"Shit," Finley groaned.

"What is it now?" Lina asked.

"We must have tripped a silent alarm when Nord left the room. The cavalry is coming."

"Shit," Lina repeated. "We'll have to try to lose them."

The five of them started running, not paying attention to whether they were going back the same way they came or not. They were just trying to get away from the Guardian horde. They'd just turned down another hallway when Lina skidded to a stop behind Crombie. Six Guardians were bounding their direction.

Lina and the rest of the group turned, preparing to run back when three more Guardians came from the other direction. Nord let out a savage roar, his berserker responding to the threat, but Finley gripped his arm.

"Wait. You can't kill them. These men haven't done anything wrong. They aren't our enemies."

"Well, that's a matter of opinion," Crombie muttered.

Finley ignored him. "Nord, mate, you know they're just doing their job."

Nord growled, clearly not appreciating being restrained.

Knowing they didn't have time to stand around and debate, Lina took matters into her own hands. Since they'd left the halls containing the containment cells and their neutralizing magic behind, she summoned her magic and was rewarded with a sharp crack as a wall split in two and pieces of ceiling started raining down.

Pieces turned to large chunks, and within seconds, there was a wall of rubble between them and the Guardians coming up behind them.

Turning to the ones still blocking their escape, Lina thought of an earthquake and the way the ground seemed to rise and roll during the worst of them.

"Hold on."

It was the only warning she gave her friends as the hallway surged up. A second later, it crashed down like a wave hitting the shore, except the shore in this case was a group of Guardians. The movement knocked them off their feet and sent them tumbling down the hall until they landed in a tangle of limbs.

Knowing they'd be able to use magic as soon as they came to, she tried to buy more time by creating another blockade of fallen ceiling.

"Let's go," she shouted, racing down the now clear path. Without realizing it, her group had somehow found their way back to one of the three initial hallways. She could just make out the elevator doors as they came barreling down the central lane.

The sight of their means of escape brought a burst of speed, and they raced into the open chamber. Lina frantically started pressing the call button, irate that they were so close to freedom and held up by another goddamn elevator.

"Come on, come on," she cried, pressing the button harder.

She almost wept with relief when the little chime rang out.

The doors opened, and Crombie, Quinn, and Finley piled in.

Nord and Lina were brought up short by a voice that cracked like a whip shouting in her mind. Lina's hands lifted up to her ears as she cried out in pain.

"You can try to run, Gunnar Bloodaxe, but there is nowhere on any world where you can hide. The Brotherhood's reach is absolute. I will find you, and you will be punished for your crimes."

For a split second, Lina didn't know who was speaking or who they were talking to. But the pieces fell into place when she noticed the lone figure standing at the other end of the room and caught her Viking's reaction to the man's presence.

That's when the last piece clicked. Nord *was* Gunnar.

He bared his teeth, his face twisted with hatred.

"Nord," she called softly, tugging him toward the elevator. "We've got to go."

He let out a low growl, the malice in it sending chills skittering down her spine. Nord's intent was clear. This man was definitely an enemy.

"I cannot presume to know what he did to you, but I do know what it's like to need to avenge a wrong. But, Nord—"

At the sound of his name, he dragged his eyes to her face.

"—if we don't leave now, we may not get out. Is his death worth all of ours?"

Nord visibly trembled as he fought against the needs of his nature and her plea. He drew in a sharp breath and clenched his hands into fists. Then he pulled her into the elevator with him.

"Come after us, and I will kill you and anyone else you send," he called out in a voice that boomed with menace.

"I do not fear you, berserker."

"You should."

"A lone man is nothing against the might of the Brotherhood."

Lina found and held the Director's angry gaze. "He's not alone."

Just before the door closed, she called on her power one last time and sent the ceiling crashing down.

CHAPTER THIRTY-ONE
LINA

Not sure what was waiting for them, Lina was ready to summon another earthquake, but Crombie was faster. He froze the room as soon as the elevator door slid open. The twenty-something Guardians looked like statues as the group wove their way around them and headed straight for the door.

Lina's group was out of the building and halfway down the street before the shouting started.

"Where to?" Finley asked, eyes burning with power as he prepared to make a portal.

"We need to get to Alistair's place. He should be back by now."

"Is that safe?" Quinn asked. "Won't they look for us there?"

"They know about him and his involvement with us," Nord said. "His place will be one of their first stops, but he'll be safer with us than on his own."

Lina nodded. "Once we get him, we'll figure out where we can hide out and decide our next move. Either way, we're going to need somewhere to stay for a while. The entire Brotherhood is going to be gunning for us. After what we just pulled, there's not a snowball's chance in hell they're going to let us go on our merry way."

Finley had the portal ready by the time she finished speaking. Quinn had already gone through.

Lina glanced back at Crombie. "You coming?"

He shook his head. "This is where I leave you. I like my odds better on my own. Don't worry, I know how to find you when things die down. You have a promise to keep."

"What's he talking about?" Nord asked.

Lina shook her head. "Later," she told him. She turned back to say something to Crombie, but he was already gone, and the Guardians had started pouring out of the door.

Before they could spot her, Lina dove through the portal, pulling Nord through with her.

They stumbled out in front of what Lina assumed was Alistair's door. She hadn't actually been to his home yet since he was always meeting up with them at the penthouse.

Lina lifted shaking hands to her face and scrubbed back the hair that had fallen free.

"Jesus, I need a drink," Quinn groaned as she pounded on the door. "Open up!"

"You and me both," Lina agreed. "I can't believe we actually made it out of there."

Nord banded an arm around her hips and pulled her back into him. His arm tightened as he pressed his face into her neck. "Remind me later to yell at you for putting yourself in danger like that."

"Don't be surprised when I conveniently forget."

She felt him smile against her skin. "Then remind me to properly thank you for saving my ass once we're finally alone."

"Now that I'll definitely remember."

He chuckled as Quinn started a second round of banging.

She turned back to look at them with scrunched brows. "Is it possible he's not back from his trip yet?"

Lina frowned. "He called last night to say he was on his way."

Finley produced a key out of his pocket. At Lina's questioning glance, he explained, "He gave me a spare when I brought him home from Crombie's the other night. Said it might be good for us to have in case of emergencies. I feel like this counts."

"What if he's naked or something?" Lina asked, worrying they'd barge in while he was in the shower.

Finley shook his head, opening the door and calling out, "Alistair, you here, mate?" When there was no reply, he looked at Lina. "I think you're safe."

Lina shook her head with a small smile. "Let's just go in and sit down," she said, exhaustion starting to set in now that the adrenaline was fading.

"Good plan," Quinn said, already brushing past Finley and heading to the right. "I know where he keeps the good liquor, too."

Finley shook his head as he moved into the living room and flicked the lights on. Lina's smile grew at the familiar smell of cigars and leather. This was definitely her uncle's sanctuary. Bookcases filled with leather-bound tomes lined the walls, and there was a massive fireplace with a beautifully crafted mantle.

A startled gasp left her lips as she recognized the woman in the crystal frame set in a place of honor in the center.

"Is that your mother?" Nord asked, following her as she crossed the room.

Lina nodded mutely, letting her fingers graze the glass. "Wasn't she beautiful?"

"You look just like her," he said softly.

She curled herself into his side and hid her reaction to his words in his shirt.

Maybe it was the lingering excitement of the past couple of hours, but when the sound of shattering glass hit her ears, Lina's stomach bottomed out.

"Can't we have three damned minutes of peace before the world goes to shit again? Is that really too much to ask?" Finley said, pushing back up off the couch he'd just sat down on.

"Quinn?" she shouted, as the three of them took off in the direction of the crash.

"L-Lina," came Quinn's broken sob.

Lina's mind blanked, the reason for her friend's ravaged voice too painful to decipher.

Quinn was standing in the doorway of a room near the back of the apartment, her hand pressed to her mouth. She didn't have to see to know what her friend was looking at, but she forced herself to keep walking anyway.

Quinn turned at the sound of their footsteps, her face grief-stricken. "Maybe you shouldn't—"

"Move," she demanded.

Quinn stepped away so Lina could enter what turned out to be her uncle's study. The first thing she noticed was the smoky scent of whiskey from the broken decanter Quinn had dropped. Then, her eyes lifted, and she took in the room's focal point: a hand-carved wooden desk that was centered in front of a massive bay window.

A window with a message scrawled across it.

A message written in blood.

WAKE THE DRAGON, SUFFER HIS WRATH

Positioned just beneath the message, seated in his high-backed chair, was her uncle. His throat slit; his shirt ripped open to reveal the massive figure of a dragon taking flight branded into his chest.

The Drakes hadn't bothered to disguise their handiwork.

There was no need.

They'd just declared war.

LINA AND NORD'S STORY CONTINUES IN WORLD OF DANGER.
AVAILABLE NOW!

BONUS SCENE
FINLEY

Finley set one foot into his room before stopping dead in his tracks.

"What in the actual fuck…"

The chaos within was so absolute, he wasn't sure where to look first. He took another step, hanging his jacket off the back of his suit rack by sheer habit.

His initial reaction to the defiling of his private space was outrage, but as his eyes found the message scrawled on his mirror, his anger became amusement.

Quinn. He'd recognize her lipstick anywhere. But even so, the words were clue enough to their author.

I know how much you enjoy putting things in their place.

And then in smaller script a bit further down:

You can start with these…

(that stick of yours deserves a break)

Finley eyed the offering she'd laid out on top of his dresser, his eyebrow raising at the creative display. She'd left him a half-dozen plugs of various sizes and colors ranging from the absurd to extreme. One had to be the size of his forearm. It was also hot-pink, sparkly, and in the shape of a unicorn horn. He inspected a large black one that had a thick tail—with a white and red polka-dot bow—attached to the back of it.

He shook his head and let out a low laugh. "You little minx."

The chance of him using either of those was less than zero, but he entertained himself with the idea of bending Quinn over and sliding one of the more reasonable sized ones in to find out how she'd respond.

His imagination ran away with the idea—as it usually did when he gave himself permission to fantasize about the sharp-tongued memory weaver. Never had a woman managed to piss him off and turn him on quite so effortlessly. Half the time he wasn't sure if he wanted to fuck her or spank her. Or spank her and then fuck her.

Finley huffed out a laugh. Who was he kidding? It was definitely the latter.

Her smooth, ivory skin was made to be marked. He could practically feel that perky ass of hers warming beneath his palm as he punished her for her cheekiness. Could perfectly picture the rosy shade of pink his hand would leave behind and the sound of her muffled cries—which of course she would try to hide from him.

Quinn Satori was the kind of woman who would make him work for every ounce of her submission. But oh, what a prize it would be. And how he would enjoy taming her.

Finley bit off a curse, the mental image having a very real effect on his body. It had been far too long since he'd indulged in that particular vice. His current flat mates had put a definite damper on his sex life. Not that he was complaining...much. He just didn't seem to have the time these days to properly vet and break in a new partner. Not with the never-ending parade of emergencies he seemed to be involved in lately. Or the near-constant company.

Neither of those excuses touched on the fact that there was only one woman, with her bewitching wine-colored eyes, who currently starred in each and every one of his fantasies.

Finley wasn't one to deny himself anything he wanted. So he had every intention of making the Satori heir his. No one else would do.

But that was a game that required the kind of time and attention he didn't currently possess. Anything less than his best would result in failure. And when the time finally came to claim her, he wasn't about to fail.

Scrubbing a hand over his half-day growth of beard, Finley took inventory of Quinn's destruction, walking slowly through his room and picking up the various shirts and ties that littered the floor. He had to give it to her, she was thorough. There wasn't a section of his room untouched. Every drawer or concealed space had been rummaged through.

Except for the closet, which was suspiciously closed.

He made his way over to that side of the room, pausing to toss the items he'd picked up onto his disheveled bed. His fingers lingered on one silk tie, unable to resist a second, indulgent scenario. This one involving Quinn lashed to his bed, her arms tied above her head, her legs spread.

Finley groaned. Imagining all the things he wanted to do to her was its own special kind of torture.

Curious what surprises awaited him in his closet, Finley forced himself away from the bed and opened the door with a little more force than strictly necessary.

He frowned as his eyes moved over the pristinely arranged suits and shirts, and perfect stack of shoe boxes. There wasn't a single item out of place. Not even the little black chest he'd tucked safely back in the corner.

For a second, Finley wondered if she'd managed to unlock it, of what thoughts ran through her mind as she discovered that particular secret. If it made her heart race or her cunt wet at the thought of him using one of those items on her.

Fuck.

Finley cleared his throat and adjusted himself, not able to recall the last time he'd been this hard from the mere thought of learning a woman's body. Of discovering what made her breath hitch and her legs shake. Of what it sounded like when she came.

Down, boy.

Finley started to back away from the closet, from that box and all its various temptations. As he did, his eye caught a flash of familiar crimson.

"Quinn, you naughty girl."

He pulled the shirt from its wooden hanger, staring long and hard at the kiss she'd left for him. Unable to resist, Finley lifted the shirt to his face and inhaled deeply. He could just make out the scent of her. Jasmine and something else. Vanilla maybe. All Finley knew was it was warm, feminine, and had him ready to devour her.

He took another breath, drawing the scent of her deep into his lungs. There was a niggling at the back of his mind, there and gone. The ghost of a memory. Of that scent.

For just a second, Finley's mind was filled with the sight of Quinn on her knees. Of her luscious lips wrapped around his cock, eyes hooded as they peered up at him, her lipstick smeared and her face flushed.

It didn't feel like one of his fantasies, though he knew it was going to be one now. The details were too real. Too real...and familiar. The slight sheen of sweat on her brow. The silky feel of her hair as he fisted it in his hand. The damp heat of her mouth as she took all of him.

Finley's hand spasmed, and the shirt started to fall to the floor.

No. She wouldn't.

But she absolutely would. He'd seen her do that very thing. Rob people of their memories. If Quinn wouldn't hesitate to use her gift on her best friend, what were the odds she'd give even a passing thought to using it on him?

The harder Finley tried to hold onto the image, the faster it faded. He dropped to his knee, lifting the shirt back to his nose to try and bring it back through scent, but it was no use. The memory, if that's what it was, was gone.

Finley stayed there, half-kneeling in his closet with his shirt bunched in his hand.

If Quinn really had stolen his memory of them being together, why go to all this trouble to get his attention now? Clearly, that's what her innocent vandalism of his room was. One blatant attempt to get his attention. Much like her constant barbs.

Finley grinned as the answer came to him.

Because she couldn't get him out of her system, any more than he could get her out of his.

His eyes dropped back to the kiss as he contemplated his next move. Quinn would obviously expect retaliation of some kind.

He already knew how he wanted to respond. He wanted to go to her and demand that she return any and all memories she'd taken. And then, he wanted to make her re-enact them all, just so he could properly relive their creation.

Finley knew exactly how she'd react to that demand. Quinn loved to bait him. She'd practically made it her life's mission to push every single one of his buttons.

He'd make his demands of her, and she'd lean in close, probably hold his gaze, or even more likely, pretend like she was about to comply. If he was lucky, she might even deign to kiss him, before pulling the rug out from under him. Because she absolutely would.

She'd move to his ear, her voice dropping to its most seductive purr as she whispered, "Make me."

God, how he'd love to do just that. Hell, right now he couldn't think of a single other phrase that would turn him on more.

But every dominant worth his honorific knew there was only one way to deal with a brat. If it was attention Quinn was after, then the best punishment was none at all. He'd ignore her prank and keep her off-balance by not reacting to or mentioning it.

It would drive her absolutely insane, and likely push her to try harder to get a rise out of him.

Finley snorted. Well, in that, at least, she'd succeeded.

He couldn't wait to see what antics she came up with next.

Standing, Finley started to smooth out and carefully fold his shirt. He moved to the small bedside table, pulling open the top drawer and laying the shirt inside. She might have considered it a joke, but to him it was a gift. The first, he hoped, of many.

As he closed the drawer, he briefly wondered what Quinn would say when she realized he'd kept it. And just how long it would be before she found out.

Then he glanced back around at his room, a slow smile curling his lips.

"Keep playing your games, love. And I'll play mine." Finley chuckled. "I just hope you know what you got yourself into."

A NOTE FROM MEG

I'm just going to wait right here and let you get it out of your system.

That one was a bit of a doozy, huh? Even if you knew the cliff was approaching, most of you probably weren't quite ready for it. I hope you don't hate me too much.

For those of you currently cursing my name, I'm sorry. Don't give up on me just yet, I have a few tricks in store for Nord and Lina. Things are just getting started!

As always, I will keep folks posted in my reader group and via my newsletter first with series updates and exclusive sneak peeks. If you want to stay up to date on everything Nord and Lina, or just share some epic Viking memes, I hope you'll join us.

Until next time, stay safe and happy reading!

XOXO,

If you enjoyed this book, please consider writing a short review and posting it on Amazon, Bookbub, Goodreads and/or anywhere else you share your love of books. Reviews are very helpful to other readers and are greatly appreciated by authors (especially this one!)

Want to know when I have a new release or get exclusive access to my newest works? Join my mailing list: MegAnneWrites.com/Newsletter

ALSO BY MEG ANNE

THE CHOSEN UNIVERSE

THE CHOSEN

A FATED MATES HIGH FANTASY ROMANCE

MOTHER OF SHADOWS

REIGN OF ASH

CROWN OF EMBERS

QUEEN OF LIGHT

THE CHOSEN BOXSET #1

THE CHOSEN BOXSET #2

THE KEEPERS

A GUARDIAN/WARD HIGH FANTASY ROMANCE

THE DREAMER (A KEEPER'S PREQUEL)

THE KEEPERS LEGACY

THE KEEPERS RETRIBUTION

THE KEEPERS VOW

THE KEEPERS BOXSET

THE FORSAKEN

A REJECTED MATES/ENEMIES-TO-LOVERS ROMANTASY

PRISONER OF STEEL & SHADOW

QUEEN OF WHISPERS & MIST

COURT OF DEATH & DREAMS

ABOUT MEG ANNE

USA Today and international bestselling paranormal and fantasy romance author Meg Anne has always had stories running on a loop in her head. They started off as daydreams about how the evil queen (aka Mom) had her slaving away doing chores, and more recently shifted into creating backgrounds about the people stuck beside her during rush hour. The stories have always been there; they were just waiting for her to tell them.

Like any true SoCal native, Meg enjoys staying inside curled up with a good book and her fur babies . . . or maybe that's just her. You can convince Meg to buy just about anything if it's covered in glitter or rhinestones, or make her laugh by sharing your favorite bad joke. She also accepts bribes in the form of baked goods and Mexican food.

Meg is best known for her leading men #MenbyMeg, her inevitable cliffhangers, and making her readers laugh out loud, all of which started with the bestselling Chosen series.